© Morgan Roberts

About the author

Dr Anita Heiss is an award-winning author of non-fiction, historical fiction, commercial women's fiction, books for children and blogs. She is a proud member of the Wiradyuri Nation of central New South Wales, an Ambassador for the Indigenous Literacy Foundation, the GO Foundation and Worawa Aboriginal College. Anita is a board member of Aboriginal Art Co, the National Justice Project and Circa Contemporary Circus, and is a Professor of Communications at the University of Queensland. *Bila Yarrudhanggalangdhuray (River of Dreams)*, Anita's epic historical novel about the 1852 Flood of Gundagai, received numerous awards, including the NSW Premier's Literary Award Indigenous Writer's prize, and was longlisted for the Stella Prize. Anita enjoys eating chocolate, running and being a 'creative disruptor'.

Anita HEISS

Manhattan Dreaming

SIMON & SCHUSTER

London · New York · Sydney · Toronto · New Delhi

MANHATTAN DREAMING
First published in Australia in 2010 by Bantam
This edition published in 2023 by
Simon & Schuster (Australia) Pty Limited
Suite 19A, Level 1, Building C, 450 Miller Street, Cammeray, NSW 2062

10 9 8 7 6 5 4 3 2 1

Sydney New York London Toronto New Delhi
Visit our website at www.simonandschuster.com.au

A catalogue record for this book is available from the National Library of Australia

ISBN: 9781761109959

Cover design: Christa Moffitt, Christabella Designs
Cover image: Woman, Shutterstock/Bibadash; New York City silhouette, Shutterstock/Pavlo S
Printed and bound in Australia by Griffin Press

The paper this book is printed on is certified against the Forest Stewardship Council® Standards. Griffin Press holds chain of custody certification SCS-COC-001185. FSC® promotes environmentally responsible, socially beneficial and economically viable management of the world's forests.

Contents

1

The quickest way to get over a man is in the arms of another

'You look dreadful!' Libby said. I hadn't slept, hadn't had my caffeine hit for the day and hadn't really prepared myself for the conversation I knew was coming.

'Didn't you see yesterday's article?' I said, passing her my phone. I'd read it a hundred times the night before and I knew it off by heart. I felt sick.

Libby read the headline out loud: 'Adam Fuller does a deal with the devil!' Then she read to herself, shaking her head and tut-tutting. 'I can see how this kept you awake. A man who keeps you awake when he's NOT in your bed can't be good for you.'

'I have insomnia anyway, you know that. The wonders of concealer,' I joked, pointing to the covered-up dark circles under my eyes.

'Don't make excuses. Your insomnia is probably due to his behaviour. Aren't you tired of having insomnia? No pun intended.'

'Yes, I'm tired. Of everything.' I sat down at my desk, put my glasses on and tried to focus on my list of things to do for the day, starting with a project meeting at 9.30 am about the new exhibition we were planning.

'Just admit you're not sleeping because of him, while he's obviously not sleeping because of *other* people.'

She handed me my phone back. I looked again at the photo with the caption 'Adam Fuller heads to the sin bin on and off the field.' In the photo he had his arms around a woman dressed up, or rather, half dressed up, as the devil. I put my head in my hands and started to cry. It was all too much. I hadn't slept. I hadn't heard from Adam all week even though I had left him voicemails and texted him and left him messages on his socials. I didn't know what was going on with us anymore. I'd never really known.

'Lauren, tidda, please don't cry. No man is worth your tears and the one that is won't make you weep.'

'I'm just tired,' I lied.

'First thing we need to do is sort out something to help you sleep.'

'I've been trying to read.' I blew my nose.

'That's good, what did you read last night, then?'

'Adam's Instagram.'

I *was* pathetic. But I was in love, and that's what Libby didn't understand.

'What? So he's out partying with the trashy she-devil, and you're analysing and obsessing over his Instagram feed. And let me guess, it's full of bikini-clad girls all posting suggestive comments and pictures. I know his type. They only have female friends. Makes me sick.'

Libby was right. It was something that had always bothered me, but when I questioned Adam about the bikini girls and their comments, he always laughed it off.

Libby was on her phone now, scrolling through Adam's Instagram.

'Here he is, Chubby Neck. Jesus, it looks even fatter in this photo.' She spat at the screen.

'What are you doing?' I said, shocked.

'Just cleaning the screen,' she said unconvincingly, running a tissue over it.

'Stop it. And don't call him that.'

'That'd be right. All his friends are young, half-naked women. Why do you think that is?'

I felt like I was being interrogated.

'How can you even look at his feed, really? It's borderline offensive to decent women like you. And what about his bio, "Simply the Best"? Jesus, he's got more tickets on himself than they sell at a home game here.'

'Stop it now!' I said.

I reached over and grabbed her phone, closing the app. Libby didn't get it. I needed to check up on Adam's Instagram because he was away a lot and it helped me keep track of him, kind of, and what he was doing. I could read the comments and then read what he posted on other women's pages.

I walked back to my desk and logged on to my computer. 'I know you don't like Adam,' I told Libby, 'but I know a different side of him. The kind, gentle, generous side. He's a good guy, mostly. You don't know his private side.'

'You mean the private side that doesn't make the papers?'

'Look, he's a guy – a good-looking guy and a public figure. Of course he's going to have women on his Instagram and around him for publicity shots. It's what football players get paid for, to be friendly in public. It's marketing.'

'Really? That's what they get paid for? Are you trying to convince me or yourself?'

'For your information, Adam was raised well, he went to a good school and I know he's not interested in those women. He says they're just fans anyway. He's expected to have lots of female followers. All the players do.'

'Because they are *players*! Can you hear yourself? Are you really that naive?' She held up her phone screen right in front of my face. 'Is this what your man is *supposed* to do for his job?'

Although I had looked at it over and over the night before, seeing him with his hand right on the devil woman's breast turned my stomach as if I was just seeing it for the first time. I felt humiliated. I put my head back in my hands. Libby sat next to me and put her arm around me.

'Loz – I'm your friend. I'm just looking out for you. This has been going on for too long.'

I nodded.

'A year of you following him to away games, watching him at training, answering his late-night booty calls – when he's not with someone else. I'm sorry, but it's clear he's not committed to you. Or your *relationship*, if that's what you want to call it.'

'I wish I'd never told you anything. You just throw it back in my face,' I sobbed.

'Well, why do you tell me everything if you don't want me to comment?' Libby was annoyed.

'I just want you to listen and support me, is that too much to ask?' I said angrily.

'So you want me to listen to you telling me about a man who constantly neglects you? No real friend would stand by and remain silent. Anyone in their right mind, friend or otherwise, would tell you that you're too smart to stay in this situation, Loz, really.'

'But I love him.' I looked at Libby with tears streaming down my face.

'I know you do. And I know it's hard. And I also know he's an idiot for not loving you back, because you've got so much to offer him, or any man for that matter. You're gorgeous and vibrant – when you've had some sleep' – she smiled – 'and witty and sexy. You've got the best smile and every woman here at the gallery wishes she had your legs and your hair. And the men just wish they could touch either. You're only thirty and you've gone from the tiny town of Goulburn to the National Arts School in Sydney to get your masters. You've got a CV of exhibitions that shows you can mix it with the best in the art world, you're one of only a handful of First Nations Senior Curators in the country, and you've got the best golf swing on any woman I know. *And* you're the only woman I know who can shop in op-shops and look like a million bucks.'

I wiped my tears as Libby continued. 'And what's Adam got to offer a woman other than a thick footy player's neck?'

She was serious, but I couldn't help laughing. Adam did have a thick neck. He played in the forwards.

'How can you be so wonderful and mean in the same breath?'

'Seriously, I don't know what you see in him. I mean aside from his sixpack?'

Libby knew as well as I did that Adam was hot. He had one of those washboard stomachs that we perved on in Libby's firemen calendars. She loved firemen, and bought every edition of every state and territory's firemen calendar every year. Adam looked like those fireys. It was why so many women threw themselves at him. Of course it was what I noticed about him when we first met at the Goulburn Little League fundraiser. His team, the Canberra Cockatoos, had donated their time and some merchandise for raffling. It was love at first sight for me, and I'd loved him ever since. All of him, not just his sixpack.

'He's got a gorgeous head of hair,' I added, trying to lighten the mood.

'Hair eventually falls out,' Libby argued.

'And he can dance.'

'Oh please, any man can have dance lessons.'

'I was talking about *horizontal folk* dancing.'

'Well, *I* don't know about that, but I'm sure that for someone so young he's had enough practice, so he *should* be good at it.'

I sat down, shattered again. If I didn't know Libby better I'd think she was being a bitch. But I understood she was trying to tell me what I already knew and had chosen to ignore. Adam was a player, on and off the field. He didn't want to settle down. He was three years younger than me and in the prime of his career. I just didn't want to believe that he didn't want me as much as I wanted him. I was all those things that Libby had pointed out. How could he *not* want me? Maybe I needed to get a devil's outfit or something. I blew my nose hard and Libby looked over at me repentantly and began to apologise.

'I'm sorry, that was harsh. Okay, I can see some things that would make you love him, and what you might see in him. But what I don't understand is why you put up with his behaviour. He's not even worthy of you. And you know it. And so does he, which is why he needs to have groupies around him, to stroke his ego when he feels inadequate.'

Libby opened her mouth to speak, then shut it again, shaking her head sideways. She sat at her desk and shuffled papers around.

'What? Say it. Why stop now? What else do I need to hear for my own good?'

'Just tell me why you don't end it. Whatever it is you have with this fella can't be worth all the pain and humiliation, can it? You have other options.'

'I don't want other options. I want Adam.' I flicked through my diary to let Libby see I had work to do, hoping she'd drop the subject.

'You know what they say – the quickest way to get over a man is in the arms of another. And by my calculations, you'd be over Adam in no time at all.' Libby's tone at least had become gentler.

'I just can't control my heart. I can't control the way I feel about him.'

'No, you can't control the way you feel, but you *can* control your *mind*, and your *thoughts,* which in turn control your emotions.'

Libby was always right. But even so, it was just not that easy to let go.

'We seriously need to detox you of Adam. And the detox needs to start today.'

Libby walked around to my computer and immediately changed the desktop photo of Adam and me together on the night we met. It was our first photo.

'Do you think he has a photo of you two as *his* background? Of course not, he'd have a pic of *himself*. A big profile shot with his chubby neck.'

I had to laugh, Libby had Adam's ego sorted out. He did have photos of himself all over his house and his zoom background was probably an action shot of himself.

'Actually, can he even *use* a computer? I mean he *is* a footballer. And while we're at it, where's your phone?' Libby picked up the phone lying face-down on my desk. 'I know you save his messages and re-read them.'

'Get out of it, you psycho.' I grabbed my phone from her.

'You know I'm right. They HAVE to go. No more over-analysing messages from Mr Chubby Neck.'

'Stop it!'

'I can't believe a woman of your age and accomplishments saves his stupid messages. I mean, it's not like you're never going to hear his voice again. I've never met a man who talks so much.'

Libby had nailed it again, Adam was a talker. But I didn't mind it. We got on well, because I was a good listener.

'Seriously, Loz – that man could have his own talk show with no guests!'

'God, you're cruel sometimes. Adam can talk, but he's smart and articulate and you know it.'

Libby raised one eyebrow. 'Well, I concede, he is articulate for a *footballer*.'

'And he's well educated – he went to uni.'

'My dear tidda, he went to uni but didn't finish his degree – I'd say that he's not one for long-term commitment and goals.'

'Well, he still reads widely.' I felt like I was back at school on the debating team.

'Reads what? Picture books?'

I'd had enough. 'Stop it! You're talking about the man I love.'

'Who, my dear friend, looks like he loves a few other people as well.' Libby made a devil horns gesture, then put her hands on her hips.

'Is it just Adam you hate or all men?' Libby's recent history with men was depressing – the last three were so bad she had sworn off men altogether.

'Hey, don't make this about me – you started this,

coming in here looking like death warmed up because of His Highness, the Royal Chubby Neck.'

'Stop calling him that, please. It's rude *and* offensive. You'd never say that about a woman with a thick neck.'

'You're right, so let's just call him Adam Full-of-himself. Anyway, it's probably fair to say I hate all men. I can certainly understand why Canberra has the highest proportion of same-sex couples – female couples – in the country. The men here are enough to turn any straight woman—' Libby stopped mid-sentence as a hot young maintenance guy walked past the window with a ladder.

'Is that true?' Emma, the director of the gallery walked in. She was in her signature look – a chocolate brown suit with a white tee underneath and a white flower in her poker straight dark brown hair. Same style, just different colours, every day. I really admired her ability to look elegant, professional and feminine at the same time.

'Sorry, Emma, just considering the dating opportunities in the great capital,' Libby said.

'Really?' Emma sounded interested. 'I have no idea about the dating scene anymore. When you're married with kids and everything is about the soccer and excursions and homework and so forth, you really don't keep up with the perils of single life.'

I glared at Libby. I didn't want my boss knowing my personal business.

'Did you get a chance to consider the "Urban Voices" exhibition proposal I gave you?' I asked Emma.

'Yes, and I love it!' she replied. 'I'd like to talk about it now if you're free.'

After our meeting, I went back to my desk, thinking only about the tasks at hand and the amount of work I had in front of me. My job consumed much of my waking life. But then my phone rang and it was Adam.

'Hi. Where are you?' I said accusingly.

'Hi, babycakes, I'm home. You want to come around tonight after I finish training?' I melted every time he called me babycakes. That was the gentle Adam I loved.

'Okay.' I caved immediately, forgetting about the tears of sixty minutes prior.

Libby was frowning at me. I waved her away so I could have some privacy. She didn't budge an inch, rather stood with her feet apart and hands on hips. 'Hang up!' she mouthed aggressively.

'Half past seven, okay.' Adam hung up, but I held on to the phone, pretending I was still talking, because I didn't want another lecture. But I think she guessed that Adam was no longer on the line so I put the phone down.

'Before you say anything, I'm going over there to tell him it's over. To point out all the things I have to offer, and to explain that I want a loving, committed, exclusive relationship, and that if he can't give it to me, then I'm moving on,' I said, but I was still warm from having just heard his voice.

'Oh yes?' Libby looked unconvinced. 'All I'm going to say is don't go to his place to do it. Meet somewhere public so that there's no chance of falling into bed. And be strong.'

2

The exotic other

'Where are you off to on a school night?' my housemate Bec asked. She was a teacher and rarely went out during the week.

I couldn't tell her I was going to see Adam. I knew she'd seen the article, even if she hadn't said anything about it.

'We've got an artist in town, just going to check they've settled into the hotel all right, might take them out for dinner if they're up for it.'

'Cool, have fun!' she said, going back to watching the news. I hated fibbing, but I'd already had Libby on my case. I just wanted to talk to Adam, no-one else. Against Libby's recommendation, I hadn't asked him to meet me in a public place. I wanted to be alone with him, and I would lie to Libby about it if I had to.

Adam was amazing in many ways, especially as a sportsperson. Without him knowing, I often watched the Cockatoos train at Canberra Stadium, parking my car as far away in the car park as possible and hiding behind a hat and dark glasses. He looked drop-dead sexy in the red, black and yellow team colours. Adam was a whitefella, but his playing for a team in the Aboriginal colours was a sign we were meant to be together. The fact he had so many friends in Goulburn, where I was born, was another one. There were lots of little signs like these that Libby just didn't see or want to know about. She always said that I stretched everything to make it seem like a sign, that the team colours were just a coincidence and that Goulburn was the next town to Canberra so it was normal for a Canberra boy to have friends there.

Unlike Libby, my housemate Bec had always liked Adam. When he'd come to our place, he was polite and generous. If Bec was home when we ordered food in, he invited her to join us and paid for everything. She saw his gentleness towards me, and she treated him the way he treated her – kindly. In reality, Adam was kind and sweet most of the time. When I was at his place, he often cooked for me. And he always had apple pie or cheesecake in the fridge when he knew I was visiting, because I had a sweet tooth. I wasn't a big drinker; sweets were more my vice. When I go out with my friends, I'm always checking the menu for desserts while the others read the wine list.

Adam was my first real love. I'd dated a few guys in Goulburn, but nothing was ever that serious. When I studied at NAS and lived in Sydney, all the men I knew were gay, so I never even went on a date, but it never bothered me. Then I met Adam, and it was love at first sight for me.

After work, I drove to the stadium and sat alone, as usual, and it was typically cold and already dark at 6 pm. I shivered as I watched Adam pass and kick and tackle. I hated seeing him hit the ground during a game or at practice and was glad for his chubby neck at those times. At least there was no chance it would snap. I looked around the boundary of the oval and noticed other girls hovering around shouting out players' names, including Adam's. A pang of jealousy burned right through me, but I convinced myself it was heartburn from the rich Indian lunch I'd had.

As soon as his training session was over, I raced from the stadium to my car. I freshened up my makeup, fixed my hair and noticed the look of sadness on my face reflected in the rear-view mirror. As I drove towards Adam's house, I felt nauseous at the thought of the conversation we had to have, but I was still looking forward to seeing him. I'd missed him. But as I walked to his front door and put my keys in my bag I remembered the article and immediately became angry again. When he opened the door I said firmly, 'We need to talk.'

'It's never a good thing when a woman says that.' Adam pulled me close and kissed me hard on the mouth, his tongue teasing mine before I had a chance to pull away and remember all the things I had to say. The heartburn jealousy was momentarily gone.

'I need to get out of my training gear. I had a good session – you should've seen me,' he said, pulling his clothes off. 'I must be the fittest guy on the team, seriously. I work the hardest in the gym – can lift more than any of the other guys.' I tried not to look as he flexed his muscles, but it was true that he was in good shape.

Adam walked around starkers a lot. I found it odd at first. But I came to expect it and appreciate it, and there he was, all ripply and still sweaty and naked. It was hard not to look at his body. But I was going to keep my clothes on tonight. If for no other reason than to save a lecture from Libby on Sunday when I saw her at the markets.

Adam came towards me and grabbed me tight.

'You stink, get off me. Take a shower.'

'You want to join me, babycakes?' he asked.

'No, I'm not dirty.' I was being cool. I was being strong.

'Well, I can make you dirty.'

I remembered the devil woman in the photo. 'Go shower so we can talk.'

'I might be a while.' He was stalling.

'Go,' I said as I pushed him away.

'I'll wait for you to come wash my back, babycakes . . . and then I'll wash your front.' He left the room singing 'Sex on Fire'.

While I waited, I looked at the action shots of Adam on his fridge and a pile of autographed photos on the coffee table in the lounge room. On them was a post-it note saying, 'Queanbeyan High School'. I loved that Adam did a lot of work in schools, building the kids' self-esteem. It was the kind of thing that Libby wouldn't give him credit for and I never bothered to tell her. Libby would say that being good in the daytime didn't give him the right to play up of a night.

Adam came out with his towel around him and beads of water still on his chest and arms. He sat on the couch and tried to cuddle me.

'Get off, you're all wet.'

'And what about you, babycakes, are you wet?'

'Oh, for god sake, stop it.' I jumped up off the couch. 'What happened when you were out the other night? You haven't returned any of my calls, or my text messages, all week. You haven't answered my DMs either but I see you managed to make new slutty friends on the gram. And what's with your bio line being "Simply the Best"? You sound severely up yourself.'

Adam shook his head like a dog shakes itself after a bath, and sprayed water all over me. He started talking but didn't look at me.

'What's with you lurking my Insta all the time? It's marketing, that's all. And I love that song, it was so written for me, don't you think?'

I liked a man with self-esteem. I just didn't like that every other woman liked it too, and that he liked them liking it. I was confusing myself by this stage.

'Why don't you have me up there as your girlfriend? In fact, why don't you ever refer to me as your girlfriend? Am I your girlfriend or not?' I grabbed his face gently so he had to look me in the eye.

'You told me you don't like labels,' Adam said, playing dumb and rubbing my thigh.

'I don't like racist labels, and you know that's what I meant.'

He moved towards me and smiled. 'Or labels on your clothes, right?'

He tried to look at the tag on my top. I flinched away.

'Don't change the subject. I read the article.' I pulled my phone out of my bag, brought the article up and shoved it in his face.

'And?' He played dumb again.

'And? *And?* And what have you got to say for yourself?'

'Don't believe everything you read. You know the media manipulate everything, it's all clickbait.' He was behind me, snuggling into my neck. 'I missed you.'

I could feel myself go weak, but I was still angry. 'Your hand was right on her breast. I saw it, the whole world saw it. How do you think that made me feel? Did you even know her?'

'I wouldn't call the readership of *The Canberra Times* the whole world, babycakes.'

'You know what I mean,' I said through gritted teeth.

'She's just a friend is all, like you and me.'

'What?' I pushed him away hard. 'So we're friends? We're *FRIENDS*? That's not what we are at all. We're lovers. We're together. I don't want to be just friends. Friends don't sleep with each other.'

'Babycakes, we're *special* friends.'

'Like friends with benefits? Is that what we are? Is that what you're saying?'

He didn't answer me directly. He was as good at sidestepping an issue as he was at sidestepping on the field.

'Look' – he stroked my hand – 'you get more of me than any other woman in my life, even my mum.'

'Great, now I'm in the same league as your mother.'

'League, that's funny, like football,' he laughed.

'It wasn't meant to be funny, Adam,' I scowled.

'Well, I love your sense of humour anyway – god knows you need one with me.' He started kissing my neck again.

'How do you feel about me?' I asked.

'What do you mean?'

'How. Do. You. Feel. About. *Me*?' I pronounced every single word slowly and clearly so he couldn't confuse the question, or his answer.

'You know how I feel. Why are you asking me?'

'If I knew, I wouldn't need to ask, would I?' Sarcasm had crept into my voice.

'I like you.'

'That's it? You *like* me?'

'Liking someone is good.'

'I *like* apple pie, but I don't need it every day. I don't miss it. I don't care if other people eat it.'

'What are you getting at, babycakes? You want me to eat apple pie instead of you? I don't know what you're talking about. I'm just a dumbarse footyhead.'

'What?'

'I know that's how your friend Libby talks – in fact, I think she may have said it to my face one night at your place, but the music was loud, though, so not quite sure.'

'You're doing it again, trying to change the subject. What I am getting at is I want us to be together properly.

I want to be your girlfriend. Your *only* girlfriend. And I want you to stop ending up in sleazy shots like this one. It's the third one this season already, and it's only June!'

'What's brought all this on? I thought we were having a great time together. That you were as happy as I was with our situation.'

'Our *situation*? You think I'm happy about booty calls, and you in photos like this, groping the devil herself for the whole world to see?'

Adam laughed but when I looked at him with dagger eyes he stopped immediately.

'We've been seeing each other for a year, Adam. That's a long time. I want us to be exclusive. I don't want to be with anyone else, only you. I think we should move in together.'

'Whoa, back up, babycakes. There are a lot of *I's* in that last statement. You want to move in? You want to be exclusive? That's a bit much, isn't it? I mean, what next, marriage and kids? I'm younger than you, remember? Is this about your biological clock thing? Cos, babycakes, I'm not telling time that way.'

'It's not about that. It's about our future.'

'*Our* future? Right now I'm focusing on the next few months of *my* future. I've got the finals to work towards. I need to focus on the game – this is my career, my livelihood. It's important.' Adam stood up, readjusting the towel around his waist.

'So I'm not important to you?' I stood up too, and I burst into tears.

Adam dropped the towel and put his arms around me. 'That's not what I said – you women are good at twisting things, aren't you.'

'I didn't twist anything. It's what you *don't* say that matters,' I sobbed. I wanted him to say he loved me, that he only wanted to be with me, that I was important to him, and I didn't want to have to extract it from him like a splinter. My heart sank – I didn't seem to figure in his future at all.

He wiped the tears from my cheeks with his fingers. 'Don't cry, babycakes, you know I hate it when you cry. Your eyes are too beautiful to be full of tears. You're the loveliest woman I know. That's why I don't have you on my Insta, because you're too lovely to be up there with the others.'

'Lovely? I'm lovely? That's it?'

'You're more than lovely. You're exotic.'

'I'm *what*?'

'You're my coffee-coloured princess.'

'Oh god, you're unbelievable! Is *that* the only reason you see me? What am I, your own personal reconciliation project or something?' I grabbed my bag and stood up, dizzy with anger. 'I'm exotic all right, especially compared to all those other botoxed bimbos you get around with. Goodbye!'

Adam grabbed onto my arm firmly, but I yanked my wrist free and ran for the front door. He followed me, still just in his underwear. I ran into the driveway, got in the car and pulled the door shut quickly behind me. I pulled out onto the street with him standing there in his jocks looking surprised, speeding away like a crazy woman.

As soon as I turned the corner I pulled over, because my eyes were so full of tears I couldn't see the road. I leaned on the steering wheel and sobbed like a child, my heart heavy in my chest. I rummaged through the glove box looking for a tissue and stopped abruptly when my phone rang. It was Adam. I didn't want to answer it. I didn't want him to hear the tears and sadness in my voice. I didn't want to go backwards. I didn't want to disrespect myself, again. I didn't want Libby to be right about me putting up with his crap. But I couldn't help it. I answered.

'What do you want?'

'I want you to come back, babycakes. You can't run off like that. I'm worried about you driving when you're so angry. Just come back, we need to talk.' Adam sounded concerned. Perhaps he'd realised what he was losing. Perhaps he'd move in, and promise not to end up in any more of those awkward situations that he said the media manipulated.

'Come back, please,' he said again, breaking the sound of dead air on the phone. 'I'll wait outside for you. I'm walking back out the front right now, so come back quickly. It's cold. I'll get frostbite and my chopper will fall off.'

'Good. I hope it does.'

'Lauren, please. I'm going to stand here until you come back. Even if I have to wait until tomorrow, I'll be here.' There was silence. Adam never called me Lauren. I could feel myself weakening. I didn't really want his chopper to fall off, but if it kept him away from other women, then so be it.

'Where are you, Lauren?' he asked gently, and it pulled at my heartstrings. I hit 'end call' and started the engine.

I drove back to Adam's house to find him shivering on the front lawn. He had a big black coat on with nothing but his jocks underneath. He opened the car door and I got out slowly, hoping that in the dark he couldn't see my red blotchy face.

'Come inside. I'll make us some dinner.' He tried to put his arm around my waist but I pulled away.

'Don't touch me. Just don't.'

It was warm inside, but I was freezing.

'Can I take a shower?' I asked softly.

'Of course, you want me to come in with you?' Adam asked gingerly.

'No, leave me alone for a while. I'm cold, I want to warm up,' I half-lied, as I really didn't want to be near him just then. 'And I want you to stay out here and think of something intelligent to say about all of this.'

'Okay,' he said, hesitation in his voice, like saying something intelligent might actually be difficult for him. 'I'll make us something to eat. You go shower.'

I stood in the shower and let the hot water cascade down my body. I wanted it to wash all the pain away. I wanted a real relationship. I wanted to walk back into the kitchen and have Adam tell me that he wanted a relationship too. That he wanted us to live together. That he wanted us to eat dinner together every night. I wanted him to be happy for me to hang pictures of us in his home with the same care as I hung the artwork in the gallery.

I turned off the taps and grabbed a warm towel that Adam must have snuck into the bathroom without me noticing. It had just come out of the dryer. He often did that for me. These were the thoughtful gestures that made me want to forgive him for his indiscretions – the little things that I didn't bother telling Libby about, because in my heart I knew the little thoughtful things didn't make up for the big painful things.

'There you are. I thought you'd gone down the drain hole.' He smiled cautiously at me. 'Are you feeling better, warmer?'

'I'm warmer.'

'Sit down and I'll serve up.' He pulled a chair out and put a bowl in front of me and poured a glass of red. I was so emotionally spent I could barely sit up straight. I didn't want to talk. I just wanted to eat and sleep. I stared at my bowl of noodles and contemplated what to do and say next.

'Are you all right?' he asked.

'No.'

'I'm sorry.'

'For what?'

'For upsetting you.'

'But you're going to keep doing it, aren't you?'

'I don't know. It seems lots of things upset you, so perhaps I accidentally will.'

'I can't do this with you anymore, Adam. I can't live like this. I wasn't raised to be a booty call girl.'

'That's not what you are. I've never thought of you like that.'

'But that's how you treat me. You treat me like you don't care at all.'

'I just cooked you dinner. I warmed up your towels. Doesn't that prove something?'

'What?'

'That I do care about you.'

'But?'

'I just don't want to be in a relationship with anyone. It's not you, Lauren. If I did want to be with someone, properly, then it would be you for sure. But I just want to be single right now. I like my life. I like what we have. I don't want to change it.'

I drank my glass of wine in one go. I was never a big drinker because I got hangovers too easily, something about the tannins. But now I felt reckless. I pushed my glass into the middle of the table so he could pour me another one.

'Are you sure, babycakes? You know you'll be sick tomorrow.'

'I'm sure.' He poured and I sipped it slowly, watching – but really not watching – the television behind him in the background. I finished as much of the noodles as I could and left the rest.

'I need to lie down,' I said, already feeling woozy. I pushed my chair back and stood up.

Adam stood up too. 'I'll clean up and check on you in a minute. I don't have anything sweet for you tonight. I didn't have time to get anything after training. Sorry.'

I went into his room, took off my shoes and lay down, feeling drunk and tired. I wasn't designed for emotional turmoil, but then was anyone?

I must have fallen asleep because the next thing I knew, Adam was trying to get me under the covers. 'Come on, babycakes, time to sleep properly.'

'I can't sleep in this dress. It's the one designer dress I have.' I started to wriggle out of it.

'Here.' Adam eased the woollen dress over my head and hung it up on the door. 'Would you prefer I wore some pjs to bed tonight?' He really didn't seem to know what he should do; he was like a child who knew he was in trouble but didn't know what his punishment would be.

'Do whatever you want. You do anyway.'

He put on some pyjama pants and crawled in next to me. I was half asleep when he turned off the bed lamp. I had my back to him and he cuddled in behind me.

'Is this okay, babycakes?'

I could feel his breath on the back of my neck and I prayed he wouldn't get any closer.

'Are you all right?' he whispered into my ear, sounding genuinely concerned. I didn't answer.

'I'm sorry, really. I'm sorry I hurt you.' And he kissed the back of neck until I let out an involuntary moan. I turned over to face him but couldn't see anything.

'We can't do this anymore. *I* can't do this anymore. It's not healthy.'

'I'll miss you, Lauren.' And he put his hand on the back of my head and pulled me towards him and it was too late. We kissed long and lovingly and before I knew it I was straddling him as he tugged my silk slip up over my head and pulled my face down to his mouth.

'I love you,' I whispered as he undid my bra.

'I love you too,' he said, burying his face in my cleavage. It was the first time he had said it, and I wasn't sure if he meant my breasts or me.

I woke up and my mood was dark like the early morning. Break-up sex may be hot, but it is bad for the heart. Adam was still asleep when I dressed, and I sat on the bed for a while just watching his chest move slowly up and down. I looked around his room. It was grey, dull, cold. It needed a woman's touch. It needed my touch, but would Adam ever realise it?

As I drove down the street I saw frost on the lawns and knew the day would be heavy with winter weather. I felt sad and confused, and I wasn't even sure we'd said 'Goodbye' properly or that we'd even agreed it was over.

3

Men behaving badly

On Sunday I met Libby for our usual stroll around Kingston Bus Depot Markets. The weather was fierce and we were rugged up. We strolled aisle after aisle looking at locally made arts and crafts and funky pieces of jewellery. I bought some wasabi and seaweed macadamias for Bec and caramel peanuts and chocolate to satisfy my sweet tooth. Sunday was my day of indulgence and sweets my only vice.

'See?' Libby said, pointing to two women holding hands, as we headed towards the muffin stall.

'What?'

'Lesbians. Canberra is full of them. I told you so. Statistically proven by the ABS.'

'And your point would be?'

I turned from Libby to the stallholder and said, 'A raspberry and white chocolate muffin, please.'

Libby leaned in close and whispered in my ear, 'There

are so many lesbians because men are jerks.' She raised one eyebrow, as if to say, *And by men I mean Adam.*

'Please don't start. Aside from the fact that no-one chooses their sexuality, and I know you know that, I haven't even had a coffee yet, and I'm freezing. What is it, six degrees?' I scanned the stall for something else that looked delicious.

'And a banana caramel fudge muffin too, please.' The stallholder smiled and put it in a bag for me.

'Don't change the subject,' Libby said. 'You're behaving like a man.'

'And I'll have two double chocolate muffins, thanks,' I added to my order.

'After coffee you're going to talk, Loz. In the meantime, there's a hottie. Ooooh, I bet he's a firey.'

'I thought you weren't interested in men anymore.'

'I'm still interested in perving, I'm just not interested in letting any of them close enough to me that they can destroy my not-so-easily rebuilt heart and head. Now, hold my hand.'

'What the hell are you doing now?' I said, playing along and taking her gloved hand in mine like we were schoolkids crossing the road. We walked towards the 'hottie' and stopped at a stall with coasters, placemats and jewellery boxes adorned with classic images.

'Straight men love the thought of women together. Trust me, he'll be over here in a flash.'

'I thought you were just perving.'

'He's not for me, this one's for *you*. You did break up with Full-of-himself on Friday night, didn't you?'

I let go of her hand and picked up a wooden box covered with images of Audrey Hepburn. 'I love this,' I said, admiring her absolute beauty.

'Okay, if you didn't break up then you must have sorted it all out. He's going to be the proper boyfriend now, is he?'

I put the box down and picked up coasters made in the same fashion, only with Klimt images on them.

'We're still seeing each other. But he's not moving in. He's got the grand finals to focus on. It's his career. His livelihood. It's important. I need to support him.'

'Oh my god. He's *still* pulling the strings. And you're just doing the puppet dance. Why? He must be a good lay, because seriously, there is no other reason a woman as deadly as you would or should stay with a man like that. Where is the hero today anyway?'

'He had an away game on the Gold Coast yesterday. They won, thankfully. He scored three tries. I was so proud of him. I would've liked to have gone but I just couldn't afford it.' I loved working in the arts but the pay was poor.

'Don't suppose he offered to pay, did he? I mean, big shot footy star that he is,' Libby mumbled under her breath. She was shaking her head.

'It's time for breakfast,' I said. 'I'm starving. The usual?'

The winter chill had cut right through us as we walked to Manuka from the markets. We sat scrolling the news and reading bits of articles to each other, drinking our coffee and feeling the warmth return to our bodies. Breakfast at Caph's was a regular Sunday morning ritual for Libby and me. We'd been doing it for three years, since we first started working together at the gallery. I liked Libby the first time we met because she drank her coffee just like me – skim mocha in a mug. But more importantly, she was the strongest woman friend I'd ever had. When someone gave her a hard time she was always quick with comebacks, sharp but not sarcastic, and always sensible. Everyone went to her for advice – women and men, young and old alike. 'Loveable Lib' – that's what everyone called her at work. She often gave advice you didn't want to take, but she was the most honest and generous person you'd ever meet. Adam even liked her – she just didn't like him back.

Just as our food arrived at the table, Libby gasped.

'What?'

'Nothing,' she said, and she put her phone face down on the table, looking shifty. 'Let's eat.' She ate a bit of dill sitting atop her eggs Benedict.

'Show me,' I ordered and she reluctantly picked her phone up again and handed it to me.

There it was: 'THREE TRIES AND THREE WOMEN – FULLER'S TRIFECTA!' I was devastated. They were triplets. One was almost wrapped around his thigh, another was pushing her crotch into his right leg. The third was standing behind him with her arms around his waist.

One dignified tear ran down my cheek as I handed the phone back.

'I don't want to talk about it, Lib. Please.' I took my reading glasses off and put my sunglasses on to hide.

'You know why men do this, don't you,' Libby said gently, taking my hand.

'I said I don't want to talk about it. Really.'

'Okay, then I'll talk, you listen. Men behave badly like this when they know they're not good enough for you, and they can't measure up, even though they wish they could. As soon as they realise it they behave so badly that you have no choice but to break up with them, so they won't look like the idiot dumping a good catch. Instead, they'll be the wounded party. They'll get the sympathy vote from their mates and other women who'll go out with them.'

'But why? Why would anyone go to so much trouble to get out of a relationship?'

'Because men – *some* men – have egos the size of Lake Burley Griffin. None of them are going to admit they're not good enough for you. And lots of men just don't have the balls to break up with a woman. If they can hurt you with actions like that' – she pointed to her phone – 'they don't have to say *I don't want to be with you.*'

I picked up my cutlery and put a forkful of eggs into my mouth without looking at Libby, who kept right on.

'All's I'm saying, tidda, is that it's *him*, not you. You are the best and you deserve the best and you deserve some respect . . . and that . . .' she said venomously, pointing at the phone again, 'is *not* respect.'

'Can you stop, please? I just want to eat my breakfast without a major crying scene in public. I like it here. I want to be able to come back.'

We sat in silence eating our eggs. I stared out into Franklin Street at the grey sky, and wanted to be back in Goulburn with Mum. She'd make me a roast dinner and apple pie for dessert and the fire would be burning, and I would feel loved. I just wanted to feel loved.

When the waitress came and cleared the table I smiled insincerely and then hated myself for doing it. It was the Canberra smile. It had taken me a while to get used to it. People just turn the corners of their mouths up to make an empty gesture of hello or thanks or whatever. I was feeling empty, though, and it was the only smile I could offer anyone. Libby was quiet.

I picked up Libby's phone and had another look at the man I loved being mauled by three strangers.

'Mum always liked Adam. She thinks he's handsome,' I said softly, sadly.

'Loz, we know he's handsome, but we also know he's not good for you.'

'I know, and Mum would actually be mortified. She didn't raise me to be treated this way. And my dad would send my brothers over to look after him old way if he knew about this. I'm just glad they don't read *The Canberra Times* at home.' I sighed with some relief. 'What now, then?'

Libby put her coffee down, placed her hand on mine and looked me square in the eye. 'You *have* to tell him it's over, properly. Once and for all, forever and ever, amen. Do it now.'

'What? He's probably not even awake.' And I felt a

pang of heartache, knowing that he was probably not in bed alone.

'I know you, Loz, you'll spend the entire day moping about sad and miserable. It's time to move on. You know it is.'

'Yes, I know.'

'Call him. I'm here with you for support.'

I took a deep breath, grabbed my phone and shook as I hit 'Adam'. I imagined bringing my eggs Benedict up right at the table.

'There's no answer. It's gone to his voicemail.'

'Hang up. Don't leave a message. Text the bastard instead. Men do it all the time. Say something like . . . *It's over, Chubby Neck, you bastard*.'

I wasn't sure if Libby was being serious or not.

'I'm not sending a text. It's not my style and it shouldn't be anyone else's either. I'm not a man, and I'm not that bad mannered. I'll wait until he gets back and tell him to his face.'

'That's dangerous, tidda, breaking up face to face when you're both still attracted to each other. Lust can be a real break-up killer, trust me, I know.'

I just looked at Libby without responding.

'I'm going to pay the bill,' she said. 'I'll meet you out the front.' I could tell she wasn't impressed with my idea of telling Adam to his face. She didn't believe I would do it. And she had every right to be angry. She'd let me cry on her shoulder for over a year. She'd come over to my place the nights he hadn't shown up. She'd seen him treat me badly again and again, and she'd seen me put up with it. But she didn't realise that this time I was determined to be strong. I was going to break free once and for all – and keep my clothes on while doing it.

It was already dark at 5.30 when Adam answered the door in his jocks. The central heating in Canberra meant you couldn't tell how severely cold it was outside most days. He smiled when he saw me.

'Babycakes, this is a surprise.'

'Don't call me babycakes,' I said angrily, trying to look past him. 'Are you alone?'

'Yes, come.' He grabbed me around the waist and pulled me into the house, slamming the door behind me and pushing me up against it.

'Get off me.' I pushed him away.

'What's wrong?' he asked, surprised by my reaction. I shoved my phone in his face, showing him *The Canberra Times* article. 'Well?'

'Well what?' He looked at the paper and shrugged his shoulders. 'I've already told you – don't believe everything you see online, babycakes.'

'So you *weren't* caught half-naked on the beach in Surfers with these three . . . I won't say *ladies*, because clearly they are not.'

'It's not what you think.' He smiled as he looked at the photo and I wanted to slap him. I was furious.

'Oh, you don't want to know what I think.'

'By your tone, I'm pretty sure I don't either.'

I took the deepest breath I could and lunged into my prepared speech:

'I am gorgeous and vibrant and witty and sexy. Every woman at my work wishes she had my legs *and* my hair. And that's just the straight ones. And apparently the men just wish they could touch *either*.'

'And I know why,' Adam said, reaching for my thigh.

I pushed him away. 'I've got a masters from the National Art School in Sydney and you didn't even finish your degree. My CV shows I can mix it with the best in the Australian art world and I'm *only* thirty. I'm at the top of my game as a Senior Curator in the country, *and* I've got the best golf swing on any woman you're ever going to know! I'm the *only* woman I know who can turn op shop buys into stylish looks. I am amazing, and you're a fucking idiot for not realising it.'

'Babycakes, why are you swearing, you never swear.'

'YOU ARSEHOLE!' I yelled, shaking. Adam stood still in his jocks, looking stunned.

'I want a man who can appreciate and respect me and that's not you! It's over.'

'You're not my friend anymore, Lozzie? Babycakes? But I need you.'

'You NEED me? You didn't NEED me when you were at Surfers, did you?' I had found a lung capacity I didn't even know I had. 'You don't fucking NEED me. You need some sense knocked into you, that's what you need!'

4

It's not stalking because I love him

'I did it,' I declared at morning tea the next day.

'What did you do?' Libby asked.

'I broke up with Adam.'

'What? When?' She let go of her mouse and looked around the side of her computer with a half-smile.

'Last night,' I said, feigning pride and hiding heartache.

'Are you serious? Why didn't you tell me! I mean, before now? It's 11 am already.'

'You've been glued to the phone since I got in. Aren't your ears ringing?'

'What's that you say, Loz? Can't hear you. Seriously, this is good news for you, tidda. We're going to find you a good man, with a normal neck. I promise.'

'I'm not looking for a man for a while. One heartbreak is enough for me.'

'Oh, tidda, you'll have plenty of frogs to kiss before you find that prince, and as for your broken heart, you'll get over it. The heart is like the liver, it mends itself eventually.'

Libby still didn't get it. Adam was the only one I wanted. And I was the best woman for him, he just hadn't realised it. I still hoped that he would, one day. Until then I would just try and be strong and stay away and wait for him to come back to me.

'I really think this calls for a celebration.' Libby stood up.

'I'm not really in the mood for celebrating. Can you at least let me have a mourning period?'

'No, sorry, no mourning the loss of losers. Really, you're amazing, and you've got a great career and friends who love you, so I think we can at least celebrate that. Why does your happiness rest on what Adam brings or doesn't bring to your life?'

Libby looked at her watch and back at her computer. 'Come on, we've both been working nonstop, let's have a cuppa and something sweet to eat. It's my treat.'

We went down to the gallery's eatery – Courtyard Cafe, on the ground floor backing onto the lawns of New Parliament House – and saw Emma in a meeting with one of the bean counters from the gallery. They both looked at me with a funny smile, as if they were talking about me.

'So?' Libby asked as she devoured her chocolate, hazelnut and espresso trifle.

'So,' I repeated, focusing on my pavlova with passionfruit and kiwifruit. 'My dentist would die if he saw me eating this.'

'Are you okay?' she asked.

'I think so.'

'You look okay. Actually you look really good. Are you sleeping all right?'

'More or less the same, really. Bec has given me some herbal stuff to help. I think it's working. I got about five hours last night, which is almost a marathon. She's a great housemate!'

'Has he contacted you since you told him it was over?'

'Just a text this morning.'

'You're not going to text him back, are you?'

'Of course not,' I lied, but I wasn't sure how convincing I was.

'I know you, Lauren. If you start texting he'll suck you back in. He does it every time. One little *babycakes* and you'll be right back into it.'

'I won't text him. I'm not *that* stupid.'

I wasn't stupid – I was just in love.

Libby raised an eyebrow. 'At least you don't drink much, so there's less risk of you doing the drunken dial or text. And that can only be a good thing. Most of us have been guilty of that at one time or another.'

Bec was a chronic drunk dialler, always texting her ex-boyfriends when she'd had a few drinks, but I used to help her script the messages, so I was an accomplice.

'You know you need to delete him from Instagram, don't you? Actually, you need to block him altogether so he can't find you. And so you can't find him. I'll help you do it if you don't know how.'

'Thank you for all your practical and moral support,

Libs, and I know you're really happy that it's over, but I'm sure I can figure out how to delete or block him or whatever. Can you at least let me wean myself off him? It's like a twelve-step plan – no phone calls, no texting, no seeing him – there's three already.'

'No stalking on the internet – there's step four,' she said with a tilt to her head.

'Oh, I wondered what step four was – thanks,' I said. Truth be known there was no way I was going to delete Adam, and I'd certainly never block him. It was the only way I could keep track of him, of what he was up to and with whom. Eventually he would come to his senses. Until then I still wanted to know what was going on in his life. I had scrolled through his feed three times already that morning. Libby would be mortified if she knew, but our desks faced each other so she couldn't see what I was doing on my phone.

Libby stood up. 'We're not done with this little chat, Loz, but I think we need another coffee. I'll go order it.'

As soon as Libby had moved from the table I grabbed my phone to see if there was a text message or missed call from him. There was nothing. I snuck the phone back in my bag as Libby arrived back at the table.

'I was thinking,' she said, sitting down. 'I reckon you need to make a pledge to yourself.'

'A what?'

'A pledge – a commitment or promise to yourself that you will allow your heart to detox properly, and *not* let Mr Full-of-himself weasel his way back into your life. *You* are in control now.'

'I can't believe we're still talking about it. Please, just let it go now.'

'Trust me, I wouldn't mind talking about me for a change, Loz, but we need to just finish this and then we can *all* move on.' Libby sipped her coffee.

'Okay, what do you have in mind, then?'

Completely seriously, she said, 'Repeat after me – I, Lauren . . .'

I started to giggle. 'Don't be ridiculous.' I had no intention of reciting a pledge to a heart-detox and was grateful when our waitress, Amy, arrived at the table with our coffees.

'Double dose for you girls today, must be serious!' Amy joked.

'It is, Amy, trust me, it is!' Libby said, staring at me hard. 'As I was saying, Lauren—'

'Ooh, it does sound serious, I'll leave you to it,' Amy said, and left.

'I, Lauren . . .' Libby repeated. There was just no point in not cooperating. This was how Libby got people to do things for her that no-one else would have a hope in hell of getting done. She just refused to give up when she set her mind to something.

'I, Lauren . . .' I said, grinning at my friend and *her* commitment to *my* happiness.

'Will not call, DM or text Mr Chubby Neck Full-of-himself . . .'

'Will not call, DM or text . . .' I paused and Libby eyeballed me until I continued, 'Mr Chubby Neck Full-of-himself . . .'

'I will delete . . . no!' she corrected herself. 'I will *block* him on Instagram.'

'I will *block* him on Instagram.'

'And I will stop stalking him at training sessions . . .' Libby said sternly.

'How did you know about that?'

'You know I go to CIT three times a week for my Spanish class. I'm usually driving behind you as you go up Barry Drive. I wondered where you were going one day so I followed you to Canberra Stadium. You just never see me because you're driving like an obsessed stalker.'

'It's not stalking!' I was angry and defensive. 'I love him!'

'You *did* love him, but now you need to move on.'

Staying away from Adam was the hardest thing I'd ever done. It required more discipline than my masters had. I felt sick and sad and alone all day and all night, even when I was head down at work. I tried not to contact him but it was difficult. Every time my phone went off I jumped in hope that it was him. I left it on 24/7 in case he wanted to talk. But he never called, though he responded to my texts, because, if anything, Adam had good manners.

I tried to keep busy at work, focusing on pulling together the exhibition, and I spent lots of time at the gym, working off the increasing amount of sweets I was eating to compensate for no love. Bec, Libby and I had a couple of movie and pizza nights, which is all that Canberra is really good for in winter. I couldn't tell if they were keeping an eye on me or not, but it helped to have people around so that I couldn't easily get online.

Occasionally when I was with the girls, I would sneak to the bathroom and check his Instagram, just to see what he was up to, but at one point, even *I* thought using my phone while sitting on the loo was a bit OTT.

I thought about getting loads of photos with some young hotties and putting them on my own Insta, but that wasn't my style, and I didn't really want to risk jeopardising anything that still may have been possible with Adam. I didn't *really* want to make him jealous anyway. Childish, tacky women did that. I was neither of those. I had class, brains, and dignity. Or so I thought.

The quickest way to get over a man is in the arms of another one. Libby's mantra rang in my head. The problem was I didn't want another man, and I didn't even want to get over Adam. I just wanted him to get over his party-boy ways.

Late one night, when I checked Adam's Instagram, I was shocked to see a story of him at a barbecue, wearing an apron and flipping a burger as he smiled at a girl who could be heard giggling from behind the camera. *I* was the girl he cooked for. *I* was the one he called babycakes. When I saw a pic of him in his stories, sitting in a restaurant clinking glasses with another girl, I felt like I'd been stabbed in the heart. I desperately wanted to see him, I *needed* to see him, to remind him of how good we were together. I got up to make a cup of tea to calm myself.

'Can't sleep either?' Bec was behind me almost immediately. 'You know there's an ear here, two actually, if you want to talk. And I'm always good for a late-night drive by.' She winked. Bec never commented on the photos or articles about Adam unless I said something first, and I'd always tried not to. We got along well as housemates, and I didn't want to taint that by having her know absolutely everything about what was going on with Adam. Now I told her the bare minimum about us breaking up and she sat and ate cheesecake with me in sympathy. Bec was good like that. I think being a kindergarten teacher made her very gentle in her approach to people generally. Then I told her how upset I was about his Instagram story.

'People post all kinds of rubbish on Insta. The girl could have been a friend, or a cousin or something.'

I ignored that comment and moved on to more important things. 'Were you serious about doing a drive-by of his house with me? Really? Could we go now?'

'It's late, Lauren, and what good would it do?'

'I just want to know if he's got someone else, if there's a woman there now. If he has, then that would make me let go, for good.'

'Come on, then,' she said, grabbing her car keys.

We cruised up to Bruce at 11 pm, both of us in our pjs giggling like schoolgirls, me holding our keep cups of tea, both of us sipping at red lights. I loved that Bec didn't judge me and let me sort myself out my own way. We turned into Adam's street and I crouched slightly. His car was in the drive. No other cars were around, and the lights were out. I told myself that he was alone and we drove home.

Libby had a dental appointment late afternoon and was going straight home from the surgery without coming back to work. I was glad, because it meant I could go and watch Adam train without having to worry about her seeing me. It was one of several 'steps' I hadn't yet mastered in my heart-detox.

I left work at 5 pm in the cold and wet. It was already dark – nightfall arrived quickly during winter in Canberra. Anyone in their right mind would have gone immediately from their office to their heated home for a hot shower and a seat in front of the fire, but the weather didn't stop me. It was the first chance I'd had of seeing Adam in the flesh since we'd broken up. I turned into Hayden Drive, parked the car and braved the weather. I had my long black coat on, and a blue hat and matching scarf wrapped halfway up around my face to hide as much of me as possible. I felt like a spy. As I held on tightly to my lolly-pink umbrella I just hoped it didn't blow inside out. I made my way to the entrance, where only a few fans were gathered to watch. I stood right back, shielding my face from the weather and recognition.

I felt a hot rush the minute I saw Adam. His dark brown hair was thick and needed a cut. He wasn't wearing a mouthguard and I could see his wide smile as he joked with the other players. I was frozen to the core by the time I left, but I cruised back down Barry Drive feeling warm in my heart for having seen him.

'Morning, how's the mouth?' I asked Libby as she came in carrying a portfolio of scanned pictures for me to go through.

'Mouth is fine, thanks. How's your chest?'

'My what?'

'Your chest. Didn't get a chest cold last night, standing in the rain at the stadium?'

'I don't know what you're talking about.'

'Really?' She walked over to the door and got my umbrella out of the brolly stand. 'So there must be another woman who wears a blue hat and scarf, carries a hot pink umbrella, and would be mad enough to stand in the rain and watch meatheads do footy training?'

'There must be,' I said, embarrassed.

'Just because I went to the dentist doesn't mean I couldn't go to my Spanish class. I had to park in Hayden Drive because I was running late, and I saw you walking to the stadium.'

I felt like an idiot. And worse, I felt like Libby thought I was an idiot.

'This is going to stop, Lauren, today.' Libby put the portfolio of pictures on my desk, grabbed a folder from her own desk and walked out.

We both had meetings back-to-back for the rest of the day, and by the time I returned from the National Gallery of Australia she had gone home. I was relieved.

5

The intervention

When I walked in the door at home Libby was sitting in the lounge room with Bec. Libby and I hadn't spoken since our unpleasant exchange that morning, and to find her at home made me suspicious, and a little nervous.

'Oh, this is a surprise. Did we have plans for tonight? I was going to go to the gym, but pizza and a movie is a much better option if that's what you had in mind.' I hung my coat on the hallstand and walked through to the kitchen. Neither had said anything yet. I put the kettle on and went back into the lounge room.

'What's wrong?' I asked, looking at Bec and then Libby. They were propped up on two dining chairs like they were about to interview me.

'Did someone die? Someone's dead, aren't they?' I put my hand over my mouth as my stomach started to churn. 'Is it Mum?'

'Your mum's fine, Lauren,' Libby said.

'Oh god, it's Dad?' I sat down.

'Your dad's fine, too,' Bec said.

'It's Adam, isn't it, what's happened? I knew it. I could feel today that something was wrong. He didn't post anything on Instagram. What happened? Tell me. Where is he?' I was almost hyperventilating with fear that something had happened to him.

'It's not fucking Adam. Stop it. You're behaving like a crazy woman!' Libby was furious.

'So he's fine, then?' I looked to Bec for reassurance.

'I . . . I . . .' Bec tried to speak. She looked like she felt sorry for me but was too scared to say anything.

Libby turned to her angrily. 'We agreed we'd do this together. You can't always be the good cop, for fuck's sake. I'm sick of seeing an intelligent, gorgeous, creative woman behave so appallingly over a bloke who's not interested in her.'

I stood up and walked around in a circle, shocked, annoyed, confused. I still didn't know why the girls were both there, and why Libby was being so brutal with me.

'Why are you doing this to me, Libby? You're supposed to be my friend. You're supposed to support me when I'm hurting, but you seem to enjoy humiliating me.' I started to cry and sat down again.

'I'm not doing *anything* to you, Lauren. You're my tidda, but someone needs to tell you that you're humiliating *yourself!* And when *you're* not doing it, *he's* doing it. I'm just trying to help you. I *am* supporting you.'

'You're helping me? You're supporting me? How exactly are you doing that? You only ever make me feel like shit.' I felt overwhelmed – the walls were closing in on me.

'This is an intervention,' Libby said calmly.

'A what?'

'An intervention to help you move on.' Libby was being matter-of-fact.

I heard the kettle boiling in the kitchen, then whistling loudly until it turned itself off. 'I don't need an intervention. I hardly drink, I don't take drugs, I don't gamble and I don't eat any more or less than you guys. Okay, so maybe a little bit more cake. But I don't have addictions.'

'So you understand that interventions are about addictions, then?'

'Yes, I'm not an idiot.' I'd had about as much as I could take.

'Well, interventions are for all kinds of addictions, like for people who are addicted to the internet, for example. Or to other people.'

'What are you talking about?'

'Lauren, the gallery is going to block Facebook and Instagram because *some people* are abusing the internet privileges we have.'

'Are you suggesting that I'm responsible for that? That I'm to blame for the entire gallery losing internet privileges? As if.'

'The powers that be have decided that only the marketing team is going to have access from now on.' Libby held a piece of paper in her hand. 'I got the memo from Emma because I'm the administrator. I thought it would be better that I tell you than someone else.'

'So you're all talking about me, are you? You two and Emma, and god knows who else.'

'No, it's just us. Emma doesn't know what's going on. She just knows you're on Instagram for an obscene amount of time, and that it's not work related, and it has to stop.'

'So people are questioning the amount of time I put into work, then?' I felt like I was being bombarded.

'God no, we all know you work your arse off and give far more hours than are expected of you. Our concern' – and she dragged Bec in again – 'is that your Instagram addiction is directly related to your Adam addiction, and so we want to do an intervention to help you with both.'

Bec smiled sympathetically at me and finally said something. 'Lauren, I totally get your addiction to Adam, I really like him. But don't you think that maybe, just perhaps, your behaviour is just a *tad* self-destructive? I mean, staying up late at night and compulsively checking his Insta? That much blue light before bed probably isn't helping your sleep issue either.'

Everyone had been watching me and I hadn't even known.

'Lauren, you need to think of how wonderful your life is right now. How wonderful it has *always* been, with good friends and colleagues and a job you are not only brilliant at, but that you love. And you need to behave like you value yourself, like you love yourself . . .' Libby's tone was softer.

'But you came with me on drive-bys.' I accused Bec of being my willing accomplice. I wanted Libby to know that she had encouraged me in my addiction.

'I know, and it was okay once or twice but, Lauren, you are out of control,' Bec said.

Libby was shaking her head in disbelief at Bec's role in my bad behaviour. 'You have to believe us, tidda,' she said, looking directly at me, 'when we say you are wonderful and loving and thoughtful, and a good friend.'

'And a great housemate,' Bec added.

And then there was silence. There I was sitting at the dining table in front of my two closest friends – the good cop and the bad cop – who loved me so much they wanted to do an intervention.

'It hurts,' I said softly and started to cry.

'What hurts?'

'Rejection. It hurts. I don't understand why he doesn't want me.' I cried more. Both Libby and Bec stood up and guided me over to the couch where they sat on either side of me, putting their arms around my shoulders.

'Tidda, it's not that he doesn't want you. He just wants a different life to what you want.' Libby was being gentle with me.

Bec dabbed at my cheeks with a tissue to mop up my tears. 'It makes me worry that you can't sleep,' she said. 'I'm really concerned about your health. I want you to eat and sleep properly – you can't just survive on cakes and the gym and no sleep.' She rubbed my back.

Libby stood up and I was relieved. I was feeling slightly

claustrophobic on the couch being affectionately smothered by my two dear friends.

'We want to support you in your post-relationship rehab, tidda.

And that's why we're both here. Just let us know if there's anything we can do. I can be your sponsor if you like. When you feel like texting him, text me. When you feel like calling him, call me.'

'And when you feel like lurking his Instagram . . . well, we need to find an alternative.' Bec wasn't sure what the answer was and looked to Libby.

'Here, when you feel like lurking, look at one of my calendars.' Libby handed me the entire set of 2022 firemen's calendars from every state and territory and a couple from overseas. I laughed and cried at the same time.

'But you love these calendars.'

'Desperate times call for desperate measures. You need the distraction, I don't.'

I flicked through one and paused on Mr April. He was hot and had the same sixpack as Adam.

'Why don't I go and re-boil the kettle and we'll have a cuppa?' Bec headed out to the kitchen.

'God, I feel like something sweet,' I said to Libby.

'Don't think I didn't come prepared, tidda. I brought some of that pavlova from the Courtyard Café.' She stood up. 'Oh, and we're going out on Friday night just to celebrate life, okay?'

'Oh, just what I feel like – pav and a party.' I rolled my eyes and shook my head.

Libby joined Bec in the kitchen and I sat with the calendars in my lap. I could see a library book sticking out of Libby's bag titled *Addiction Intervention: Strategies to Motivate Treatment-Seeking Behaviour.* I knew then that this was serious. That *she* was serious. That my behaviour was serious. To have my friends borrow library books and learn about interventions and confront me like that meant they loved me, but it also meant they were worried about me. Even though I wasn't quite sure how I was going to do it, I knew I had to change my behaviour. It was going to end, today, somehow.

6

There's a man drought in Canberra

'Everything all right?' Emma asked as Libby and I sat silently in her office.

'Yep.'

'Yep,' Libby echoed. We hadn't mentioned the night before.

I hadn't slept at all – not because I was on Instagram, but because I was lying in bed trying to work out how I had arrived at a place where my happiness depended on another human being. Where my self-esteem had disappeared and I had forgotten all my achievements in life. Libby and Bec had offered me support but I still needed to believe in myself – that I was worth much more than Adam was giving me. That belief was the only thing that was going to help me move on and be the woman I was capable of being.

Emma looked from her computer to her diary to the whiteboard on the wall and then back to us. 'I need an update on how we're going with the schedule for the exhibition next year. Have you decided on the artists? Is there a short list we can discuss?'

'We've come up with a few artists: we're thinking Judy Watson and Joanne Nasir, Blak Douglas and Vernon Ah Kee.' I always included Libby by saying 'we' but I was the one who really made the decisions related to the curatorial side of things. Libby was the program manager, dealing with artists' agents, estates and other galleries and controlling the budget.

'They sound great. I like the mix of mediums and states and you've got some strong women in there as well. And Libby, I know you've been getting on to some regional galleries – who's showing interest so far?'

'Moree Regional Gallery, Wagga Wagga and Newcastle. Once Lauren has confirmed all the artists I'll approach the galleries in each of their home towns where possible, as well. In terms of major cities I'm aiming for Boomalli in Sydney and Aboriginal Art Co in Brisbane. I'm still in talks with galleries in Victoria and Tassie. Some of the smaller regional galleries require funding assistance, and I've offered to help them with applications.'

'Excellent. I love working with you girls. You just get in and do it. Sounds like we're on schedule for a March opening, then.' Emma looked at us for confirmation.

'Indeed we are,' I said, and that ended the meeting.

The lead time for exhibitions was long but we needed it. Libby and I worked well together and we liked working with Emma too. She was a considerate manager of staff and a visionary director. Emma was in her early 20s but at the forefront of the fight to get the site of Old Parliament House as the National Aboriginal Gallery back in 2006. She said she knew the government would never hand it over for an Aboriginal embassy but they could be persuaded to hand it over for a national gallery because of the success of our visual arts movement internationally, and the revenue our artists were bringing into the country every year.

Emma had written so many submissions she reckoned it was like doing a PhD. As soon as we moved in she invited the Tent Embassy mob to take up residence in the old Country Party Rooms, which overlooked the original Tent Embassy site, where only a flagpole and plaque stood now in honour of the 'Tent' and activists. She turned the Senate space into a room for community meetings, and the House of Representatives into a venue for readings and launches.

The gallery now had a staff of over sixty, a growing team of curators and a number of exhibitions running concurrently, with an exhibition schedule right into the next decade. International dignitaries visiting Canberra always insisted on visiting the NAG because we had the most comprehensive collection in the country. When they entered Kings Hall they saw statues of our warriors and activists, like Windradyne, Pemulwuy and Jandamarra. There were portraits of inspiring activists, politicians and other modern-day heroes like Neville Bonner, Aden Ridgeway, Linda Burney, Pearl Gibbs, Eddie Mabo, Vincent Lingiari, Charles Perkins, Mum Shirl, Oodgeroo Noonuccal and Chicka Dixon.

Over the years we had managed to broker a lot of relationships with visiting consular officials and even prime ministers of other nations, and such meetings led to us being able to plan travelling exhibitions overseas in coming years. My masters thesis considered the appeal of Aboriginal visual arts in the international market and now helped me plan for visits by embassy officials and the like. My knowledge of international markets had helped me secure my job – during the interview process, I'd been able to rattle off the national revenue figures for First Nations visual arts for the previous five years.

I had an important job and tried not to get overwhelmed by it, although I had become more prone to panic attacks since being promoted to senior curator. But right now I had work to do, calls to make and deadlines to meet.

I looked at the schedule in front of me: confirm artists, talk to marketing, commission someone to write the text for the catalogue, speak to the education department about activities and tours, go through the budget . . . Libby was already back on the phone to regional galleries sorting out who was interested in touring the exhibition. I needed to confirm the artists as soon as possible, so I started the ring around.

The best part of my job was inviting artists to show at the NAG. I could hear their excitement and gratitude down the line when I put in the call. It took some time but I finally tracked down Gordon Hookey in Brisbane. He wanted to show something from his 'Ruddock's Wheel' collection, inspired by Philip Ruddock, once Australia's immigration minister, who had claimed that Indigenous Australians had not reached a great level of sophistication because we didn't use chariots or the wheel. Gordon was known for his political commentary and his work would add a lot to the exhibition.

I tracked down Queensland artist Tony Albert, who was enjoying a residency in Barcelona. I wanted to show his 'You Wreck Me' video clip made up of fifty collages, as well as some of the stills, because his reimagining of Miley Cyrus's 'Wrecking Ball' was both hilarious and on point in terms of the impacts of invasion and colonisation.

I had a passionate conversation with Luke Penrith from Brungle. He was a successful artist but also an entrepreneur building partnerships and creating opportunities for others, particularly in central NSW. That local connection meant we'd be able to invite his Wiradyuri mob to attend the opening as well. By lunchtime I felt like I'd accomplished loads and was back on track.

With the curatorial adrenaline pumping, I thought about what the NAG had become and what the future held for the gallery and all of us working there. Just thinking about it put a spring in my step and made me realise how great my life was, with or without Adam.

After work Libby and I met Bec in Civic, Canberra's city centre. The night was cool, but not as unbearable as it had been in weeks past. I could get by without my gloves and hat; that was always a good measure.

Bec seemed particularly excited about being out with 'adults'.

'Let's go to Highball. All the teachers at school love it, because it's plush and the menu is meant be delish.'

'What's the crowd like?' I asked.

'It's full of public servants,' Libby said, sounding critical.

'What? Like us?'

'Not as colourful or creative as us, but yes, kind of like us.' We walked into the crowded bar.

'God, it's packed here, and it's only early,' I said, feeling overwhelmed by the crowd and blindly following Bec as we wormed our way through tables with punchbowls of cocktails being enjoyed by exhausted workers, just like us.

'Most of these fellas would've been here right after 4.51 pm knock-off time,' Libby said.

'Really?' I was surprised

'Most people don't work like you, Loz. And happy hour should be every hour.' She laughed as we took a seat.

I looked around the room at the public servants, some still wearing their security tags around their necks like prized war medals or something equally out of place at Friday night drinks. It was casual Friday so there were few ties to be seen.

'I don't mind a man in a suit,' Bec offered.

'Who do we know in Canberra who wears a suit?' Libby asked.

'More importantly, who looks good?' I asked. 'Adam Bandt,' Libby offered. 'And looks good without a tie.'

'So does Josh Burns,' Bec countered.

'I also vote Jason Clare for the non-tie-suit-wearing sort. But none of them rock a suit like Julia Gillard did,' Libby said adamantly. Both Bec and I looked at her strangely.

'What? Seriously, she wore a suit better than any of those guys. Especially that purple one.'

'Yes, that's true,' Bec and I concurred.

Two old men arrived at our table and stood with their schooners.

'Let's move,' Libby said, giving the nod with her head, and we stood outside under a heater.

'Why did we have to move? It was warmer inside.'

'It's not a good look, us three stunners with those two fellas who should be home with their grandchildren.'

'Oh, for godsake, you're being ageist, who cares how old those fellas are?'

'Look, I've been out with a sex fiend, a gay guy and a man in love with his mother. I'm not dating someone's grandfather. They were too old for any of us.'

I'd been eyeing the menu. 'I think we should eat something?

It started to rain and we went back inside and ordered charcuteria and a cheese board to get us started. Libby and Bec decided on wine and we settled in for the night, doing a running commentary on the men in the room.

'See, I told you, there are NO men in Canberra at all,' Libby said.

'What are you talking about, there's blokes everywhere,' Bec argued.

'They're all twenty years old and drunk. The older ones

who were here earlier came straight from work, had their beers and went home to their wives and families in the wastelands.'

'The what?' I laughed.

'Nappy Valley – Tuggeranong, you know, where all the families live. The ones left here now are all too young.'

'You two are mad. I'll be back in a minute.' I stood up, then added, 'I read it's now more "mature valley" out that way, as the population is aging, just as an FYI.' I winked at the girls and then escaped to the ladies with the intention of sending Adam a text, and was just about to take out my phone when I was distracted by the conversation of a drunken woman at the basin.

'I shouldn't have sent that text,' she slurred.

'No, you should've,' her friend disagreed.

'No, I shouldn't have. I only did it because I was drunk. He never sends me messages like that. I'm sick of my boyfriends having other girlfriends. God, take my phone.'

I realised I was just like her – but I wasn't drunk enough to use that as an excuse. I let go of my phone and grabbed my lipstick from my bag instead.

7

Rambo's eyeballs are cosy

When the director of the National Aboriginal Gallery calls you to her office, you go. And so I did, scurrying along the corridors of Old Parliament House wondering what could possibly be so urgent. There'd been budget cuts, but my exhibition had already been locked in, so it couldn't be that. I hadn't been on Instagram at work at all to spy on Adam since the internet audit, so it couldn't be that. I was so far ahead in programming that I was planning exhibitions for 2026, so I knew it wasn't my work performance – and yet I still felt sick with anxiety.

'Hi, Lauren, sit down. I've got a proposition for you,' Emma said. She waved a sheet of paper in front of my face. 'I've just received an email from the National Museum of the American Indian at the Smithsonian in New York City. They've got a visiting curator fellowship available for a First Nations curator.' Emma was so excited she couldn't get her words out fast enough. 'The fellowship allows the chosen curator to work on their own *original* exhibition *and* curate within the museum generally.'

'Sounds interesting.'

'Interesting? Lauren, it's the chance of a lifetime for a young curator! And I want *you* to apply for it. I think you'd be perfect for it.' Emma smiled the hugest, widest grin, showing off her perfectly straight teeth.

'Me? But it's in New York. That's in America. And America is so far away, from *everything* and *everyone*!' This had come out of the blue.

'I don't think you understand what I'm offering you,' she said. 'Lauren, this is a dream opportunity for anyone in your field. You'd get the chance to network with other curators internationally and work with American Indian artists across artforms and communities.'

'Emma, I'm so honoured you think I'm even up for the challenge, but what about my work here?'

'We both know that you're scheduling so far ahead I haven't even been allocated my budgets to cover the exhibitions you're planning in three years' time. I'm glad you're on top of everything, but I can afford to let you go right now – especially for something as important as this. I'll poach a curator from someone else to cover for you while you're gone.'

'It's really kind of you to think of me, but—'

'Look, I have to be up-front with you, Lauren. I'm not doing this entirely selflessly. I want to build a relationship between the Smithsonian and the NAG. We're a fledgling gallery and we need to build our profile internationally.

You're the youngest senior curator in the Pacific and having you on staff will get them – and us – heaps of publicity. Everyone wins.'

'Everyone wins,' I repeated, not at all convinced. I felt like my life had suddenly been hijacked when I'd only just started to feel like I was focused again.

'This fellowship would look sensational on your CV, Lauren. You'll be in a stronger position when you return to Australia, having had this experience. And your masters was about the internationalisation of Aboriginal art, so here's the perfect opportunity to put some of that theory into practice.'

Emma knew I wanted to go as far as possible in the art world, that I had my sights set on being the director of the NAG one day. But *I* knew I had plenty of time to work my way up the ranks, because Emma wasn't going anywhere for a while.

I moved to the edge of my seat, leaning into her desk. 'I know it's a fantastic opportunity, and that it's important to my career and the gallery – it's just that – well, it's America. I like being here, even with the miserable Canberra weather. It's my second home, after Goulburn.'

'Firstly, Lauren, it's not forever – it's twelve months, with an option to extend for another year. And secondly, and most importantly, it's not just *anywhere* in America, it's New York. The Big Apple; shopping on 5th Avenue, Broadway shows, Times Square, Central Park, the Metropolitan Museum of Art and the Guggenheim. Doesn't any of that interest you?'

'To be honest, I like what's offered here locally. I'm not unhappy living in Canberra.'

'*Not unhappy* and *happy* aren't quite the same thing, Lauren. But even if you're happy here, it doesn't mean you won't enjoy life in a big, bold, brilliant city like New York.'

I could feel myself becoming defensive.

'How do you think someone like me – Libby calls me a country bumpkin, you know – is going to survive in New York? A lone Blackfella at that. This is big city enough for me. I was out of my depths in Sydney when I was studying.'

'But there's a whole world out there, Lauren! New York is an exciting place for a young single girl like you.'

Single. I had no real ties keeping me in Canberra now, even if I wished I did. Emma had no idea I'd been seeing Adam, so she didn't know we'd broken up – or why, or how – but I felt like she'd knifed me in the heart. And I knew instantly the real reason I didn't want to go was Adam.

'Before you make a decision I want you to give it some serious thought. I want you to know there is no-one else I would even consider nominating. You are the best we have. And I don't say that lightly.' She handed me the email. 'Here's the job description and all the details. They'll fly you over, we'll sort out an apartment for you before you leave, and so forth.'

'How long have I got to decide?' I said, staring at the paper, but with Mum and Dad in my mind's eye, feeling completely overwhelmed. 'I need to talk to my family.'

Emma looked at her desk calendar. 'I need to know by Monday. You'd be leaving early next month.'

I walked the long way back to my office, stepping outside for a brief minute to get some air, as I was beginning to hyperventilate. No-one at work had seen me have a panic attack – I'd managed my anxiety well since my uni days – but I felt like one was close to the surface.

'You all right, Lauren? You're wheezing. Are you asthmatic?' Joel from security asked.

'Oh, yeah, fine, thanks. Not asthmatic. I must be just really unfit,' I said, pinching some flesh on my midriff. 'Wouldn't hurt to lay off the cakes here, either,' I laughed, motioning towards the cafe.

'This isn't a dress rehearsal, Lauren, it's life. Eat cake and be merry, I reckon. See ya.' Joel walked off chirpy and none the wiser. I looked over to the Tent Embassy monument and thought about the ongoing struggle for human rights in Australia. I breathed in, exhaled loudly, mentally slapped myself and reminded myself of my responsibilities to artists. Emma had just paid me an enormous compliment. I went back to my desk.

'Where have you been?' Libby asked, barely looking up from her computer.

'Had a meeting with Emma.'

'About?'

I handed her the advertisement for the fellowship and she immediately screamed with delight.

'You're going to New York New York? Oh my god, I'm so jealous! Take me with you.' Libby was even more excited than Emma.

'I haven't said I'm going yet. I have to think about it. What about my family? What about Bec? What about my work here? I'll be letting too many people down.'

'You won't be letting *anyone* down – unless you don't go and then you'll be letting us *all* down, including yourself.'

'What about our program here?'

'Emma wouldn't have suggested that you go if she thought it would jeopardise our program.'

'What about Bec, then?'

'You're Bec's housemate, not her girlfriend, unless you've become one of those Canberra statistics and just haven't told me.'

'Oh, you're hilarious. What about Mum and Dad, then? Dad didn't even want me to go to Sydney to study. You can imagine how he'll flip over the thought of me going to New York.'

'Lauren, you're thirty years old, you're not Daddy's little girl any more. And I'm sure Mum Jules will be thrilled you're going to New York with all that shopping.'

'Well then, I still need to think about Nick. He needs me too, even if I don't see him that much.'

'Both your brothers would be happy for you to go. You know that.' Libby was making it difficult to argue with her.

'Maybe you're right.' I sat down and tried to look at the emails that had come in while I was away from my desk, but I couldn't concentrate.

'I don't get it,' Libby said, confused. 'Don't you want to go to New York? Are you mad? Didn't you watch

Sex and the City? The place is crawling with men and bars and good fun.'

'I'm not interested in men right now, and you know it.'

'Okay, then. While Mr Full-of-himself didn't help you get much shut-eye, at least New York City is the city that never sleeps, so it will be *perfect* for Loz-the-insomniac.'

I couldn't think straight. It was only lunchtime, but I knew I needed to go home to Goulburn. I switched off my computer and finished up for the day.

'I've only got until Monday to decide. I need to go see Mum and Dad.'

As I drove around Lake George, it was good to see rain had filled the waterbed after two decades of it being mostly parched. Seeing water birds again out of the corner of my eye as I travelled from Canberra and Goulburn brought back memories of my youth along the lake. I loved this country – my country. I would miss the sense of peace it gave me if I went to New York. I sighed deeply. A few hours with Mum and Dad and my brother Max would help to clarify everything for me. I wouldn't have time to see Nick, and wasn't emotionally strong enough, but I'd write him the usual weekly letter on Sunday.

I turned off the Hume Highway, passed the Big Merino and headed into town. As I turned left into Auburn Street I saw a banner saying the Wiradjuri Echoes – my mob – would be performing in Belmore Park for NAIDOC

Week. I'd miss them if I went to New York. My heartbeat settled when I saw home. The red brick house always gave me a sense of peace and security that I never felt anywhere else. As I pulled into the drive, Jerry – our family dog – came running towards me, and nearly bowled Dad over as he worked out in the garden. I was home, and didn't know how I could ever move too far from it.

'Oh, your father and I have watched all the old movies set in New York, haven't we, Graham. I loved *An Affair to Remember* and *Breakfast at Tiffany's*. It looks like a wonderful city.' Mum was pouring tea for all of us as we sat at the kitchen table. 'You know, I always wanted to go to America, but your father wouldn't even discuss it, and we could never afford it anyway. And here you are having someone else fly you there and give you a great job with Native American artists. How wonderful. Isn't it wonderful, Gray? Max?'

Max went to speak but didn't have a chance, as Dad was already thumping his fists on the table.

'What are you talking about, woman? Romantic movies? What about *The Godfather* and *Goodfellas* and …' – he put his cup down – 'and what about all those crime shows we watch on television, most of them are set in New York!' He turned to me. 'Don't you watch the news? They shoot each other in the street in America. They fly planes into buildings in New York. They never turn the lights off in that city, waste of bloody electricity if you ask me.'

'Come on, Gray, don't be like that. Be happy for Lauren going to the Big Apple.' Mum patted Dad's hand; she was always worrying about his blood pressure.

'Big bloody Apple my arse. We've got Big Apples here, at Batlow, and there's one somewhere in Tassie and another one in Queensland, so I don't know why she'd want to go to some bloody big-noting apple in America.'

'Gray, c'mon love, you're being silly. America has everything bigger and better than we have.'

'Bigger? Better? I'm sure the Yanks don't have a Big Banana, or a Big Avocado, and you can bet your bottom dollar they ain't got a Big Mango or a Big Pineapple!'

'And I bet they don't have a Big Poo like Kiama either,' Max said, which made us all laugh – except for Dad, who took a deep breath and just kept going.

'Oh and they wouldn't have a Big Prawn, would they? They'd have a bloody shrimp, which doesn't even sound big.' Dad waved his arms in the air with frustration.

Max was laughing hard and even I had to chuckle. Being his favourite, I always took Dad's side, but this time he was just too outrageous, and Max seemed to be supporting his case anyway.

'Gray . . . stop it, please . . .' Mum looked concerned that he was going to completely overheat, but he wouldn't give in.

'There's the Big Mushroom in Canberra, and there's a Big Cow somewhere and a Giant Kangaroo, but ah, no, you women want to go to some Big Fancy Apple in America.' Dad stood up and took his cup to the sink, running water into it as he spoke. 'I'm sorry, love, but the Big Merino has been good enough for our mob for the longest time – no big piece of fruit is going to make me let any daughter of mine go to New York.'

'Gray, Gray, don't be so silly.' Mum went over and put her arms around Dad's belly. It was what she always did to make him calm down. It mostly worked. 'Come on, this is something we should be happy about. Our only daughter has the kind of opportunity we worked all our lives wishing we could give her. This is what she studied for.'

All of a sudden Max stood up, as if to give himself more authority, and put his hands on my shoulders. 'I'm with you, Dad – I'd rather the Big Merino.'

Dad tried to wriggle out of Mum's embrace. 'You know I can't think straight when you get that close to me, woman. Give a man a chance.'

That night Dad took us all to the Goulburn Workers Club for dinner. I felt sick the whole time, because it was where I had first met Adam.

As we queued at the bistro Dad ummed and ahhed about whether to have the schnitzel or the roast of the day.

'Sit down, Gray. You know you always have the lamb shanks.' Mum knew Dad better than he knew himself. 'Go grab table number forty-two, and, Max, you get the drinks.' My mum always had everyone organised and kept the family together.

'I think it would be good for you to go to New York, Lauren, to see the world, to meet new people, to move on from Goulburn and Canberra, at least for a little while.' That's all Mum said before she placed our orders and we settled into a night of keno and catching up with some friends who were also at the club.

It was karaoke night at the Workers, or what we liked to call Koori-oke night. Mum had a great voice so we both got up and sang 'New York, New York', laughing at Dad's reaction to our singing and the song. But everyone cheered us as we did the high kicks and I could see the pride on his face for his two Koori roses. I'd miss the fun we had at the Workers if I went to New York. I was starting to feel homesick even though I hadn't decided to go yet.

When Mum and Dad went to bed that night, Max and I sat in the lounge room watching telly. I had a favourite chunky olive green velvet chair I would just mould myself into.

'Mum and Dad haven't asked me any *personal* questions,' I said to Max as he flicked through a car magazine.

'They saw that jerk in the papers,' is all he said, without looking up.

'But they don't read *The Canberra Times*,' I said, confused.

'It was in the *Goulburn Post*.'

I gasped with shame.

'And not that it's any of my business,' Max said, looking straight at me, 'but I'd prefer it if you stayed away from the Canberra Cocksuckers altogether.' And that was the end of the conversation. Max rarely got involved in my personal business, but when he did, he was serious.

I didn't sleep at all, confusion only adding to my usual insomnia. I got up early and had breakfast with Dad.

'Come on, Dad, let's go to see Rambo.' That's what the locals had always called the Big Merino. We hadn't been much since it was moved closer to the highway. I had loved climbing up into Rambo's eyes when I was a kid, and did it nearly every weekend if I nagged Dad enough to swing by there. When I was little I didn't have a problem with small spaces. Now, as a grown woman, I felt much more enclosed, but it was a familiar space, a safe space. I wanted to climb into the eyes once more as Dad waited for me in the car park. He couldn't take the metal stairs anymore – he got puffed a lot easier these days. His days of climbing Rambo had ended years ago.

There wasn't a lot of room in there, it was 'cosy', as Adam had said when we pulled up at the massive structure one Sunday afternoon. He had wanted to shag in Rambo's eyeballs, but as they were shut to the public he was happy for a grope at the barrier to the stairs. I didn't feel comfortable at the thought of either and started feeling claustrophobic just thinking about being in Rambo's cosy eyeballs.

On the way back home in the car, Dad said, 'What about Nick? How are we going to tell him his sister is leaving the country?' He was worried about my older brother, who was serving time in Goulburn Correctional Facility for driving unlicensed and unregistered and then running into the back of a police vehicle at a set of traffic lights. Nick worked on a farm out of town and they never worried about a licence for the tractor. He'd never had lessons and shouldn't have been behind the wheel. I visited him once a month, wrote to him once a week and he always seemed okay. He promised Mum he was never going to drive again when he got out. Nick never mentioned that he couldn't get a licence now anyway. He was the tough one in the family. I was the spoilt girl and Max was the baby.

'Nick lives for your visits, even though they're not that often,' Dad said.

I felt a pang of guilt; he wasn't due for release until next year, and all I could do was hope that he would understand if I chose to go to New York.

'I'll make a special visit if I decide to go.'

Back at home Dad put my bag in the Ford Fiesta and with little sentimentality said, 'Do what you need to do, love. It's just I worry about you. That's my job as a father. And I can tell Nick if you want me to. Your mother said I shouldn't have made you feel bad about your brother. And you know, your mother is nearly always right.' He rolled his eyes.

'I know.' We hugged and I pulled out of the drive and headed towards Canberra with tears streaming down my face. I couldn't imagine what it might be like to have to say goodbye and leave. Just leaving Goulburn for Canberra was emotional enough.

8

Manhattan Dreaming

'Welcome to the Manhattan Movie Marathon,' Bec said as I walked in the door and collapsed on the lounge. Libby was there drinking coffee and scrolling on her phone.

'What are you on about?'

'Libby told me about the amazing offer to go to New York and we thought that some fabulous films might help you make up your mind. I've gone through Netflix and picked out all the best movies set in New York.' She turned on the TV and showed me the movies she'd added to our 'to watch' list. 'But I didn't think you'd want to see *The Godfather* and *Godzilla*.'

'You were right.' I thought of Dad.

'Now we just need to sit back and relax. I've cooked veggie lasagne for lunch, and Libs brought some of your favourite goodies from Divine and Delicious, so we're all set for the rest of the day.'

We started with the classic *An Affair to Remember*, first screened in 1957.

'This is one of my mum's favourites,' I told the girls. 'I think she likes the handsome playboy Nicky Ferrant and fancies herself as Terry McKay. They meet on a cruise from Europe to New York and have an affair, even though they're both engaged to other people. They decide to meet up the top of the Empire State Building six months later. It's such a romantic story.' I stopped myself as soon as I realised I was getting carried away.

'Spoiler alert!! But I agree, of course – stories about people cheating are always romantic, as we know,' Libby said sarcastically.

We watched the movie in virtual silence, munching on popcorn that Bec had microwaved. When Nicky and Terry planned their reunion it gave me an idea – I would go to New York and Adam would meet me at the top of the Empire State building – it would be far more romantic than shagging in Rambo's eyeballs, as long as I could keep the claustrophobia in check. Even *he* would have to appreciate that.

As the credits rolled, I lay back on the lounge and envisioned Adam waiting for me when I got out of the lift at the Empire State Building. He'd be looking hot in a suit – it was my fantasy so I could have him any way I liked – and a cashmere scarf, because I knew he couldn't make it until after the footy season was over, so it would be cold in New York. I'd walk towards him wearing a little black dress, black boots and a red coat – I'd always wanted a red coat – and we'd kiss without speaking and then just nuzzle into each other as we watched the sun set. There would be no-one else there to disturb us. It would be the perfect moment, and perhaps he would even propose.

Libby broke my private reverie. 'Hey, wake up. Ready for another movie?' she asked as she poked me.

'Yes, I was just resting my eyes. I'm good to go,' I said, with new interest in the movies and New York.

'I know you love *Breakfast at Tiffany's*, Lauren,' Bec said, queuing it up.

'It's more that I love Audrey Hepburn's style. I may have mastered accessorising my op shop numbers to look high class, but I still dream about wearing Chanel and Dior dresses and Cartier jewels.'

'And now you can dream about someone like Paul Varjak moving into your building and becoming fascinated by you – you're just like Holly Golightly – and sweeping you off your feet.'

'As if I'm like Holly Golightly! For a start, I'm way smarter than she is! And as if some hot, sexy writer would be interested in me.' I couldn't even keep a footballer interested lately.

'Why not? You're pretty, sexy and sophisticated,' Bec told me.

'And a naive neurotic just like Holly, too.' Libby was joking but there was truth in her words, at least when it came to Adam.

'Maybe if I went to New York I could learn some style

like Audrey,' I said, taking a bite of the chocolate cake and remembering the jewellery box at Kingston Markets.

'What are you talking about? You've got plenty of style! It's not what you wear but how you wear it. And, tidda, you'll be able to get all that designer stuff on sale there. We won't even be fashionable enough to hang out with you when you come back.' Libby shovelled some Moroccan date cake into her mouth, catching crumbs in her lap.

By the end of the film I didn't think I could consume any more cakes, or New York couture, culture or courtship.

'I'm ready to call it quits,' I said, yawning. 'I had a late one last night at the Goulburn Workers, if you can believe that!'

'I'm done too,' Libby said. 'I've got to get home and feed the cats, anyway.'

'What time should we resume the marathon in the morning, then?' Bec asked, picking our coffee mugs up from the floor. 'I'm thinking brunch with *Barefoot in the Park* at ten.' Libby and I nodded in agreement.

Next morning the wind howled outside and the sky was grey as we sat in our trackies, eating almond croissants that Libby had picked up from her favourite bakery, L'Orange Patisserie, and Bec made us all homemade mochas.

'This is the perfect Sunday morning. How could I leave this and go to New York? Do they even have mochas in New York?'

'Jesus, you really *are* a country bumpkin. They'll have a million coffee shops there and so many choices of coffee you won't know what to order,' Libby said, shaking her head.

We watched *Barefoot in the Park* and I was intrigued by Corie and Paul Bratter's adventures living in a tiny walk-up brownstone apartment. I wondered what Greenwich Village looked like decades later.

'I want to run barefoot in Washington Square Park too!' Libby said when the film was over, reaching for the last almond croissant. '*And* I want to live in a tiny walk-up brownstone apartment in Greenwich Village. *And* I want to go to the Comedy Cellar to see who the newest stand-up comics are too,' she added.

'You want a lot,' I accused her jokingly.

'Not really, I just want what you're being handed on a plate, Loz. So don't be wasting it.'

We watched the cheesy eighties hit *Ghostbusters* next. I took particular notice of the exorcism scenes in the New York Public Library.

'That's somewhere I'd really like to go, I mean, *if* I went to New York. The space looks so grand, like a sacred site for the literary. I wonder if they have any books on Aboriginal art in their collection. I would definitely suss that out.'

I noticed Libby fiddling with the remote.

'Now, this wasn't on the official bill for this afternoon's viewing, but before we move into the new millennium of films, I have one more eighties fave for us to watch,' she said, laughing. 'Tadaaaaah!' Paul Hogan's shiny pecs appeared onscreen.

Bec rolled her eyes and said, 'Oh God, *Crocodile Dundee*? You can't be serious.'

'Yes, yes, yes. I know we've all seen it but it's a classic – the stereotypical Aussie from the bush who hits the Big Apple. Sounds a little bit like our friend here, don't you think?' Libby laughed as she hit play.

'Excuse me, but I am nothing like Mick Dundee. I have far better fashion sense, and I may be a country bumpkin as you keep pointing out, but I'm *sure* I could work out how to use a bidet quicker than he does.' We all laughed.

We watched the movie, cringing as Dundee asked an African American limo driver his tribal background.

'Anyway, I don't have a big knife to keep the baddies away.'

'I could probably rustle up a red thong cozzie to scare away almost anyone, good or bad,' Bec said.

The last film the girls had chosen to assist my decision-making was the first *Sex and the City* movie. Libby concluded I was the most conservative, so I was Charlotte. She was Carrie because she had the most pairs of shoes, and as Bec was a party girl but also most likely to settle down first and have kids, she was a mix of Miranda *and* Samantha. We watched the film with only a platter of fruit to nibble on, to make up for all the cakes and chocolate we had scoffed.

The movie made me laugh *and* cry, especially the stood-up-at-the-altar wedding scene, a moment of absolute heartbreak and humiliation for Carrie. Perhaps New York would *not* be the place for Adam and me to reunite.

I could feel Carrie's pain and wanted to hit Big *and* Adam with more than the wedding bouquet.

'Earth to Loz!' Libby said, clicking her fingers in front of my eyes as she picked my mug up off the ground. 'You all right?'

'Yeah, just dreaming.'

'Manhattan Dreaming?'

'Yeah, Manhattan Dreaming.'

'I don't blame you, tidda, it's such a wild thought, you going to NYC.' Libby held out my cup, asking if I wanted another. 'Your Dreaming is present and future, not just the past, and the Ancestors will take care of you over there too.'

'You sure?'

'Of course, they'll take you from your Wiradyuri country, right over the ocean to another land. And my theory is we're the First Peoples of the planet, so no matter where we are, we'll be taken care of, sis. Even in Manhattan.'

'I like the way you think.'

'See if the Ancestors can help you with some men too, Lauren, because it certainly looks like New York is the city for dating – the theatre, all those classy bars and restaurants,' Bec said. 'You don't have to fall in love, though – dating is different over there. My sister Georgie lived in Brooklyn for a year and said a date can be just going to a sporting event, or whatever. You can even have three dates in a night if you want: a drink, then a show and then maybe a coffee. Three men, three dates, zero commitment – sounds good to me. No heartache necessary. I'd move to New York just for that.'

'You make it sound like all the men in New York are wonderful,' Libby said cynically.

'No, there are bastards everywhere, it's just the dating culture in New York is different to here, where, in fact, there is NO dating culture. You know what it's like here – people are either married, or single, or they just hook up when they go out. Do you know anyone who actually *dates*?'

'I don't,' I said.

'At least sporting dates in New York would be more interesting than here – they have ice-hockey and baseball,' Libby said.

'You think ice-hockey is interesting? It's just men with sticks hitting a rubber disc.' I wasn't a fan of any form of hockey.

'It's a puck,' Libby said, disgusted by my lack of knowledge. She knew much more about sports than I did – unless it came to rugby league, of course.

Bec entered the debate. 'Ice-hockey, no way, they'd have to be nude to make that interesting. Now baseball – that's a game to watch; men in tights with big round bums. Yeah, Yankee Stadium – you *have* to go there, Lauren. There'll be plenty of male action.'

I smiled at Bec, and to lighten the mood, I said, 'Mental note to self: tights, round bums, Yankee Stadium. Got it!'

Maybe New York would be the place for me after all.

With the movie marathon over, Libby went home to her cats in Ainslie, Bec went to visit her parents, and without a second thought I went to tell Adam I was going to New York, even though I hadn't really made up my mind. I needed to see his reaction, find out how he felt about me moving to the other side of the world. I felt like a child sneaking out of the house when I'd been grounded, because both Bec and Libby would be disappointed in me. But what if losing me, perhaps forever – because twelve months could become twenty-four months, could become thirty-six months or even more – would make Adam want to settle down?

I pulled up at his house slowly, creeping along the dark, tree-lined street, peering hard through my glasses to see if there were any cars outside his place aside from his own Range Rover. The lights were on in the living room, so I guessed he was probably watching the replay of the match from yesterday. He often did that; he said it helped improve his game. Libby reckoned he just liked looking at himself run the length of the field, and loved hearing the commentators rave about him. She was probably right, but who doesn't like to be praised for something when we do it well?

I got out of the car, took a deep breath and walked to the front door, trying to see through the frosted glass for any movement, particularly any female movement. There was none, so I pressed the doorbell. Adam answered the door holding a couch cushion in front of him, naked. He didn't open the door fully until he realised it was me, but then he dropped the cushion, pulling me into the house and embracing me immediately. He squeezed me so tight my glasses almost popped off my head.

'I've missed you so much, babycakes. It's so good to see you.' He started kissing my neck and running his hands down my body, trying to get me out of my jeans.

'Wait,' I said reluctantly.

'What is it? Haven't you missed me too?'

'You know I have.' I closed my eyes and allowed myself the momentary pleasure of him nibbling my ear, but then pried him off me as my glasses started to fog up.

'What is it, babycakes?'

'I didn't come here for this.'

'Why did you come here then?' He spoke gently.

'I'm moving to New York,' I said. 'Next month. I've got a great job offer. They'll fly me over, help me find a place and I'll be curating my own exhibitions. It's a dream opportunity.'

'Wow.' He rubbed his head. 'This is out of the blue.'

'Not really. If you'd called me sometime, you'd know.'

'You broke it off with me, babycakes. You ended it, remember?'

'You were splashed all over the media fornicating with triplets on the Gold Coast,' I yelled, because it still infuriated me.

'You can't believe everything you read in the press, babycakes, I told you that already.'

'So, you weren't with triplets?'

'Not technically, no.'

'What the hell does that mean?'

'They were twins and just another girl who looked a lot like them. That's all.'

I shook my head in disgust and knew I should've walked out, but I wanted to give him one last chance.

'I'm going to New York – the dating capital of the world.' I wanted him to get jealous. 'People go on dates there – to classy bars, and restaurants and the theatre.'

'Classy bars and theatre, not really my cup of tea, but I'm sure you'll love it.'

My plan wasn't working.

'I just want to be clear about something. You don't mind if I go, then, to New York? All the way over there in America? It's like a twenty-three-hour plane ride away. That's a lot further than from Manuka to Bruce.'

'Do I mind? Why would I mind? It's a great opportunity for you – you should go and have a good time. I would if it was me.'

'You would?' I glared at him angrily.

'Of course, it's New York. It's a 24/7 party town.'

'But wouldn't you miss anything here? Or *anyone*?'

'There's nothing in Canberra I would miss enough to turn down a trip to New York.'

At that very moment I hated Adam, and I hated myself for being so stupid.

9

Start spreading the news, I'm leaving today . . .

'I'm going to New York,' I declared, walking into the office.

'YES!' Libby nearly flew across the room and hugged me so tight her enthusiasm made me laugh. 'What? I'm excited for you. And for me.' I saw a cheeky look in her eye.

'How does that work? You're not getting my job while I'm away, if that was your sly plan.'

'Hell, I don't want your job, but I do want to visit you in New York, and *that,* my dear tidda, *was* part of my plan. I'm going to take some leave and I'll meet you there for New Year's!! And we're going to shop and go to bars and the theatre and shop and go up the Statue of Liberty, and the Empire State Building, and shop some more.'

'Wow, you've been thinking about this more than I have!'

'One of us had to be excited about all the opportunities

coming your way.' And she pulled a Lonely Planet guide out from her handbag and handed it to me.

'I got this on the way home yesterday. I knew that after the films there was no way you could stay here and not go explore the Big Apple.'

When I told Emma she was so happy that I agreed to go she punched the air like a gold medallist Olympic swimmer. Everyone else's excitement was starting to infect me, but I only had two weeks to prepare. I got on every website possible trying to learn about New York – some facts and figures, the layout of the city.

I read and re-read the National Museum of the American Indian website – otherwise known as the NMAI – and googled galleries in New York, looking for the ones that showed Native American art. I didn't even own a decent set of luggage so I went shopping for that and other bits and pieces I'd need.

HR arranged to get my passport processed quickly and sorted out my accommodation for the first week I was there. I started communicating with Maria, my new boss at the NMAI, by email. It was all systems go and I was glad, as it gave me less time to think about Adam. In fact, I was too busy to think about him during the day at all.

Emma said she would also line up meetings for me with other key Native American organisations while I was there so the NAG could establish relationships outside the art sector as well.

'Wow, you're making me feel very important,' I said to Emma, feeling proud.

'You're a VIIP – a Very Important Indigenous Person.'

Joel from security emailed me to say his cousin Kirsten was working at the United Nations in New York and was always glad when Blackfellas were in town. He gave me her email address, so I dropped her a line and told her what I was doing.

Kirsten had a room to let in Chelsea. She had just advertised, but if I wanted it, it was mine. She sent me some photos and it looked great. The area was home to hundreds of galleries, so I'd be right in the arty district. It was on a subway line, too, so it was convenient. I could walk to Macy's and Madison Square Garden, and you could see the Empire State Building from the bathroom. It was meant to be.

I emailed back immediately, telling her I'd love to move it, that it sounded perfect.

Kirsten and I agreed to meet at the NAIDOC event at the UN the week I arrived, and I'd move in the following weekend.

'I'm so happy all my accommodation is sorted out – I was getting a bit stressed about it,' I told Mum down the phone.

'And how wonderful you're moving in with another Koori. I mean, what was the chance of that happening?' Mum echoed my thoughts. New York was a massive city. I was lucky to connect with Kirsten, but that was the Blackfella way, looking after each other, especially when there's only a few of you.

'I know your father will be relieved, that's for sure.'

My last day at the NAG arrived too quickly. I couldn't believe how fast I'd tidied up loose ends, packed most of my personal belongings in the Manuka flat and organised my gear for America.

As I wasn't actually leaving the gallery completely, I insisted on a low-key farewell, so Emma, Libby and I just went for lunch together.

After lunch Emma handed me a box. 'It's not really a farewell gift – after all, you have to bring it back. I convinced the purchasing officer to order something practical but at least a little arty.'

I admired the stylish wrapping of gold paper and red and black bow and then tore it all off. 'Oh my god, it's great.' It was the newest, sleekest, fastest laptop around. And it was pink! 'Mine has just about worn itself out.' The wear and tear, no doubt, from my endless Insta scrolling.

'This is from me,' Libby said, and handed me another box that was much lighter. Inside were a pair of beautiful leather gloves. Before I had the time to tear up, Amy was at the table with sparklers blazing on the biggest pavlova I'd ever seen.

'What? How did you know? This is my favourite dessert here.'

'Yes, all the kitchen staff are aware of that. We've gotta get extra passionfruit when we know you're coming in.'

'You do realise I can probably eat all of this myself,' I said to Amy.

'Yes, we know that too. We just wanted to wish you well.' I looked past her to see the kitchen hands hanging out the kitchen door blowing kisses. I blew one back. I was a very good customer.

Before I left the building completely, I went to the sculpture garden one last time and just stood still, admiring the community mural on the western wall. It carried the handiwork and stories of Kooris from right across Canberra, expressing their ownership of the space. I smiled, knowing I was helping to develop the cultural heart of the nation's capital. Since we were the national space promoting Aboriginal art and culture to the world, I knew that my work helped artists from right across the country. The adrenaline started to pump through me at the thought of being able to develop more international links for our artists as well.

Libby and Bec had planned my one last hurrah in Canberra before I headed back to Goulburn and left for the US. We had dinner at Sammy's, my favourite restaurant in Canberra.

'Thank you for booking this for me – I'm going to miss this place,' I said through a mouthful of san choy bow.

'New York has an entire China Town – you won't miss anything,' Libby said.

'I bet they don't have rock salt squid like this, though, and pass me that san dong chicken, please.'

'Drink up.' Bec refilled her wineglass.

'Yes, drink up,' I said, holding my glass of water up to say cheers.

We spent the next hour eating and chatting until the serving dishes were all empty.

'I'm so full,' I said, pushing my bowl as far away from me as possible.

'Now, we drink cocktails.' Libby could eat and drink like no-one else I knew.

'You can but I really have to have an early night. I have to finish packing tomorrow.'

'Packing schmacking, we're having cocktails – and no mocktails tonight, Loz, we're not going to see you for a year. Come.' Bec dragged me to a groovy bar, Molly, that many talked about but could rarely find. On the way, we passed a firetruck at the end of a job, and Libby pulled her phone out and started taking pics.

'I'm on fire,' she said sleazily, sidling up to one of the men.

'Scrubba dub dub, three firemen in a tub,' Bec added.

I grabbed each by the hand and pulled them back on the footpath. 'Oh, you girls really *are* on fire, aren't you? I'm glad I'm going to New York, you're both bad news.'

Inside Molly, and several drinks later, I was so tired and drunk I could've made my bed on the bar there and then.

'Who can manage to drink one more Cosmo?' Libby asked.

'I CANNOT drink another cocktail. Actually, I can't drink anything at all. You know I'm not a drinker. Please, I want to lie down.'

'You drink or we go to Mooseheads.' Bec was surprisingly chipper, and I wondered if we were all drinking the same amount.

'No-one's going to Gooseheads. It's dodgy and full of bogans,' Libby said sternly.

'You're a boganist,' Bec told her.

'Yes, I am. Let's just go back to Manuka, have a cocktail at Public.'

Back at the upstairs bar in Public, Bec and Libby ordered strawgasms and I had a peppermint tea. Depression was setting in. I wouldn't be saying goodbye to Adam properly before I left. I could feel tears welling, so I took my glasses off and rubbed my eyes as if I were just tired. I didn't really want to leave the country having not made peace, but I had no choice.

'What's wrong with you?' Libby slurred. 'You need a strawgasm, let me buy you a strawgasm, please.'

'No, I can't, really. And stop saying strawgasm.' I laughed.

'It's a going-away present. Waiter, I need a moregasm . . . strawgasm please, for my sad, bad, mad friend here. She's going to New York New York and leaving me alone here on this barstool.' The waiter looked at me and I shook my head and mouthed the words: '*No more drinks for her.*' He smiled and winked back.

'Why don't I bring you a special drink on the house, with more straw than gasm.'

'Oh make it more gasm than straw,' she slurred.

The waiter walked off and Libby's eyes followed him.

'I'm scared, Libs.'

'Why, tidda? What you scared for?'

'It's New York City, there's like fifty million people there.'

'There's just under nine million, across the five boroughs,' Bec corrected me.

'Well that's twenty-two times more than Canberra and hell knows how many more than Goulburn.'

'Ah, but it's a bigger place, so more room for all those Yankee Doodle Dandies.'

'It's just I've got five days before I move into the apartment after I arrive, and I don't want to bother Kirsten before then either. She seems like she's got heaps on her plate as it is.'

'I'm sure Kirsten will be thrilled to have another Blackfella in the city with her. Maybe she's been lonely the last couple of years? I reckon you should call her as soon as you arrive.'

Libby was practical, even when she'd had too many drinks. 'And,' she said, rummaging through her huge tote, 'I'm going to help you work out a schedule of things to do until you start work, so you can get a feel for the city and the subway.'

'What? Not now, it's two in the morning. Let's do it tomorrow.' I was ready to leave.

'You're right, too late for scheduling meetings. Waiter!' Libby clicked her fingers and the waiter came over. 'I need a multiple strawgasm, please, with extra strawberries and double gasms, pretty please.' The waiter looked at me for approval. I nodded and mouthed, '*Half everything.*'

'Are you flirting with that waiter? If I didn't know better I'd say you're into him,' Bec said to Libby.

'Don't be ridiculous. I'm on a man-fast, forever!'

'Me too, then!' I said.

'Me three!' Bec raised her glass.

'You girls are mental. It's seven-thirty, why aren't you in bed? And why am I the only one who ever gets a hangover?'

'Sit, drink mocha, listen,' Bec ordered.

The kitchen table was covered with maps of New York City and tour books and butcher's paper covered with what looked like lists being created.

'*I'm* working out which touristy sites are where, so we can narrow down sections of the city you can do a day at a time.' Bec put a mug in front of me.

'And *I'm* working out the main sites you have to see before you start work, and what you *have to* leave until *I* arrive,' Libby said.

'Okay, where are you up to then?' I was intrigued and impressed.

'I'll be there in winter, so we'll skate in Central Park. I want to go to Ellis Island and of course the Statue of Liberty. We need to do Macy's and 5th Avenue, naturally—'

'Naturally,' Bec and I echoed.

'We can walk from Bergdorf Goodman to Tiffany's, Brooks Brothers, Givenchy, Cartier and then do Saks.' Libby was so excited anyone would have thought *she* was moving to New York.

'Have you been given a massive pay rise that I don't know about, Libs? Because there's no way we're ever going to be able to afford to shop in those places.'

'I know that, but what a novelty, two Kooris strolling from Central Park along 5th Avenue. It will just be fun. It's free to dream. And there's also Saks off 5th for designer bargains.'

'Thank god for that, because otherwise we'd be running up some serious dream debt here.'

Libby was treating the exercise like work, flicking through a travel guide and making notes at the same time. Without looking up she said, 'I'll get online soon and look at what's showing on Broadway, because let's face it, the Canberra Theatre is never going to do *Hamilton* like Broadway will.'

'I am sooooo jealous, you guys. My teacher's wage won't get me to New York, not this year anyway.'

'Sorry, love, but as I was saying. . .' Libby laughed. 'I want to go on the carousel in Central Park because I really am a kid at heart, and love the nostalgia of it. But if you want to do it with some gorgeous Yankee before I get there, that's cool, you can do it again with me.'

'I'll be back before I have time to do all that.'

'Oh, I forgot!' Libby nearly jumped out of her seat.

'What?' Bec and I echoed again.

'We HAVE to do the Empire State Building. I'll be looking for the ghosts of Cary Grant and Tom Hanks for sure.'

'Oh, it could be a bit crowded with all those ghosts, don't you reckon?' I tried to make light of it, but I couldn't tell Libby that she wasn't part of my plan for the Empire State Building. I sat back and watched the girls comparing lists and maps and started to feel sad again.

'Brooklyn she should probably do with a local. We should just focus on Manhattan at this stage, okay?' Libby was advising Bec and I was just an observer.

'I need to go finish packing.' I walked out of the kitchen and left the girls to it. In my room I had a pile of clothes for Vinnie's, a bag of clothes for my cousin Terri, half-a-dozen odd socks, a box of recycling and another box ready for the bin. My room was a mess. I opened another drawer and found three cards from Adam: one for my birthday, one for Christmas and one postcard from when he went to Hawaii for a holiday. I sat on my bed and felt a hot rush of disappointment and emotion. I couldn't bring myself to put them in the recycle box, so I slipped them inside the book beside my bed.

Bec suggested I sublet my room for twelve months so all I had to clear out were my clothes and knick-knacks. On the day I left I was emotional about leaving my beautiful Manuka home and my mate behind. But Bec was so full of excitement for me it was impossible to be sad. She helped put almost everything in my little Fiesta and what didn't fit we piled into Libby's car. 'Don't be a stranger around here, Libs.' Bec hugged Libby.

'Are you kidding? Now Miss Goody Two-shoes is going, we can get into some serious partying.' Libby smiled and winked at Bec so that I could see.

'All right, it's not like I expected you to stop hanging out because I wasn't here, but can you at least pretend you're going to miss me? Please!' I tried hard not to cry as Bec hugged me. Libby revved her car loudly.

'I better go. I'll text you as soon as I land.'

Libby followed me back to Goulburn and stayed with me at Mum and Dad's overnight, insisting on coming to the airport to say goodbye the next day.

'Why would you even bother coming all the way to Sydney to see me off ? It's really not necessary.'

'To make sure you get on the bloody plane, that's why.'

Dad took us all to the Paragon for dinner; it was where we always went on special occasions – birthdays, anniversaries, new jobs, leaving jobs, family reunions – but mostly I went there on Sunday afternoon for cake and coffee. It was our traditional place, just like it was for many Goulburnians.

Libby and Max had a great time talking about me going away.

'Yeah, I get to do burnouts in the little blue Fiesta for the next twelve months. The fellas in the footy club will probably flog me for driving such a woosy car, though.'

I interrupted. 'You have a problem with the Fiesta, do you? And what are you driving right now, oh brother of mine.'

Dad laughed a big belly laugh trying to get the words out. 'He's driving your Mum's Rio when she's not using it.' And then he got serious. 'Or *I* have to drive him everywhere.'

'I rest my case.' I was glad that Dad was holding his tongue about me going away. I knew he still felt the same, but Mum must've warned him to keep the peace.

We filled up on huge meals, which included the chips that came with almost every dish on the menu. I would miss the Paragon: Dad with his standard mixed-grill, Mum with her after-dinner Jamaican coffee, me and my Mars Bar cheesecake. The restaurant had been refurbished over the years but I remember the pendant lighting, brown vinyl chairs and laminated tables of the past; they were part of my family history, my life in Goulburn, just as much as Rambo was.

Max left the table without excusing himself and walked out of the restaurant, but before I had a chance to say anything, locals were coming up to us and saying hello, wishing me well – they'd read something in the *Goulburn Post* about my fellowship in the US. Dad seemed suddenly proud of his daughter heading off to the Big Apple he had once loathed.

Max came back into the restaurant with a huge box. Inside were a whole lot of gifts Mum had picked up at the Big Merino: Billie Goat Soap, Ugg boots, a chocolate brown merino mink hat with matching gloves, and a gorgeous wool scarf.

'I love the scarf, Mum – it's really stylish and good quality.'

'And it's fire resistant,' Max said. 'I read about it at the shop.'

'Good, don't want to catch on fire,' I said, smiling at Libby, knowing she'd be thinking of firemen immediately.

'And it's natural, biodegradable and sustainable, just like you, my sista.' Max was a kind brother when he wasn't being a joker.

'Ahah! You *are* going to miss me.'

'What else is in the box, Mum?' Max tried to change the subject.

I pulled out a stuffed toy Merino sheep that baaaa-ed when pushed in the stomach.

'That's from Nick,' Mum said. 'He wanted to give you something fun as a reminder of home and of him.'

I swallowed a lump of regret that I wouldn't be seeing him for a year.

'And this one is from me.' There was no box, or wrapping, just a card that Max handed me to open.

'Why are you giving me . . . a QR code?' Everyone started to laugh.

'Seriously, sis, you really needed to update your tunes, so I put some of the latest deadly Blackfella music on a Spotify playlist so you won't get too homesick, eh?'

'I think that will make me even more homesick.'

'See, men just can't win,' Dad said to Max.

'Yeah, not even brothers!'

I took out my phone and used the QR code to pull up the playlist. I scrolled through the albums he had saved: Thelma Plum, Emma Donovan, Emily Wurramara, Baker Boy, Briggs, Rochelle Watson, Electrical Fields, Spinifex Gum, and the now defunct (but my all-time fave) band, Tiddas. There were a few hip hop bands I'd heard of as well.

'This is too deadly, dear brother, but you know I don't do hip hop.'

'And you wonder why we don't hang out, sis.'

'Come here.' I grabbed him and gave him a huge hug but he resisted as best he could. He was his father's son.

We all got up early in the morning to head to Sydney. Dad was standing at the kitchen sink drinking a cup of coffee and I went and hugged him. He gave me an envelope and said, 'Mum said to buy yourself something from Marcie's.' I knew he meant Macy's.

'You don't have to do this, Dad.' I got teary.

'C'mon now, you can't be crying today, your mum won't cope.' We both knew it was him who wouldn't cope.

'And you might want to buy something from Marcie's for your mum too, or else she's gonna be on my back about going to New York, and there ain't no way I'm flying to America. No way.'

'I'll get something from Marcie's for Mum, no worries.'

I could've taken a domestic flight to Sydney and then boarded the international flight to New York, but I wanted to do the road trip with Mum and Dad, to see the countryside before I left. They were going to Aunty Sonia's after they dropped me off and Libby was going to check out the latest exhibition at the Yiribana Gallery before they'd all drive back later that afternoon.

Kooris'll drive three hours for a cuppa, Mum always said.

As we drove slowly along Auburn Street, I took in my last view of the gazebo in Belmore Park and saw a couple having their wedding photos done. I swung my head from one side of the car to the other looking at the shops and wondering what new businesses would pop up while I was away. I made Dad cruise past the Regional Art Gallery and I could feel homesickness setting in already.

Inside the international terminal at Mascot Airport, Dad manoeuvred the trolley with my two big red cases, strategically piled on top of each other, while I carried my laptop and Libby took my carry-on suitcase. The air buzzed with emotion as families, friends and colleagues prepared for pending departures and sad farewells. Dad was jittery, Mum was flapping about, running through a checklist of things I should have in my hand-luggage – clean underwear, toiletries and so on – and Libby had her arm linked in mine as we walked. We all stopped at the area leading into customs. It was time to say goodbye.

'Now don't be ringing us reverse charges all the time, okay?' Dad joked.

'Don't listen to your father, we can Zoom whenever you like,' Mum countered.

'And don't talk to strange men.'

'Yes, Dad.'

'In fact, don't talk to anyone. And buy some of that mace stuff to spray in their faces, but don't get any in your own.'

'Yes, Dad.'

'And don't take a drink from a stranger. I've seen those shows – the men over there spike drinks and then take advantage of innocent girls.'

'Mum, can you stop him, please?'

'Gray, stop it. The girl's in a state as it is.'

'Tidda, you better go, you gotta get through customs.'

Thank god Libby was there being practical, else I'd never have left. I missed her already. I started to cry the minute she hugged me. Mum hugged me next, and by the time I got to Dad I was a blubbering mess. He couldn't handle it.

'Stop crying, won't it ruin that stuff you put on your eyelashes, macasa?'

'Mascara,' I laughed through my tears. 'And no, it's waterproof.'

I hugged Mum and Dad again, at the same time. We all cried some more. I almost changed my mind with the sadness of it all. How would I cope without them?

'I love you,' I sobbed, and as I wiped my face with my hands, Dad pulled a hanky from his pocket and handed it to me. How would I last in New York when I couldn't even find myself a tissue?

'I better go,' I said, pulling away reluctantly. 'I'll call you when I land.'

Mum, Dad and Libby stood there waving me off. As I walked through the glass doors into the customs area I felt sick, but it was too late to turn around.

10

From the Big Merino to the Big Apple

I had a thousand butterflies in my stomach as I boarded the Qantas plane. I'd never been overseas before, only Canberra to Sydney or Melbourne or Brisbane and the occasional remote community. They were mostly short flights, and I was nearly always with someone else – Libby or Emma or one of our artists – for gallery meetings. I'd never seen the inside of a 787 Dreamliner before, and wondered how something so big could stay for so long in the air. But I was on the plane named after the world renowned artist, the late Emily Kame Kngwarreye, and I took that as a good omen,

I sat in row 56 between an elderly woman clutching her bible and a chubby man who smelled like cigarettes. Within minutes I could feel beads of sweat form on my brow and it was difficult to breathe properly. I felt closed in and agitated.

'Are you okay, love?' the man next to me asked.

'I can't breathe properly – I don't know what's wrong.' I started to pant.

'I think you might be claustrophobic.' He pushed the flight attendant button and a woman with flame-red hair and a big smile arrived quickly.

'Is everything all right?' She looked at the man and then at me.

'She can't breathe properly. I think she might be a bit claustrophobic.'

'I'm sorry, I've never flown a long distance before. I'm just a bit nervous.' I felt like I was going to throw up.

'Don't be sorry – just give me one minute.'

'I'm sorry,' I said to the man and woman next to me. I was embarrassed and didn't want any more attention drawn to me.

The flight attendant was back within minutes.

'I'm going to move you to an exit row. There's more space, and a spare seat between you and the next passenger.' She grabbed my laptop and my carry-on case from the overhead locker, and I crawled out of my seat mumbling an apology.

'This happens a lot, Miss Lucas. Don't be embarrassed. Next time when you check in be sure and tell them that you're an anxious flyer, then we can look after you properly, okay?'

In my new seat I breathed deeply and closed my eyes. I had a million things going through my mind. I still felt sniffly from all the crying I'd done at the airport and my heart was breaking at leaving Adam behind. I hadn't even had time to call or send a text before I left. It didn't feel right, I didn't feel right.

The captain's voice came back over the loudspeaker. 'While we are refuelling please do NOT have your seatbelts fastened. I repeat, do not have your seatbelts fastened while we are refuelling the plane.' I looked around me to see if anyone else was confused by this announcement. What did refuelling the plane have to do with not having seatbelts on? I convinced myself it was because if there was an emergency with the refuelling we would have to escape quickly and seatbelts would just slow everyone down. What other reason could there be? I wanted to ask someone to tell me why, because I felt more and more nervous, but no-one else seemed worried so I just let it go and shut my eyes. I felt a hot tear streak down my left cheek and I didn't even bother to wipe it away. *Tears are the best water for your face*, my mum used to tell me when I cried.

It seemed like forever before we took off and I was silently praying that there were no holes in the plane and that we got safely to Los Angeles. I started to think about Adam, trying to focus on pleasant memories, and that calmed me down. I soon dozed off, waking as the meals were being served, and I found that I was starving. I never liked airline food, and having such a sweet tooth and eating the best pastries in Canberra, airline desserts could never measure up for me. For the first time ever, I had a little bottle of wine with my dinner, and toasted myself for being brave enough to go to New York.

When all the post-dinner queues for the bathrooms were gone I finally stood up and stretched. I was concerned about DVT, and hadn't really done enough of the seated exercises. I wanted to do a lap of the plane and was glad the hotel I was staying in had a gym so I could get on a treadmill as soon as possible after I arrived.

The smell of the airline toilet nearly made me sick, the disinfectant was so strong. I hated public toilets at the best of times, but on a plane with no ventilation it was a nightmare, and I cursed the grubby man before me who'd left the seat up. I got the desperate urge to wash my hands and I pushed the soap dispenser so hard it came right off its wall hinges and fell straight into the garbage unit below.

As I rummaged in the bin, fishing for the soap dispenser, I was glad Libby wasn't with me. I knew she'd be thinking I was a country bumpkin who couldn't even survive the bathroom on a plane. There was a knock on the door.

'Everything okay in there?' It sounded like the flight attendant who'd helped me before. I washed and dried my hands and walked out.

'All okay, thank you.'

For a while I sat and tried to watch a movie. I was so tired from all the lead-up to the trip that I really had to sleep, but there was a baby that just wouldn't stop crying. Libby used to freak out when we flew if a baby was crying. *If I wanted to listen to a screaming baby I would have one myself!* she would say, loud enough to embarrass the parents and me at the same time. *Babies cry*, I would tell her. Libby reckoned she was going to write to Richard Branson and ask him to start up a 'no-children' airline.

I tried to read the in-flight magazine, but I was too antsy to sit still and concentrate, so I pulled out my phone and listened to all the new music Max had put on Spotify for me. The sounds of Blackfellas singing about culture, land, history, relationships, politics and the future soothed me. The songs carried me to my dreaming tracks back home, and I knew they would carry me safely to America, just like Libby had said.

I was relieved to finally arrive in New York. It was good to have my feet on the ground after spending too many hours in the sky. As I walked out of the customs area at JFK I struggled with my trolley, which was piled high with two big red suitcases, my matching carry-on suitcase, my laptop and my handbag. It had been so much easier back in Sydney with extra hands.

I was weary from the flight, and anxious at the same time about being alone. I was on the verge of tears again but sighed with relief when I saw a black-suited man holding a sign with my name on it. Emma had organised a car to meet me. I didn't feel like a VIIP, more like a rock star as the black town car pulled out of Terminal 7 and drove to my hotel. I liked sitting in the back of the huge car with its tinted windows and air-conditioning that blocked out the stifling summer day.

'Are you in the movies, ma'am?' the driver asked me as he peered in his rear-view mirror.

I laughed. 'Oh no, far from it.'

'You look like a movie star.'

I was wearing black pants and a sleeveless black top with big black-framed sunglasses Libby had made me buy. I felt like a big blowfly.

'I think it's just the big glasses, they kind of make anyone look that way. I'm just a girl from the country really.'

'Are you from South Africa?'

'No, Australia.'

'Oh, you're an Ossie. I've seen *Crocodile Dundee*.'

'Yes, I've heard it was big here back in the day.'

'You've got a lot of luggage, like a movie star.'

'I'm going to be here for a while, so I brought as much as I could carry.'

'So, your husband is here?'

I felt sad at that question. 'No, I don't have a husband.'

'Don't men marry beautiful women in your country?'

'Apparently not.' I liked the cheeky driver.

'Surely not *every* Ossie man is intimidated by a beautiful woman.'

'Apparently they are.' I was getting embarrassed by the compliments, but assumed it was standard repartee between drivers and passengers. After all, Libby had told me that everyone in the US is sugary sweet because they're working for tips.

'Actually, I'm going to work at the National Museum of the American Indian.'

'Yeah, there used to be Indians here, but they're all gone now.'

'Really? There's plenty on staff at the Smithsonian.'

The conversation seemed to die down at that point and I took the opportunity to check my phone for messages. The first was from Libby, saying:

> Hope you arrived safely! Miss you already. Have fun, and let's Zoom when you can xx

There was a message from Emma, too:

> Car will be at airport. Email me when you've settled. I'll call you next week. Have fun.

And one from Max:

> Mum said to Zoom us when you arrive. She's told Dad it's cheaper than reverse charges, lol. Burnouts are fun! Luv ya 😃

There was nothing from Adam even though I'd emailed him my itinerary before I left. Maybe he hadn't got my email. I looked at my phone and contemplated lurking his Instagram, but realised I couldn't. I hadn't got a new simcard yet, so my phone was useless without wi-fi.

I peered out the window and looked in awe at the size of the city, the amount of traffic and all the yellow taxis. The yellow cabs alone gave New York more colour than anything ever could in Canberra, except maybe Floriade in Spring. I could feel the adrenaline rush begin. It finally hit me: I was in New York, New York.

As I got out of the car at the Millennium Hilton UN Plaza Hotel, the sun hit my face. It was like a heat wave compared to the frosty Canberra weather I'd just left behind. I felt colour come back into my cheeks almost immediately.

'Hello, how are you?' The valet greeted me as though we were old friends.

'I'm good, thank you, how are you?' I thought perhaps that's how they greeted all their guests.

'I'm wonderful, thank you. It's good to see you again, welcome back.'

'Oh, you must have me confused with someone else. This is my first time here.'

'Really? You look just like a woman who comes here often from England.'

'Sorry, but it's not me.'

'Don't be sorry, she's beautiful too. It's a compliment that you look like her.'

'Well, thank you for the compliment then.' I giggled like a young girl. A movie star from England, that's who I looked like. I was already having fun.

As I stood in the lobby waiting to check in, I was conscious of the energy in the air. I saw people from around the globe in sarongs and saris, burkas and business suits, all speaking dozens of different languages. They were in huddles planning their day, greeting each other, saying goodbyes.

Some carried laptops, others folders and clipboards, one had a guide dog, and a couple had impressive-looking cameras. For work or pleasure, in the people I'd seen New York so far all looked like tourists on holidays.

Libby said I should've stayed Downtown or near Central Park or somewhere more touristy, but Emma wanted me in the same hotel as the artist showing at the UN, just in case he needed something, and so we could talk about a potential exhibition at the NAG in 2025. Tony Anum was from Kununurra and doing linocut designs that were already gaining popularity on the international scene. Logistically, it was easier to have me travel to New York earlier than try to get me up to the East Kimberley for a meeting before I left. We'd spoken briefly before I'd left Australia, but we'd never met.

I looked at the growing number of people entering the hotel and wondered what everyone else was doing there. Were they diplomats or consular guests or UN members? I felt like I was among some very important people, some *real* VIPs.

The longer I stood in reception and saw the smorgasbord of cultures represented, the more I got excited about meeting new people in New York. Canberra seemed like an entire planet away, not just half a world.

My junior suite on the twenty-eighth floor was furnished with sleek modern pieces in a light-coloured wood. There was a small round glass-top coffee table and bright scatter cushions that would look perfect in the apartment back in Manuka. I walked straight to the full-length windows and gasped at the spectacular views of the East River. I couldn't wait for it to get dark so I could see all the lights of the city, and I knew I would never shut the curtains.

In a hurry to unpack, I put my passport and jewellery in the safe, showered and put on a blue flowery summer dress. Back home I'd call it a frock but Libs would always say I sounded like one of the old aunties. I grabbed my Lonely Planet guide and my map, and the lists Libby and Bec had drawn up for me. I put the 'Lauren's Everyday Reminder List' in my purse so I would always have it with me. It read:

- Get photo of firemen for Libby whenever / wherever possible. Send updates on dating opportunities regularly to Bec.
- Seek out perfume / make-up bargains.
- Look for potential art projects / partnerships. Stay away from footballers of any description.

And then I looked at my 'Lauren's New York To Do List – Day 1':

- Go to Grand Central Station and get a MetroCard.
- Have a bagel with cream cheese – this is VERY New York.
- Go to Duane Reade or Rite Aid for 'Tylenol PM' to help you sleep.
- Get a US sim card – send Libby, Emma, Bec and your family new phone details.
- Don't talk to strangers unless they are firemen.

Around 1 pm I went down to the lobby and must've looked confused, as the concierge came out from behind his high counter and directly towards me.

'Are you okay, ma'am?' It felt weird being called 'ma'am'. I looked at his name badge.

'Hi Bob, I'm Lauren,' I extended my hand. 'I want to go for a walk, here's my list.' And I showed him the page.

'Grand Central Station, bagel with cream cheese, sim card and Duane Reade or a Rite Aid. That is all doable and in walking distance from here.'

'Cool – can you point me in the right direction, please? I have no idea where I am right now, and should probably be in bed, but—'

'But it's New York, Lauren, you can't sleep here.'

'I'm sure of that.' I laughed. My insomnia guaranteed I'd be right at home in the city that never sleeps.

'Okay, Lauren.' Bob grabbed a map from his counter and drew on it. 'This is where we are. Go out the doors and make a right. Walk two blocks and turn left. Duane Reade will be on your left two blocks down and Grand Central on your right. You can get a bagel there and probably sort your phone too – there's stores surrounding the station and inside.'

'Um,' I hesitated, 'is it completely safe to walk around here? By myself, that is?'

'Yes, very safe this time of day. Well, as safe as any city this size can be, but don't be walking too far alone at night. Any time you need a cab, we'll get one for you.'

'Right, well, I should be fine then. I'm just a country girl so this is a big thing for me, coming to New York.'

'Country girl from . . . let me guess . . . Australia?'

'Hey, you're the first one to get it right.'

'This is the UN Plaza, we have people from Australia stay often – I've always wanted to go there, but it's so far away.'

'It's just a plane ride. You lose a day going there and you gain it coming back, so you don't really lose at all. You'd like it. Come visit.' I smiled as I walked through the revolving doors out onto 44th Street.

I took Bob's directions towards Grand Central. I couldn't help but smile feeling the sun again. The Canberra winter had been so brutal; it was the one thing I wouldn't miss. I caught a glimpse of myself in a shop window and my big round glasses *did* make me look like a movie star, and I liked it. I'd never noticed it before back home.

I tried to keep pace with the fast walkers in the street, but I couldn't, and I wanted to absorb every minute anyway, to consider the different types of people passing me by – all their sizes, shapes and colours. I wondered where they were all going and what they were doing in New York. I passed little cafes and restaurants, hairdressing salons and banks. Along the way I could smell garbage, and sometimes urine and then hot donuts. This was the smell of the Big Apple. I'd have to get used to it.

I turned left onto Lexington Ave and could see the entrance to the station across the road. I was excited. I walked up to 42nd and was taken aback to see police lining the entire entrance to the station like a guard of honour. I wondered if it was because someone important – that is, a real VIP – was staying in the Hyatt Hotel there. I walked through the upper concourse looking like a tourist. For at least a week during the NAIDOC celebrations, that's what I was. I didn't want to take my camera out but I had to. It was beautiful. I took photos of the ornate ceilings, the huge clock, the arrivals and departure boards and the crowds.

Grand Central Terminal sounded rather grand and it looked even grander. It was nothing like Kingston Station back in Canberra and it was far bigger and more glamorous than Central in Sydney.

I looked at my watch, realising I still hadn't turned it back fourteen hours. I counted backwards and worked out that it was 2 pm. I hadn't eaten for eight hours.

I found a take-away place that had bagels and then struggled with what version to try – blueberry, poppy seed, wholemeal and so on.

'Blueberry, please,' I said before the guy could go on listing the choices. I'd never had a blueberry bagel, even though I'm sure they had them in Manuka. I felt authentic having my first ever at Grand Central Terminal, New York.

I watched the server lump a chunk of cream cheese on it – one centimetre, two centimetres, three centimetres – but before I had time to say anything it was wrapped and I was paying for it. My coffee was handed over in a cup the size of a small bucket. I walked through some arches and found somewhere to sit, trying delicately to scrape most of the cream cheese off without looking wasteful.

'You need to ask for a *schmear* of cream cheese if you don't want that much,' said a hot guy in jeans and a Led

Zeppelin T-shirt from the table next to me. I was taken aback, but Bec had told me that New Yorkers were known for being friendly. Besides, I was already lonely, so I was thankful for the conversation.

'Thanks. This is enough for about four bagels. It would give anyone a heart attack, right?'

He smiled. 'Yeah, and people wonder why there's so many fat Americans. Everything is upsized, all you can eat for $10, and a year's worth of cream cheese spread on one bagel.'

I couldn't help but laugh, showing him my humungous coffee. 'And your small coffees are the size of our large ones. We'd call this a bucket back in Australia. No chance of any sleep with this much caffeine.'

'That's the plan – this is the city that never sleeps, didn't you know?'

'So I've heard.'

'Are you here on holidays?'

'I'm here working for a while.'

'That's cool,' he said, suddenly looking at his watch. 'Oh, my train's leaving soon – gotta go, but it was nice to talk to you.' He got up and wiped his table over with a serviette. 'Welcome to New York.' He smiled as he walked off.

I couldn't believe how friendly people were. I didn't know what Dad was worried about, really. I already felt comfortable.

I crossed the road from the station and went into Duane Reade; it was a pharmacy the size of a small department store. I strolled aisle after aisle, upstairs and downstairs, and was fascinated by the range of hair products for African American women. There was a whole section of 'relaxers' and straighteners. I'd never seen anything like it back home. Like the over-abundance of cream cheese on my bagel, everything in Duane Reade was also en masse; there were so many varieties of Tylenol it took me almost ten minutes to find the one I was looking for. But it was locked behind Perspex so I needed a staff member to get it for me.

On the way back to the hotel I found a phone store and secured a cheap plan with enough data to allow me to call the girls and family whenever I wanted. I was getting myself organised for life in New York.

I was hallucinating by the time I got back to the hotel. I finally understood what jet lag meant. I made it to my room just in time to get out of my clothes and collapse on the bed. When I woke up, it was night, and the lights of the city were beaming into my room. I stood at the full-length window in awe of the colours. I could see the Empire State Building, the Chrysler Building – the whole scene was beautiful.

I turned on the telly and switched from station to station, amazed at the number of channels and shows. I stopped on *The Late Show*; Bec and I used to watch it back home. We both liked Stephen Colbert's politics and he was a hoot. I ordered room service – a green salad and a piece of New York cheesecake.

I watched TV and scrolled on my phone, finally bringing up Adam's Instagram to catch up on his movements. He had some new action shots on there from his most recent game. They'd lost 24–12 to the Parramatta Pythons. I knew Adam would be furious about that and decided to send a message of support. It was something I could do once a week, just to keep reminding him of how I was always there for him – so he could remember what he was missing. As soon as I sent the message, though, including my details in New York, I knew I'd messaged myself into my own pathetic corner – the one where I'd wait for him to respond.

And so I did, for three hours. I checked and rechecked but no messages from Adam at all. I received a few from the girls, though:

From Libby:

I think you should hit up the nearest karaoke bar and start singing New York, New York 😉

From Bec:

I've got a new housemate, but she's nowhere near as cool or as much fun as you. Miss you heaps.

From Max:

Mum said to say hello and she misses you. Dad too. I'm okay and the car's great! 😃

A couple of local artists who knew I was coming to New York had dropped me a welcoming line as well. Following Libby's suggestion, sort of, I put on Frank Sinatra as I read my messages and emails. I started doing high kicks around my hotel room and then wondered if anyone could see me from across the city. A naked Koori girl 'spreading the news' that she had landed in the city that never sleeps would have been an interesting sight for any voyeur. I finally shut my laptop and got into bed at midnight, annoyed with myself. Expecting something from Adam had only led to disappointment, again.

11

Black Tee guy

I woke up groggy at about 10 am, disturbed by the sound of housekeeping knocking on the door. I opened it, sticking only my head around, as I was naked.

'Sorry,' I said through half-closed eyes, 'I'm a bit jet-lagged. Can you come back in about an hour?'

'Of course,' the staffer said. I quickly checked my messages but there was nothing from Adam. I needed to get energised so I went to the hotel gym and ran for thirty minutes. It was all I could manage, even though I was sure the cream cheese bagel and the New York cheesecake for dinner were already making a home for themselves on my thighs.

Downstairs an hour later, I said hello to Bob the concierge and showed him my 'Lauren's New York To Do List – Day 2':

Museum of the City of New York
Slice of pizza and / or pretzel
Evening walk in Times Square

'Okay, Lauren, take the 4, 5 or 6 train from Grand Central uptown to 103rd Street and then walk to 5th Avenue near the park and you're there.'

'Thanks, mate,' I said.

'No worries, mate.' And he gave me the thumbs up.

I said hello and goodbye to Barney the valet and Joe the doorman and strolled up the street feeling good about the warm weather. I ducked into the shop on the corner to grab a Red Bull, as it was too hot for coffee.

I already felt confident walking to Grand Central Terminal and couldn't believe I had been so nervous before leaving Canberra. Everything was a street or an avenue and they all ran in numerical order so it wasn't that hard to follow. Even for a country bumpkin like me.

Not wanting to act overconfident, I double-checked at the information booth for the line I needed to get to 5th Avenue and the museum. The information officer politely confirmed Bob's directions and handed me yet another map. I was becoming the 'map lady'.

I headed to the platform, following the crowds and the signs, and was anxious as I took an escalator down. I breathed deeply and I didn't stand too close to the tracks, in fact a metre back from the painted yellow line. I started to feel claustrophobic being underground, and among so many people. How would we get out if there were an emergency? Like flying in the sky, it really wasn't normal to be travelling under the city. It was stifling hot, like there was no air. What if there was an accident or a terrorist attack? We'd all be stuck under the ground with no easy escape. I'd never even been in the Sydney Harbour tunnel or the M5 tunnel, even though the M5 tunnel knocks about twenty minutes off the Canberra to Sydney drive. Mum and Dad just laughed when I made them drive the long way up to the airport. 'It's not normal to be driving under the sea or the earth,' I tried to tell them. And that was exactly what I was thinking as I boarded the train.

I sat nervously, unsure of train etiquette and concerned about getting off at the right stop. I tried not to look too much like a tourist and hid my many maps in my bag. I'd download a google map when I got back to the hotel. I glanced around the train for anything or anyone that looked suspicious and laughed to myself, knowing Dad would have thought it was *all* suspicious. I read and re-read the 'Emergency Evacuation Information' in the carriage. The sign was near a young man's head. I think he thought I was staring at him as he smiled big and gave a nod of acknowledgement.

But then I did stare – at a middle-aged woman who kept sniffing her hands and her fingers. She was strange. Actually, lots of people looked strange in New York, but I liked the strangeness. It made Canberra seem even blander by comparison. Everything about New York was antithetical to Canberra. People looked busy in New York. They moved faster down the street. They smiled more.

They talked to strangers as friends, they talked to themselves. Men smiled at you in the street. If this happened back home it would be thought odd. If you were alone and mumbling and didn't have Airpods in your ears, then you'd be unhinged. Not in New York. People were just people.

The carriage wasn't full. There was no-one standing and there were free seats, but I still felt closed in. Sweat started forming on my upper lip and I was hot and wheezy. I almost lost my breath when I saw someone familiar-looking opposite me. He caught my eye and smiled. It was a smile I recognised. And a neck too. He looked so much like Adam, I couldn't help but stare at him.

We finally reached my stop and I got off the train, fought my way through the turnstiles and found myself up on the street again. I breathed in lungfuls of relief.

I walked three blocks to 5th Avenue and then up the stairs to the Museum of the City of New York. Libby and Bec thought it would be the best place to get some background about the city before I hit the galleries and other museums. I smiled as I was greeted by volunteers just inside the huge doors, and went to check out the Activist in New York exhibit which highlighted social activism in the city, covering many themes including immigration, civil rights, and sexual orientation. It helped to give me some understanding of the politics and diversity of NYC.

Moving to the next exhibit, titled New York: Home, I felt the photographic exhibtion was meant just for me. It was about New York in a contemporary context, through the lens of photographers and their definitions of 'home' in the big city. It really helped inform my own lens moving forward with my life here for the next twelve months.

A guy in a black fitted tee and jeans walked past me as I left the exhibit. From behind he was the image of Adam. The same height, the same thick brown hair, the same broad shoulders and grabbable arse in jeans. His biceps looked massive like Adam's did in a T-shirt as well. I followed him into a new exhibit – something about theatre in New York – without even thinking, just trying to see his face.

I stopped and glanced at him as we both paused to read about African American theatre at the same time. He caught my eye and I swung immediately to the text, focusing hard on the words. It said that *A Trip to Coontown*, a show put on in 1898, was the first full-length musical written, performed and produced by African Americans – Bob Cole of Georgia and Billy Johnson.

'Interesting, isn't it,' Black Tee guy said, with a huge white smile. I'd noticed many Americans had really good teeth and wondered if it was a symbol of the wealthy and healthy in society.

'Yes, it reminds me of some Black theatre we have back home.'

'Are you South African?'

'No, Australian, Aboriginal Australian. We refer to ourselves as Blak, with a capital B and without the c.'

'Ah, the Aborigines. I've seen *Crocodile Dundee*. Can you tell time by the sun too?'

'No, I rely on my Garmin for the time.' And I held up my watch.

'You're funny. That's sexy.'

I immediately felt uncomfortable.

'Have you checked out the City of Faith exhibit? It's about the connection between religion and public space in New York.'

'Thanks, I will.' I walked off, but I couldn't help looking behind me and found Black Tee was looking back at me too. I was distracted to the point of walking into a group of schoolkids and near knocked one over.

I was so worried about giving off the wrong impression that I didn't even know how to talk to straight men anymore. I didn't flirt back in Canberra because I had always considered myself in a relationship with Adam, and most of the guys I worked with in the arts were gay, so there wasn't even any fun flirting at work. I just didn't know how to react to the rush of male attention that I'd already experienced on my second day in New York.

My feet were killing me by the time I left the museum, and jet lag had kicked in. I couldn't face the underground so I got in a cab; there were yellow cabs everywhere, so I didn't even bother booking an Uber. The driver didn't speak to me at all, but he talked the whole way back to the hotel, on his mobile. I watched the small television screen in the back of his seat, fascinated by the technology available in New York cabs.

Back at the hotel I logged in and checked Adam's Insta because I felt guilty about flirting with the Black Tee guy, but I needn't have. Adam had a whole new swag of busty women commenting on his posts. Why was I even worried about a few words with a stranger, when we were both fully clothed? Nothing had changed at Adam's end and I owed him nothing.

I took a nap and woke up at 8 pm. Times Square was the next thing on my list, so I got dressed and went downstairs.

I introduced myself to another guy at the concierge desk.

'It's safe to get the underground at this time, Lauren, and you can get it back too. People ride the subway late into the night,' Raph said from behind the desk.

'I'll see how I feel. I'm still a bit knocked around with the time difference, and boy, the heat is exhausting, isn't it?'

I felt flustered on the train but didn't have to go that far. I walked around Times Square and the lights were breathtaking. There were so many lights and billboards and neon signs: the ABC's Good Morning America, American Eagle, LG, *The Lion King*. More interesting to me was the installation of new signs going up declaring that the area was a gun-free zone. I took my phone out and photographed all the bright, flashing lights and felt like I was on a movie set. I couldn't stop smiling, but it would have been so much better to have someone to share it with.

I was hungry and kept walking, trying to find the right place to stop. I had to have a slice of pizza as per Libby's list, but walking along 7th Avenue, I was confused. Every cafe claimed to serve 'the best coffee in NYC' and similarly, every pizza and bagel house sold 'World Famous' pizza or bagels. I didn't know where to stop for my slice.

Finally, I stopped at John's Pizzeria on 44th Street, which was in a deconsecrated church and celebrating twenty-five years of being in business. They didn't serve pizza by the slice and I had to buy a whole one for myself, but I somehow managed to eat it, and wash it down with Bud Light. I thought it meant low alcohol content but it was also low calorie.

Back at the hotel I messaged Libby and Bec to fill them in on the day's events and thank them for my lists.

> You guys were right when you said men were more assertive and interested in women in New York than in Australia. They are and they're hot. There was one on the train today, let's call him 'Train Guy'.
>
> He had gorgeous bone structure, a very square face. He'd be the perfect model for a portrait sitting. He caught me staring at him. I looked away embarrassed and found a small child to watch instead. He got off and walked away with a sashay that would have worked well in Sydney.
>
> Anyway, I went to the Museum of the City of New York as you ordered and there was another hot guy, let's call him 'Black Tee Guy' – they had a fabulous 20th century in Times Square exhibit and a Eudora Welty photographic exhibition with photographs of and about Mississippi. I stood and pondered a photo of two black girls carrying white dolls, others of men and women

strolling, laughing, posing, dressed for pageants, hanging out, living in poverty, 'making chitlins', packing tomatoes. They were taken in the 1930s and it made me think of the photographic exhibition we were planning for 2025. There's inspiration everywhere here. Anyway, it's really late and I'm really, really tired but will write again when I have time. There's just so much to do here . . .

Miss you xxx

Libby replied:

I was laughing when you wrote about the sashay guy – Bec can have him. I'm so glad you're having a great time and I can't wait to get there too, yay! It's flat out here, talk soon. Miss you. Xx

There was still no message from Adam.

12

Love needs faith

My day three list included the Metropolitan Museum of Art, otherwise known as the Met. The place was so huge I kept getting lost and winding up back where I started. It reminded my of every time I went to IKEA back home and needed to google map myself out of the place. It didn't seem to matter which way I looked at the Met floor map, I never really knew where I was, and so I just walked around aimlessly.

There were a lot of marble statues and busts and torsos – Roman and Greek – which made me think of Adam and his rippling six-pack. I started to feel sad, and then angry with myself for wasting my time on a man who hadn't contacted me since I left his house weeks ago in the middle of the night.

I headed towards the Oceanic art section, but was sidetracked by an exhibition titled 'Art and Love in Renaissance Italy'. As soon as I read the sign at the exhibit entrance – '*Amore vole fe* / Love needs faith' – I just knew that it was a sign meant for me, to give me faith in the notion of love – real love, ideal love, romantic love. The love I had not had with Adam but that I still wanted. I was in New York to work but perhaps my time here would renew my belief in relationships. 'Love needs faith' would be my motto from now on.

The exhibit included lavish gifts like rings, vases and bowls, given as part of courtship, and I wondered when both those traditions had stopped – courting and the associated gift-giving. I didn't know anyone back home who had been courted. Most of the younger girls at work told stories about how everyone just went out these days and hooked up in bars and pubs. Adam never courted me, and rarely gave me gifts other than cakes – though I guess that was better than nothing.

Near the end of the exhibit I couldn't help but laugh out loud at '*Te do la mone / Dame lae fede*', translated on the wall as: 'I give you my hand / Give me the ring'. That summed it up for so many women, and I wondered if Adam thought I was the same. Surely he knew it wasn't about the ring or material things. I really wanted his heart and that didn't cost anything but trust and time.

There was a huge gift store at the Met and smaller gift outlets on each floor. Libby and I had a tradition where we would buy something at every gallery we visited – whether we were there for work or pleasure. We knew that if artists had licensed their works to be turned into gift cards and the like, then it was another way to support them. It was generally a gift for ourselves, but Libby had stipulated on my list for today that I should get her something too. 'Don't forget a gift for me!' she'd written.

I found a heart-shaped pendant with the phrase '*Amore vole fe* / Love needs faith' on it. I put it on immediately and wore it as my love talisman from then on. It took me only minutes to find the perfect gift for Libby – a Greek palmette velvet scarf that she would look deadly in back in frosty Canberra. I could just hear her explaining to admirers that the palmette was one of the most frequently used motifs in classical art in every medium and in all periods. I was looking forward to giving it to her at Christmas time.

Next, I took in the Oceanic exhibit. Just like the Roman and Greek areas, I thought the Aboriginal collection was a very male space, with a boomerang, spear thrower and shields, all related to men's roles. There was also artwork by Pintupi artist Long Jack Phillipus Tjakamarra. I started to think about how our material culture is often considered artefact rather than art and displayed in museums rather than art galleries. The Met did well to showcase both.

The local First Nations display included clothes and bags made by the Plains people, and some 'Eskimo' dolls and ceremonial instruments like Haida rattles used by spiritual leaders from the peoples of the west coast of British Columbia in Canada to harness spirits. I wondered what my new colleagues at the NMAI thought about this collection. I didn't know enough about North American art to have an informed opinion. I wondered how many people who visited the Met were then inspired to head down to Bowling Green, to the other great institution that would soon become my working home.

'Hi, Tony,' I said, pleased to see another Blackfella and even just another Australian.

'Hi, yes, sorry, I didn't see you coming – I'm so tired,' he said as he stood up and towered over me at six foot three. With a huge smile and warm hazel eyes, Tony looked like a gentle giant in his unironed check shirt and black pants. He seemed relaxed and casual, and not like some of the eccentric visual artists I'd met in Sydney and Melbourne. I could picture him at his work bench in Kununurra doing his linocuts.

'We don't have to go out if you want to stay in. We can get food in the hotel.' I pointed to the hotel restaurant to the right of us.

'Nah, sis, it's the big city. I haven't got long here, got to go straight back home for another showing. Let's go see the Big Apple, eh?'

We went to a lively and loud Mexican restaurant, walking distance from the hotel. There were lots of funky places and restaurants with good vibes nearby. I would have found it difficult to decide, if it was just me, but Tony said it was hard to find Mexican in Kununurra, so the choice was easy.

It was noisy and the crowd was young and hip. The restaurant was dimly lit with tea light candles on mosaic-tiled tables set close together. There was music in the background and every bar stool was taken. I couldn't think of any place back in Canberra with the same energy. I'd never had a mojito before, but it was on my list so I ordered one as soon as we were seated. Tony ordered one too. I sat on the bench and faced the restaurant proper, and Tony only had me to look at and the mirror behind to see the reflection of other patrons.

The drinks arrived almost immediately and the conversation flowed easily.

'Who's your mob?' he asked me.

'I'm a Lucas from Goulburn, but my mob is all around the area. Most of us have migrated to Canberra for work – and the braver ones have moved to Sydney and Melbourne.'

'How long are you here for?'

'I've only been here for three days, but I'm staying a year.'

'A year!' Tony was shocked. 'Wow, that's a long time to be away from country, and your mob.'

'I know, don't get me started or I won't last a week. It was really hard for me to leave, but I'm here now, so—'

'You're single, then. I mean if you're here for a year, no brother would've been that stupid to let you come here all alone for that long, eh?'

'Oh, some fellas are stupider than you imagine sometimes.' I could feel the mojito kick in. I sucked hard on the straw until there was only ice and a mint leaf left, making a loud slurping noise.

'Sounds like you need another one.'

'I don't usually drink much – one is probably more than enough.'

'Don't be silly, we're in New York.' And he threw his arms up in the air as if to say, *look around.*

'We are too.' I beckoned the waiter over and ordered two more cocktails.

By the end of the evening we'd discussed every visual artist we knew, the latest Telstra National Aboriginal and Torres Strait Islander Art Award winner, Tony's speech for his opening the next night, and the dreadfully long flight from Australia to New York. I was tired and my cheeks were flushed. I was more than tipsy. This was not exactly professional, as I was essentially on duty.

'Let's party, sis, c'mon.'

'Honestly, Tony, I need to lie down, I think I'm drunk.'

'Nah, sis, c'monnnnn – I've only got a few nights here. We can tear this town right up, eh?'

'I think I need to tear back to the hotel, but I promise I'll go out with you tomorrow night, okay, to celebrate the opening.'

'You make a man weak, sis, but okay.'

'Here's my number – call me if you need anything.'

Tony put me in a cab back to the UN Plaza and I left him to explore the city on his own.

As soon as I got in my room I tugged my clothes off and opened my laptop. I stared at the screen through blurry eyes and squinted as I tried to focus on Adam's Instagram. He had changed his bio to 'Simply Irresistible' and it made me cry. I went to my own page, tapped the new post button and uploaded a deadly selfie of me in Times Square, and then sent Adam a message::

I miss u.

I woke in the morning with the worst hangover I'd ever had. Three mojitos and two pinot noirs were five drinks too many. I didn't even want to imagine how Tony felt – I just hoped he'd be right for the exhibition opening. My pounding head reminded me why I usually chose cakes over cocktails. I might put on a few kilos eating cakes but I could still function.

I picked up my phone and there were three messages, all from Adam:

The first one read:

I'm running my tongue up your thigh . . .

The second one read:

What are you doing to me now??

The third one read:

Have you cum already, babycakes?

I was annoyed with myself, and ashamed for initiating what was essentially a long-distance, logistically impossible and meaningless DM booty call.

I had fallen asleep in the middle of sexting. Adam's last message had come in at 4 am so I'd only had a couple of hours' sleep, which wasn't usually a problem – except that this time I was hungover. I dragged myself out of bed and forced myself to the hotel gym to work off the heavy Mexican food and sweat out the alcohol. Without Libby's 'To Do' list I would have just crawled back into bed. Luckily, she had given me a relatively easy day, going to the Guggenheim and then to Bloomingdale's, to buy something to wear to the exhibition that night.

I'd googled the Guggenheim before leaving Canberra, and I was excited about checking it out. It also gave me a chance to stroll along 5th Avenue and glance into Central Park, which I was dying to walk through to suss out the jogging paths. I stopped and took a photo for a couple who were trying to photograph themselves and the building behind them. They returned the favour for me, and I realised that it wasn't that difficult to travel alone. I'd never done it before, but here I was in New York City, visiting world-acclaimed galleries and meeting other tourists and having my photo taken. It wasn't that hard at all, even for a country bumpkin. I'd still rather have been there with Adam, but I knew he'd only want to be checking out the sporting venues anyway.

After all the hype from Emma and Libby about the Guggenheim I was looking forward to going through the space. I was so moved to be up close to artworks by such geniuses as Van Gogh and Picasso but I was less impressed with seeing Gauguin's, having learned he fathered children with teenage girls in Tahiti and considered Polynesians 'savages'. I was pleased that the article I'd read about him in the *New York Times* before I left Canberra had been asking whether or not it was time the artist was cancelled.

More interesting than the exhibitions themselves, though, were the visitors viewing them. The gallery was brimming with studious-looking characters with French, Italian and German accents wafting through the space. Everyone was young and good-looking, and someone smelled so delicious that without even noticing I found myself following him from painting to painting just to breathe in his scent. He was wearing Beckham Signature, just like Adam wore, and I allowed myself to drift mentally back to the last time we made love.

'Bill, Bill, come and look at this one.' My daydream was shattered by a loud woman pointing to a work by Cézanne. It was the only American accent I'd heard in the exhibition space until then, challenging the almost sacred atmosphere. It was as if they didn't realise the value of the artwork came from viewing it and not screeching about it across the room.

I kept moving but still had my mind on Adam, and what it would have been like to have him with me. I knew he would've made some crass comment if he'd seen the brass sculpture by Edgar Degas titled *Seated Woman Wiping Her Left Side*. Perhaps it was better he wasn't there with me.

I looked at my watch and realised that according to Libby's schedule it was probably time for me to make tracks downtown to Bloomingdale's but I wanted to see Ground Zero first. I stopped by to see the memorial – two deep, square pits cut into the ground where the towers had once stood. Water trickled down the walls of the pits like tears, and the names of those who had lost their lives were engraved around the raised edges.

I thought about the innocent people who died and the families left behind, and I began to tear up. I also remembered my parents taking me to the march for peace in Canberra when I was a kid, to protest the US and Australia declaring war on Iraq. I took a deep breath, sighed and turned to cross the road, wanting to focus on more positive things, like the opening of NAIDOC Week at the UN.

I looked at my watch and realised I'd have to get a move on back uptown to Bloomingdale's, because I needed a dress for the opening. I found myself a black silk dress. It was classy and elegant, but not overdone. The label was Black Halo and I liked that as much as the style. It would be perfect for the opening and any others that were coming up at the Smithsonian. I also grabbed a black suit for meetings and two tops for the gym. I wanted to get more but my budget would not allow it. And I was feeling claustrophobic in the change room. I couldn't wait to share with the girls my shopping wins.

'Nervous?' I asked Tony as we left the hotel for the UN and the opening of his exhibition.

'Nah, sis, it's all about me – I'm cool. You look hot.'

'Thanks. I got it at Bloomingdale's.' I sensed that Tony wasn't as interested in the shop as what was under the dress as he touched the silk slip against my thigh.

'Silk, on sale,' I said, stepping away obviously. I didn't want him to touch me, not like that. He was a client.

'We're going out tonight, sis, right?'

'We'll see. I'm still recovering from last night. I've got a whole twelve months here, remember? I can't be wearing myself out in the first week.'

'Don't go soft on me, you promised.'

I handed my passport to the security guard as I entered the grounds of the UN and we were met by our guide from the Australian consulate. The crowd was already strong – chatting, drinking Australian wine and champagne, exchanging business cards and viewing the exhibition. There was a lot of interest in the earthy-coloured linocuts telling stories of Tony's country back home. There were red dots on more than half the prints, indicating they had been sold, even though it wasn't meant to be a selling exhibit.

I found the bar, picked up a mineral water and looked around the massive foyer, straining my neck to see if I could find Kirsten. I spotted her in the middle of a group, where she was keeping everyone enthralled with an animated face and hand gestures. She wore a red jersey dress that showed off her lean figure. Her long black hair went down the length of her back to her bum and she had matched her dress and matt lipstick. I admired her style, which looked effortlessly glamorous. I walked slowly towards the group, listening to her voice get louder the closer I got. I hovered, waiting patiently for an opportunity to introduce myself. A waiter came by to offer people a choice of drinks from his tray and I cut in.

'Kirsten?' I smiled, extending my hand, 'I'm—'

'Lauren.' She grabbed me and hugged me like I was a long-lost relative coming home to the fold. 'It's so good to meet you finally. I'm so sorry I haven't called the hotel – I was going to drop in but I've been working flat-out and finishing too late. Come let me introduce you to some people.' Kirsten talked fast.

For the next thirty minutes before the speeches began Kirsten swept me across the room, introducing me to ambassadors and journalists, Aussie expats, local artists and consulate staff.

'And Lauren, this is Maria – your new boss – from the National Museum of the American Indian. I think you might know each other, yes?' Kirsten smiled.

Maria had short dyed red hair, green eyes and olive skin and looked very professional in a navy suit. Her plump face forced out any wrinkles she may have had, so I couldn't gauge her age.

'Oh, it's great to meet you!' I said. 'Your email said you couldn't come tonight.'

'Our meeting in Maryland finished early. It was a rush, but we're here.'

'I'm really glad we got to meet before I start work on Monday.'

Maria kissed my cheek, and waved someone over. 'I'll introduce you to Wyatt – you'll be working with him on the main exhibits and he'll show you around the NMAI on Monday.'

A dark guy with a huge white smile sauntered towards us. He wore black jeans and a black jacket, but underneath I could see a T-shirt with a purple and white flag on it. He had pointed boots and he looked like a city-styled cowboy.

'Wyatt, this is Lauren, from Australia.'

Wyatt shook my hand gently but firmly. 'Hey, it's awesome you're here. I'm looking forward to working with you. I checked out the NAG website – you guys have a lot of great stuff going on.'

'Thanks, I can't wait to get to the museum on Monday too. I've got part of an exhibit already mapped out that I want to talk through with you . . .'

'Okay, you two, talk shop later. Right now, go check out Tony's exhibition,' Maria said, waving us away.

Wyatt and I walked through the exhibition together.

'I'm Mohawk, and so is Maria,' Wyatt said. 'Actually, there's quite a few Mohawks in New York, and Mohawk iron workers laboured on many of the skyscrapers and buildings here. They were known as skywalkers because they scaled staggering heights to build some of the most iconinc bridges and buildings.'

'Wow, that's impressive, but why Mohawks in particular?'

'There are two communities of Mohawks not far from here. Akwesasne straddles Ontario, Quebec and New York State, so it makes sense to travel here for work, just like other workers come to New York. The other community is Kahnawake near Montreal, and that's a six-hour drive, and so lots of men would come and work the week and go home on weekends.'

'Is that your flag?' I asked, pointing to his T-shirt.

'This is the flag of the Iroquois Confederacy.' He ushered me forward as he talked. 'It's made up of the Mohawk, Oneida, Onondaga, Cayuga, Seneca and Tuscarora nations. As a group we're also known as Six Nations. We're pretty much the nations of upstate New York.'

'The Haudenosaunee,' I said eagerly.

'That's right, how'd you know?'

'I always google the traditional owners to pay respects when I'm visiting or speaking somewhere I don't know. It all makes sense now.'

I was enjoying the history lesson as we walked through the exhibition. And there was no break in the conversation – as soon as Wyatt stopped, I started. As we looked at the art we talked constantly. I explained some of the nuances of Aboriginal art and the different regions and reasons for art; from the Papunya Tula artists to the aesthetics of Arnhem Land right through to contemporary urban 'Blak' art, including photography and installation art, which I was particularly interested in.

I liked Wyatt immediately – he was down to earth, smart, funny and well dressed, and he was a good sort.

I also felt at ease with him straight away, and all of this set my gaydar off. I knew I could be my friendly self around him and not worry about giving off signals.

We emerged from the exhibition when the speeches began. I listened carefully to the opening words of the guest speakers, to see what level of respect was paid to the Indigenous people of New York City. I expected to hear an acknowledgement of country like we did back home, but there was no mention of the Haudenosaunee at all.

Tony walked up to us after the speeches and I introduced him to Wyatt. They did the brotherhood handshake, but Tony turned straight to me.

'So, we going out, sis? You promised, eh?' he said, looking no more the worse for wear after last night.

Before I had a chance to respond, Kirsten appeared and started organising everyone, just like Libby did back home. 'Okay, you mob, you're all coming to for a couple of drinks and maybe some koori-oke? There's a place just around the corner, but it's an English pub.' She laughed, and rolled her eyes. I knew straight away that Kirsten and I would get on well.

I was happy to be going somewhere close to my hotel, but I smiled, knowing Libby would've cringed at the thought of going to an English pub. *I'm not drinking the coloniser's brew!* she would've said.

As it turned out, the bar was really an English pub with an identity crisis, with American rock songs playing on the jukebox when we arrived, then an Irish singer taking to the stage, and a bar full of people from across the globe, including a handful of Aboriginal Australians. It really was a United Nations kind of venue, but compared to the places I went in Canberra it wasn't very fancy or flash, and nowhere near as big.

'This is where we come after all our major meetings,' Kirsten bellowed across the noise. 'All the Blackfellas from home drink here and other Indij mob come here too, because it's pretty friendly most of the time.'

Friendly it was. I stood at the bar and got talking to Cooper, a local who lived in Trump Towers.

'Here, have a seat.' He pulled out a stool for me

Even though I didn't want to be anywhere near anyone who had anything to do with Trump, I needed to sit down. 'Thanks heaps. My feet are killing me from walking in these heels and standing for hours at an exhibition tonight.' I sat, grateful to take the weight off my feet.

'What brings you here?'

'To New York or the pub?'

'Both.'

'Well, I've just been to an exhibition tonight and everyone wanted to come here, so I was dragged in with the tide, but long-term I'm working as a curator at the NMAI at the Smithsonian.' I was already tired of saying the whole name and I hadn't even started work yet.

'Let me buy you a drink. You look like a cosmopolitan kind of girl.'

Trying to sound a bit more cosmopolitan myself, I said,

'Actually, I prefer a mojito.'

'Oooh, mojito. You're my kinda girl.' And he started to rub my thigh. I panicked, not wanting to make a scene in front of one of my artists and my new flatmate, only a few metres away. While Cooper tried to get the barman's attention, his hand still on my knee, I looked desperately around the room, and before I knew it Wyatt was next to me. I pulled a face and mouthed the words 'Help me' and he put his arm around me. 'Lauren, everyone's waiting for you at the table.'

I smiled at him, thankful, hoping I didn't also look pathetic.

'Right, of course, I'll be right there.' And he walked off.

I turned to Cooper. 'Thanks for the offer of a drink, but I really need to get back to the group.'

'Are you with *him*?' Cooper said in disbelief.

'Yes,' I said, not clarifying that I was with Wyatt for work.

'Really? He looks . . .'

'He looks what?'

'Like a really nice gay . . . I mean guy.'

'He *is* a nice guy.'

'I'm sorry – I didn't mean to cause any offence.'

'I've got to go.'

I got up and walked back to the table, embarrassed that within hours of meeting my colleague I had made an idiot of myself and looked unprofessional.

'I'm sorry about that,' I said.

'Not a problem at all. I saw him' – Wyatt looked and nodded towards Cooper – 'watching you from the minute we walked in.'

'Really?'

'It's a guy thing,' Wyatt said. I wondered if guys behaved the same way with other guys.

I tried to glance at my watch casually, so I didn't appear rude, and then looked around the bar. Everyone appeared to be settling in for the night, but I was feeling jet-lagged.

'I really think I should go back to my hotel and sleep,' I said to Wyatt, who leaned in to hear me properly. 'I've had a massive week with all the travel and I move into my new place tomorrow, with Kirsten in Chelsea.' Wyatt just nodded approval and looked over at Tony, who was doing his best with her.

'I live in Chelsea as well,' Wyatt said, resuming the conversation. 'You'll love it, there's plenty of galleries there and lots of interesting bars and restaurants.'

'My best friend, Libby, she also works at the NAG, she would've loved to see me in Greenwich Village, but a move from Canberra to Chelsea is more manageable for me, I reckon.'

I said goodbye to Wyatt, feeling we'd set a good foundation for an easy first day at work on Monday. I slid around the table and said goodbye to Kirsten and we planned for me to arrive at 11 am the next day.

'I'm really glad you emailed when you first did Lauren, you're going to enjoy living in Chelsea. And we're going to have fun!' I knew Kirsten was right on both counts.

13

Working the Australian accent

I checked out of the UN Plaza and was surprisingly sad to say goodbye to Bob, Raph, Barney and Joe. I felt like I had made myself a little family in midtown, but I was ready to settle into Chelsea. I was also looking forward to a much bigger space, a regular exercise routine, meeting my other flatmate Vikki and hanging out with Kirsten.

A car picked me and my red luggage up and deposited us all on 25th Street between 7th and 8th Avenues. My new home was an apartment on the 5th floor without a lift. In New York this was called a walk-up. Kirsten came down and helped me with my bags.

'Wow, this place is so cool.' I fell in love with the apartment immediately; there was an eclectic mix of furniture, movie paraphernalia, a massive framed signed photograph of President Obama in the living room, a combined washing machine and dryer and a red microwave. My room was going to be full of sunlight all day. I was desperate to see the bathroom, and as soon as I walked in I closed the door, stood in the bath/shower and there it was, a view of one-fifth of the Empire State Building. I could tell from the layout of the apartment and all the appliances that I had scooped an up-market place in Chelsea. Even with three paying rent it was a stretch. Lucky for us, Vikki's grandma owned the apartment and it was rent-controlled.

Kirsten put the kettle on when I came out and I sat at the wooden dining table and started flicking through copies of the *New Yorker* as she fussed around making tea.

'So tell me about your work,' I asked.

'Basically, I coordinate the sixteen members of the Permanent Forum on Indigenous Peoples. I love it, but it's a massive job, pulling together four meetings a year for the leaders who advise the UN on Indigenous policy.'

'Wow, that's full-on, and so important. Should I have curtseyed to you or something when we met?'

'Very funny, no curtseying required.' She put the cups on the table. 'There's a meeting in a few weeks' time – you should come and observe. Or you could just hang out with us at a bar afterwards and meet the other members.' I was keen to observe the meeting, but I could take or leave the pub after my experience with Cooper.

'Cool,' I said, not committing myself either way.

The door swung open and a buxom woman with long legs and a short dress strolled sexily into the room. I wondered if I could ever walk that way.

'Hey there,' she said in a strong Brooklyn accent. 'I'm Vikki.' She put fresh flowers on the table. Vikki was gorgeous: taller than me, with an hourglass figure, a small diamond nose ring and masses of brown curls billowing down her back. 'Been up since four, so I just want to have a quick shower and freshen up – be back in a minute and promise I'll be normal.' She dragged a huge bag behind her into the bathroom.

'Vikki works in films – she's a freelance location manager.'

'What's that entail? I've never met someone in that job before.' I did sound like a country bumpkin.

'There's loads of films made in New York so you'll probably meet heaps of film people while you're here. Vikki's responsible for finding the locations for film and TV shows.'

'Wow, that's deadly. Do you get to meet any movie stars with her?'

'Not really, but she meets them all the time. She works really long days, though, out on shoots early in the morning until late at night. There's no way I could do it. She loves it and always comes home with the best stories.'

Vikki came back and sat down with a bottle of water. 'Now, that's better. Kirsten tells me you're going to work at the Smithsonian – that sounds cool.'

'Yeah, can't wait. I'm already loving everything about New York, I'm sure the museum will be great.'

'We did a shoot there on a history documentary last year. It was awesome.' I liked the word 'awesome'; it was like the Yankee version of 'deadly'.

'Where did you shoot today?' Kirsten asked.

'Well, I didn't know when I scouted the place out, but apparently we were in the same apartment block where Gigi Hadid lives.'

'Wow.' I wasn't a fan by any stretch but it was hard not to be impressed by being so close to celebrity life.

'It's a gorgeous day – let's show Lauren around the area. You can unpack later, eh, tidda.' Kirsten was organising the flowers and me at the same time but I didn't mind, and I felt at home, being called tidda for the first time since I'd left Australia. I knew Libby, Bec and Kirsten would get on if they ever met.

'All the action happens below 23rd Street, so let's go,' Vikki said, running her fingers through her still-damp hair. 'But others will tell you it all happens uptown. You'll figure it out soon enough.'

We strolled along 8th Avenue and I felt happy. The sun was shining on my face, I had two new friends and roomies, and as we walked along the street people kept smiling and nodding at the three of us.

A horn beeped and I jumped. 'Everyone beeps their horns here too.'

'I like to call it the New York horn symphony,' Kirsten joked. 'Took me a while to get used to it as well. I had to buy earplugs because it goes on all night.'

'It's fair to say that everyone is horn happy here,' Vikki said, 'so, I guess you could say they're horn*y*.'

'Boom-tish!' Kirsten and Vikki high-fived each other.

I liked the way they played off each other. Life with them was definitely going to be fun.

'Let me explain,' Vikki said, stopping mid-footpath. 'There are two reasons someone will honk their horn at you, Lauren. Either they want you to get out of the way, which of course we can appreciate for safety reasons. Or, if it's just a normal car' – a Chrysler drove past and honked and the driver waved – 'like that one' – Vikki pointed – 'and you're obviously not in the road or going to be hit or blocking their path, then they're just beeping to tell you they think you're hot.'

'Really? Oh my god, that's crazy.'

'That's right,' Vikki said. 'I always like to assume it's the second option, of course.'

'Well of course, we all do,' Kirsten confirmed.

The girls pointed out different businesses I might need: the drycleaners, Rite Aid, Duane Reade, the bank, coffee joints.

'There are so many pharmacies and coffee shops,' I said, having lost count of both.

'Yes, there are, but we don't go to Starbucks,' Kirsten said, not commenting on the 'drugstores'.

'Why? Bad coffee?'

'They have one at Guantánamo Bay,' both girls said in unison.

'You're kidding?'

'Nup.'

We kept walking.

'That's my favourite nail place,' Vikki said, and I smiled when I saw a man in the window drying his nails.

'Oh, the Brooklyn Bagel & Coffee Company. Now, Lauren, this place has the best selection of bagels you'll find round here. Seriously, it took me months to go through the entire list. Just be sure and ask for a schmear of cream cheese,' Kirsten advised.

'Yes, I've learned that lesson already, thanks.'

'Patisserie Chanson has amazing pastries.' Vikki pointed to a store across the street.

'I have the biggest sweet tooth so I'll definitely check that place out.'

'There's a gym just around the corner, if you just want to think about exercise.'

'No, I actually *want* to exercise – really. I'll need to go check out the gym so I can get in a routine as soon as possible.'

'Come on, Lauren, worry about fitness later. Right now we're going to initiate you into one of our favourite weekend rituals – shopping at the Chelsea Markets.'

I had read about the markets in my travel guide and fell into step willingly. As we headed towards 9th Avenue between 15th and 16th streets I looked at all the bars, cafes, grills, restaurants, and a few sex shops: the Blue Store and the Rainbow Station. It was like a mini Darlinghurst within a block. Adam would have felt out of his comfort zone here for sure – Chelsea was a world away from rugby league culture.

'This way, Lauren.' Kirsten took my arm as we entered the markets. 'Every Saturday morning, we come here together if I'm not travelling and Vikki's not working, and we do our fruit and veggie shopping.' Buskers were playing classical music and it gave the centre a peaceful, restful atmosphere, much less hectic than the Bus Depot Markets back home, where the sounds of whitefellas playing the didj always bothered me.

'It's the best place locally for seafood too.' Vikki motioned to the seafood delights on our right.

'I have a great selection of tea in the apartment, Lauren, and I get it all from here.'

Kirsten pointed out the tea shop.

'You and your tea,' Vikki joked. 'I need a coffee.'

My sweet tooth was going crazy as I took in all the different chocolate shops and bakeries.

'Could we get a coffee here, do you think?' I asked, staring into a store full of cupcakes and cookies. The sign said 'Amy's'.

'Oh, yes, this place is a treat. I usually go to Day Drinks, cos they do *really* great coffee, but we can stop here today.' Vikki was kind to oblige my request.

I walked into Amy's and there was the most delicious-looking chocolate cake that made my mouth water, an amazing range of cookies and so many different breads to choose from.

'You should buy one of those T-shirts,' Kirsten said, pointing to a staff member wearing a shirt with the slogan 'Eat dessert first'.

'That's hilarious, and I really should.'

'Would you ladies like to try one of our newest cupcakes?' a shop assistant asked, holding a tray of little cakes, each with a picture of Kate Hudson made out of icing on top of it. 'Kate popped in during Fashion Week and we all nearly fainted. She bought cupcakes, so we made a Kate cake, in her honour.'

'Oh, wow, yes please. Can I take a photo?'

'We don't allow photos in the store,' the assistant said, as the manager came out into the shop area.

'Oh,' I said, disappointed. The cakes looked incredible. 'I'm not from around here, and my girlfriends back home would love to see your shop, I just know it.'

'I guess one photo won't hurt,' the owner said, sidling right up next to me with the tray of cupcakes, and Kirsten took the picture.

'Oh my god, you are unbelievable,' she whispered as we walked out with a free sample of Kate cake. 'You are such a flirt.'

'That wasn't flirting, I was serious, and Libby and Bec would kill for one of those cakes. We watched her latest movie *A Little White Lie* together, and they loved it!

Vikki stopped and put her hands out to stop Kirsten and me.

'It's the accent, Lauren, they love the Australian accent. Kirsten, you really need to exploit it more too. I'm taking you two everywhere with me,' she said.

'Let's have a drink at Easy's first,' Vikki said as we descended the stairs that evening, heels clicking on the laminated flooring.

'Good idea, Ms V.'

Easy's was a bar only a block away from our apartment,

nestled below the street, small, intimate and dark. I wondered if it was a place where it was 'easy' to meet someone. The name left a lot to the imagination. There were lots of gay couples taking most of the seats around the horseshoe bar with a rainbow flag hanging above, so we sat ourselves at a table in the corner.

'I like it here,' I said. 'It's comfortable.' There were little kerosene lamps on the tables giving off a hint of light.

'It's mainly regulars, and after-workers,' Kirsten said. 'It's the kind of bar I come to alone and feel okay, and of course it's handy.'

'It's my shout.' I stood up, grateful for everything the girls had already done for me on my first day in Chelsea.

'You mean, you're going to buy a *round*?' Vikki smiled. 'I can see I need to give you a crash course in the American vernacular.'

'Oh, yes please, but I'm sure I can get us a *round* without too much trouble.'

I waited at the bar patiently to be served while the girls worked out the plan for the night.

'Two gin and tonics and a mojito, please.' I was being brave and thought that I could probably manage one drink for the night, just to get into the party mood.

'We don't do mojitos here,' the barman said apologetically.

'Oh, that's okay – I'll just have a soda then.' Libby had warned me about the free-pour system in the US and I didn't want to risk drinking three-nip drinks in small tumblers.

'A what?'

'A soda.'

'What kind of soda?' The barman appeared to have no idea what I wanted.

'Soda water.'

'I think she means club soda,' a guy next to me said to the barman, and then winked at me.

'Right, club soda, that's it.' I was getting flustered and feeling a little Mick Dundee-ish.

The bartender poured the drinks and placed them on coasters on the bar. I paid for them without fuss, but then fumbled over the tip I had to leave. I walked back to the table shaking my head in embarrassment.

'I need that linguistics lesson asap,' I told Vikki, handing the girls their drinks.

'We're going to an Australian bar tonight,' Kirsten advised.

'Australian? Why?' I thought about what Libby would think, she was deadset against going to Aussie bars overseas. 'But we're in New York. I'd really like to check out a local bar and meet some New Yorkers, if that's possible.' I didn't want to sound ungrateful or pushy but it was, after all, my first Saturday night in Manhattan.

Kirsten smiled and put her hand on mine as if to reassure me. 'Of course! The bar is full of New Yorkers who love Australians, that's why I go there, and for the Aussie food I miss.'

'And *I* go there because the guys love Kirsten's Aussie accent,' Vikki said. 'With both of you it's going to be double the fun.'

'I'm not really convinced that my first Saturday night in New York should be spent in an Australian bar. My tidda Libby would have something to say about it.'

'I promise you'll love it. The owner used to play rugby league in Sydney – he's friendly and the place is fun.'

Kirsten had said the magic words 'rugby league', which equalled Canberra Cockatoos and Adam. I suddenly sat up straighter and felt a rush of adrenaline.

'It sounds great, can't wait.' I couldn't drink my club soda fast enough.

It was a balmy night outside and there were masses of people in the streets, with music coming from bars and restaurants. We sauntered along 7th Avenue towards 38th Street and I thought of the girls from *Sex and the City.* I wondered if they ever went to this bar, but I imagined it wouldn't be high-end enough considering it had TV screens with footy on. I upped my pace – the sooner we got to the bar, the sooner I could speak to the owner and the sooner I could get some real information about Adam.

'You've got it all going on, Lauren,' Vikki complimented me.

'Sorry. Is that another New Yorker phrase I need to learn?'

'Haven't you seen men checking you out? Jesus, I already had a good batting average but you've just raised it. Where did you find this sista?' she said to Kirsten.

'Koori grapevine, you know how it is.'

'Well, whoever said men don't make passes at women with glasses had never seen Lauren in Manhattan. I'm glad I've got you as a roomie.'

Vikki hooked arms with me and then grabbed Kirsten as well and we walked in time together. 'I might have to get myself some glasses too then, cos if nothing else, they'll help me see better what I'm getting in a dude,' Vikki said, matter-of-factly.

'And you can match your frames with your lipstick, bag and shoes,' I said, holding my red bag up to my face to show my coordination.

Just as we got to 38th Street two teenage guys at the lights called out, 'You ladies are hot!'

'And you fellas are cheeky,' I said, like an ageing aunty.

'What did you say?' one of the teens asked.

'Yeah, that accent is mad,' said another.

'She's Australian,' Vikki said proudly.

'I'm going to *Oztraylya* then, if all the chicks talk like that.' One fella put his hand across his heart to demonstrate his affection for the girls' accent.

'C'mon, let's go,' Kirsten said, dragging us away.

'That *never* happens back in Canberra, guys talking to you on the street like that, not when they're sober.'

Kirsten spun around like a child enjoying a new space. 'And this is why I love Manhattan, Lauren. There are plenty of men here and most of them actually *like* women *and* they know how to flirt *and* they like to go on dates. And they're not tainted by stereotypes of Aboriginal people from the media. Hell, most don't even know there's Blackfellas in Australia. Here we're just women, people.'

'Wow, that is different. I hate being the exotic other back home.' I thought about Adam's comment only weeks earlier.

'And Ms V – she's the dating queen, really. She's dating three guys right now.'

'What?'

'She is! I know – greedy, isn't it?'

Vikki stopped in her tracks and feigned shock. 'It's not greedy, it's great. I haven't been to Australia, but Kirsten tells me lots of stories about how you don't really date much down under.'

Linking her arm through Vikki's again and starting to walk, Kirsten said, 'Generally, you're single and maybe hook up with someone when you go out, or you're in a relationship, but you don't really hear about people just going on dates for fun. There's always the expectation of something more – sex or a relationship, I guess.'

'See? It's different here. Lots of people date and it's normal,' Kirsten said.

'Look, you just need to know there's a hierarchy,' Vikki said.

'What? A flirting hierarchy?'

'A flirting and dating hierarchy, yes. You can't just talk to *everyone*. You don't flirt with or date the doorman, the barman or the waiter. And if you *have* to, then the doorman is the top of the hierarchy because at least he can get you into a venue. The barman is next because he might give you some free drinks. But never the waiter.'

'That's appalling. I thought everyone was equal in America.'

'This is Manhattan, and no-one is equal, girl.'

'It doesn't matter, anyway, because I'm not really here

to date. I've kind of put my relationship on hold, sort of, to come here, so I'm not really looking.'

Kirsten smiled at me sympathetically.

'The plan is' – and I began to stretch the truth slightly – 'that my boyfriend, Adam, will come to New York in a few months' time, and we'll meet up the top of the Empire State Building. I know it's a bit clichéd but it's also very romantic.'

'Very romantic, but I'd suggest meeting up the Top of the Rock – you know, the Rockefeller Center? The building itself is much nicer and it's a far more romantic place to sit and gaze at each other,' Vikki said.

'Trust her, she'd know,' Kirsten said.

'Adam plays football – for the Canberra Cockatoos – so we'll have to wait until the season is over.' I was grateful for the opportunity to talk about Adam freely, without being judged or tsk tsk'd.

Vikki took some gum out of her bag. 'All I can say is that your boyfriend was brave letting you come here to New York alone. Didn't anyone tell him this is the dating capital of the world?' she said as she popped a piece in her mouth.

'Yes, *I* did, but I'm sure he trusts me.'

'One night I counted six men – *six men* – smile or wink at me as I walked from the office to Grand Central Terminal.' Kirsten was animated. 'Of course it's not the only reason, but it's one of the reasons I don't think I can ever go back to Australia. Our men would never get a date here, because none of them ever have to put the effort in back home. Here, dating's like a game, fun. Men still like the hunt in America.'

We finally reached the bar, walked in slowly and the girls started saying hello and kissing everyone. It was good to be in a place that felt familiar. There were Aussie beers on tap, 'Hey Mate' written on the blackboard above the bar, Powderfinger playing in the background, the Australian flag flying. I stopped still when I saw football on the television screens – AFL, Union and League games – and my heart started to race. I looked for the red, black and yellow colours of the Canberra Cockatoos but didn't see them.

'This is Matt,' Kirsten said, dragging the owner of the bar over to our table. He was tall, blonde and had a baby-face with a warm smile. He looked like a friendly guy without having done anything. He was wearing a baseball cap but I didn't know the team logo on it. 'Matt, this is Lauren. She's one of the top curators in Australia and has been poached by the NMAI for twelve months, and we're showing her the Saturday night sites of Manhattan. We had to bring her here to be initiated, of course.'

'Wow, that's impressive – your career that is, not Saturday night in Manhattan.' Matt was a bit of a joker. 'Welcome to your home while you're away from home,' he said, smiling. 'Let me buy you girls a drink. Let me guess . . . a Fizzy Lizard for you, Kirsten?'

Kirsten perched herself comfortably on the bar stool. 'You better believe it,' she told him, then turned to me. 'It's made with Midori, triple sex, oops, triple *sec* and orange juice. It's to die for. You should have one.'

'Hold up, K!' Matt touched Kirsten lightly on the arm. 'You know the official Australian welcome drink is the Australian cosmo, otherwise known as the *Ozmo*.'

Kirsten nodded her head in agreement. 'You're absolutely right, my apologies.'

I clapped my hands like a child in a lolly shop. 'Ozmo, I love the name, what's in it?'

'Absolut Mandarin and fresh orange zest,' Matt said.

'I'll have one too, Matt,' Vikki said. Matt saluted her and walked towards the bar.

'He seems nice,' I said to the girls.

'He is, always looks after Aussies and I always bring Blackfellas here. He used to play for the Nambucca Ninjas and knows most of the Koori players. Turns out he went to school with my cousin Marty who plays for the Coffs Crusaders. All the players come here when they're in town. He'll probably know your fella too.'

Matt came back with the drinks.

'Lauren's from Goulburn and her man plays for the Canberra Cockatoos, Matt.'

'Really, what position? I bet I can guess his name.'

'He's a forward.'

'Forwards . . . right.' Matt was thinking. 'Is it Ben Wallace?'

'No, not him.'

'Is it Darren Holloway? Good ol' Dazza, he's a top bloke.'

'No, not him,' I blurted. 'It's Adam Fuller.'

'Really?' Matt looked surprised. 'Ol' mate Full-of-himself?'

The girls looked at Matt and then me.

'Oh, I'm sorry, that's just what the boys call him.'

'That's okay, I hear it all the time. My girlfriend Libby calls him that too,' I said, trying to hide my embarrassment. Even on the other side of the world people didn't seem to like Adam.

'Adam's a great player.'

'Yes, he is,' I said proudly.

'And you're dating him?' Matt sought confirmation.

'Yes, why?'

'Oh, nothing . . .' Matt looked like he didn't really believe me.

'Come on, why?' I grabbed him by the shirt sleeve gently but immediately let go.

'Come on, you two. There's more to-ing and fro-ing here than at the US Open,' Vikki said curiously.

Matt fiddled with his cap nervously.

'You just seem too classy for him, I mean, from what I see about him in the papers. I thought he was the bad boy of football, but if he's got a woman like you, then he must be all right, eh?'

Even in Manhattan they knew about Adam's off-field behaviour. I stared at my drink.

Matt had an embarrassed look on his face.

'I'm sorry, it's just that I read the sporting pages online every day, so kinda know what's going on. But you can't believe everything you read, can you?' Matt started to sound like Adam.

'No, you can't.'

'Anyways, he's mad for letting you come to New York.'

'That's what I told her,' Vikki said, sipping her Ozmo.

'For starters, I can tell you now that Hunter over there at the bar is going to be all over you in five seconds flat. Be careful, Hunter by name and hunter by nature. And you are way too classy for him as well. Take that as a warning. You've gotta keep an eye on him.'

Matt walked away as the girls started chatting to some guys at the next table.

'I'm just going to the toilet,' I whispered in Vikki's ear.

'Washroom or bathroom,' she said with a wink.

'What?'

'No-one says toilet here, we say washroom or bathroom. Vikki's Vernacular Course 101 starts tonight.'

'Thanks.' The Americans were strange. I wasn't having a bath or a wash. Downstairs in the toilet I took out my phone and went straight to Adam's Instagram. His latest story was a selfie in his footy shirt with the caption: *Adam Fuller is too sexy for his shirt* and 'I'm Too Sexy' by Right Said Fred playing over it. I started to cry. I was homesick, I was humiliated, and already I knew I would have a hang-over in the morning from just one Ozmo.

My night was ruined before it had started, and it was my own fault. Why did I talk about Adam to Matt? Why did I bother looking at his stories? It only ever upset me. I looked in the mirror and thought about my mum. She would have been so disappointed to see me in this state, after all it took to get me through school and uni and then to New York. 'I didn't raise you to be treated badly by men who are not worthy,' she said when I broke up with my first boyfriend at eighteen. I dabbed a tissue gently around my eyes so as not to smudge my make-up, touched up my lip gloss, and remembered Matt's words. *You are too classy for him.* I said out loud, 'That's enough. No more talking about him, no more mentioning his name.' My first Saturday night in Manhattan was the first day of the rest of my life. I could do it. *Yes, I could!*

'Lauren!' The girls waved me over to the restaurant area as I reached the top of the stairs. I took a deep breath, sat down with them and took a sip of my Ozmo. I could see how some people got lost in the bottom of a martini or schooner glass; it would be an easy thing to do if you were feeling depressed. With AC/DC playing in the background now and the girls full of Saturday night energy, I felt my spirits lifting, and when I read the menu I smiled.

'Wow, at least I won't get homesick for the food – Aussie meat pies, Aussie burgers, Aussie lamb roasts, kangaroo fillet mignon, roo skewers and wines. This place is like home.'

'I'm having Aussie nachos,' Kirsten said.

And then I saw it. 'I'm having the pavlova with kiwifruit.' I felt immediate relief just thinking about the meringue and cream.

'You really do have a sweet tooth, don't you?' Kirsten laughed at my excitement for dessert.

'It's my only vice.' That and my addiction to Adam, but they didn't need to know about that.

Just then Hunter the bartender appeared and sat at our

table. 'Hey ladies, sorry it's taken me so long to come say hello – we're soooooo busy tonight. You must be Lauren. Matt said I'd love you, and I do.' He moved his chair closer to mine. 'I'm Hunter, it's great to meet you.'

'Nice to meet you too,' I said politely.

'There's Sam and Mike – we'll just go say hello to some friends over there, Lauren, be back in a sec,' Kirsten said as she and Vikki got up.

'Be nice, Hunt,' Vikki ordered.

'Make sure that's an H and not a C, Ms Veeeee.' Hunter turned his body completely in my direction.

'How long have you worked here?' I asked him.

'About six weeks. My brother used to play for the Manly Maulers, I played reserve grade, he called Matt when I got to New York, so here I am. I love it. Lots of pretty girls just like you. What about you?'

'Just got here this week.' I wished the girls would come back.

'Fresh meat in town, the boys are gonna love you.' He ran his finger down my arm. 'You are Lozalicious.'

'Excuse me?' I pushed his hand away.

'Ooooh, touchy! Sorry, love. So what are you doing here in New York anyway?'

I wasn't touchy, I just didn't want to be touched by a sleazebag. I really wanted to walk away but I didn't want a scene on my first night out with my new roommates, so I answered reluctantly. 'I start work on Monday at the National Museum of the American Indian, at the Smithsonian, downtown.'

'Doing what? Displaying skulls and stuff like that, or bows and arrows?' He laughed.

'I'm a curator, actually, so I'll be working on some exhibitions for the next year.'

'Curator . . . I need a curator, for my refrigerator, and my carburettor, I'm no masturbator . . .'

'Pardon?' I wasn't sure where he was going with this rave.

'I'm practising my rap tunes, got some contacts here, and you know they love the Aussie accent.'

'So I've been told.'

'I'm working it the whole time I'm here, Lozalicious.'

'I bet you are.'

'So, whereabouts are you from back home?'

'Goulburn originally, but Canberra more recently. Do you know the Big Merino? The HUGE sheep?'

'Of course, I've been there.'

'I live close to that. I grew up hanging out there on the weekends.'

'I climbed right up into the eyes of it once, it was awesome,' he said.

'Yeah, it's cool.' I was grateful then, to have at least found something in common.

'Actually, I think I boned my ex-girlfriend up in those eyeballs.'

'What?' I spat some of my Ozmo at him accidentally.

'Hey, no need for that.'

'Sorry, it was an accident.' I wiped the table.

'No, come to think of it . . .' – and he looked into the

air as if concentrating – 'I'm pretty sure I *did*, on the way to Canberra for a wedding. We were both really horny.'

I wasn't surprised she was his ex if he was telling this story to complete strangers.

'Have I upset you, Lauren? I didn't mean to offend you.'

'Do you always feel the need to tell strangers about your sex life?' I sculled my Ozmo as the food arrived at the table. 'Hunter, can you please bring me another and tell the girls our meal has been served?' I just wanted to be rid of him.

'Of course, Lozalicious,' he said with a sleazy grin on his face.

As Hunter walked away I wondered how many women Adam had taken up into Rambo's eyeballs and if he told stories like that as well.

14

If a man wants to pursue you he will

I was excited and anxious about starting my job at the Smithsonian. I arrived at Bowling Green an hour early and walked around Battery Park, taking photos of monuments and breathing in the space that would be my second home in Manhattan for the next year. Vendors were setting up to sell pretzels and nuts, and tourists were arriving to catch the Staten Island Ferry over to Lady Liberty and Ellis Island. I walked around the museum building to get an idea of its size.

At 10 am I walked in the entrance and started to take off my shoes to go through security. I knew the spiky heels would probably set an alarm off. I placed my bag on the conveyor belt and smiled at the guard.

'Good morning,' I said.

'Good morning, ma'am. You have a beautiful smile.'

'Thank you,' I said, widening my grin.

'And lips.'

'Wow, now that's a good start to Monday morning.'

'I love that accent, where are you from?'

'Canberra, Australia,' I said proudly.

'Well, if all the women have lips like that in Canberra, Australia, then I'm going there as soon as possible.'

'You should go, for sure. They could use a man like you down under.'

'Hear that, boys? They could use a man like me down under.' The group of four ageing guards all laughed.

'I'm Lauren Lucas.' I gave him my hand.

'I'm Carlos. Welcome.' He put both hands around mine.

The fellas doing security back at the NAG told me that their day could be very long if there wasn't a little small talk and flirting with pretty young visitors. But was the guard flirting with me? I didn't care, I was just appreciative of the friendliness.

'Well, Carlos, I'm going to be working here for the next twelve months, so I'm glad we've got our little routine worked out already. My smile looks forward to seeing you tomorrow.'

I knew if nothing else, I was going to enjoy arriving at work at the museum every day.

'Hey there, Lauren, right on time.' Wyatt picked up my bag off the conveyor belt. 'Did you have a good weekend?'

'I did, thanks,' I said, taking it from him and noticing his gentlemanly manners. 'Did you?'

'Yeah, I had an awesome weekend, just hanging out with some friends. Left here,' he said, ushering me along. 'Maria is waiting for us, so we'll head there first and then I'll give you a tour of the building.'

We walked into an office full of light and Maria was at her desk. 'Welcome, Lauren,' she said, walking over and hugging me. I felt like I was back at the NAG again. 'Wyatt's going to show you around today, and I want you to take your time going through the exhibits and getting a feel for the building. We'll have a meeting tomorrow morning to discuss the schedule for the next twelve months. Your office is just down the hall, so drop in at any time if you need anything. Open door policy here.'

'Come, let me show you your prestigious office, Ms Lucas,' Wyatt said, taking me by the elbow and escorting me to our shared space. The desks sat like mine and Libby's back in Canberra. You could tell my desk had just been cleaned. Wyatt's was covered with postcards of American Indian art and photos of him with artists and his family and friends. I looked to see if there was a 'couply' kind of photo, keen to see if he had a boyfriend, but there were lots of different guys and a few women too.

Wyatt waited while I unpacked my meagre belongings and personalised my space: a photo of Libby, Bec and I taken on our last night out together, a family pic, some postcards of Canberra and Goulburn and an old but much loved image from Michael Riley's *Cloud* series with a boomerang set in a blue sky among the clouds. I pinned them all on the wall and put my NAG coffee mug, my mousepad and an Aboriginal flag on my desk.

'That's an eclectic mix of things, Lauren. I love the mug.' Wyatt picked it up smiling and I wasn't sure if he was kidding or not. 'What's the flag?'

'That's the Aboriginal flag. Black for the people, yellow for the sun – the giver of life – and red for the earth and the bloodshed since colonisation.'

'Your flag is a little like ours, maybe we could swap,' he said, and he reached around to his desk and held up a similar-sized flag. 'This is the Mohawk flag.' The flag was red, black and yellow and had an image of a long-haired warrior, a single upright feather, rays of the sun, and a red background. I took it from him and looked at it as he explained.

'The long hair represents the universality of the Native struggle. The feather relates to both tradition and strength. The rays of the sun symbolise fundamental Mohawk values.'

'I love it, especially because it's in the same colours as our flag. Too deadly,' I said. Wyatt look confused. 'Oh – deadly is our word for awesome.'

'I think we'll find we've got lots more *deadly* things in common over time, Lauren – like how we BOTH have to get to the media department right now!' Wyatt smiled as he motioned for us to leave the office.

The media department wanted to do a story on me for the *National Museum of the American Indian* magazine, so we did an interview and quick photoshoot, and then we began the tour of the museum, starting in the three-storey oval rotunda. 'This is pretty much an architectural icon,' Wyatt said as we both looked towards the ceiling. 'The tile and plaster domed ceiling is by Rafael Guastavino and the murals are by Reginald Marsh,' he said, waving his hands. There was a video playing in the room as well. 'You may like to come back and watch that later.'

As we entered the ongoing exhibition I read its sign out loud: 'Infinity of Nations: Art and History in the Collections of the National Museum of the American Indian.'

'We are fortunate to have seven hundred items from across the three Americas.' Wyatt paused. 'We even have what we believe to be one of the oldest wedding dresses in existence, worn by Susette La Flesche from Omaha in 1881.'

We both stopped and took in the elegant skirt and jacket trimmed in hand-stitched silk, satin, and lace. Wyatt turned and asked, 'You're not married, are you?' He looked at my ring finger.

'No, I'm not married yet. I'm not ready to settle down – but in the meantime this is the perfect place to be. Right here in New York.'

'We're so lucky to have you, then – in the meantime, that is.'

I wondered if he was the marrying kind.

'How about you Wyatt? Are you married?'

'No, not yet, but hopefully one day.'

He ushered me further through the space, talking all the while. 'The Fresh Focus on Native American Photography exhibition is one of my personal favourites of all time. Many of our professional photographers use the lens to unpack concepts of identity, gender, race and the impact of colonisation today.'

'Our artists are the same back home,' I told him. 'They have also broadened the definition of what constitutes "Aboriginal art" and who is an "Aboriginal artist".'

'It's great that the conversations around the artist and the art is being driven by us now, too.'

I nodded and Wyatt smiled as if we were on the same page and needed no for further explanation.

'Wow,' I said, as we walked in the the Native New York exhibition, showcasing stories about the Mohawk ironworkers who played a major role in building some of the city's most famous buildings from the the 1930s to the 1950s, just as Wyatt had mentioned at the opening the week before.

'What a wonderful way to acknowledge these workers,' I said.

'And the tradition continues today,' Wyatt said, continuing to walk on. 'That's more than six generations. And that's why I think your proposed urban exhibition will fit in perfectly here. Focusing on different aspects of city life and how we fit in. This is the space it will go into.'

I looked around the walls, imaging the artwork of my own artists hanging here on opening night.

'Who actually comes to opening nights here?'

'A mix of people: curators from around the city, gallery people, our artists and other local New York artists, art collectors looking to buy, university lecturers with their students. Actually, Maria was talking about getting you to give a lecture about Aboriginal art at the NYU New School. It would be great for us. It would bring more people into the Palace.'

'The what?'

'Oh, some of us call the museum the "Palace".'

'I like it. The Palace it is.'

We eventually made it downstairs, but not before I was completely confused by all the back corridors.

'I'm going to need a behind-the-scenes map to remember all these doors and back entrances.'

'I'll draw you one, you'll be right. Mind you, I'm *still* finding doors I didn't know existed. This is the Diker Pavilion, where we screen national and international Indigenous films. We have a biennial Native American Film and Video Festival – the next is in April.'

'I'll definitely check those out, too. Maybe we could think about doing a First Nations Australian Film Festival here at some point.'

'Sounds like an awesome idea, Lauren. You should mention it to Maria tomorrow.'

As we walked, I marvelled at the amount of marble in the museum: floors, walls and pylons.

'Most of the white marble is from Vermont and New Hampshire and the coloured marble comes from Italy,' Wyatt told me. He seemed to be knowledgeable about the whole building.

I noticed a lot of marine references in the architecture with carved details of seashells and boats.

'What's with the marine theme?' I asked.

'This is the old Customs House – and this used to be the country's most important port of entry, so lots of history in this site. And this is the museum shop.' Wyatt was whisking me through the building.

'I have to admit that one of my favourite parts of any museum or gallery is the shop. So many pieces to take home to remind me of an exhibition by artists I love but can't always buy.' I touched my 'Love needs faith' pendant and scanned the space quickly, taking in the book collection, dolls, posters, jewellery and cards. I knew I would be spending some of my first pay cheque here and sending quality items back to Mum and the girls.

A school group came in, bustling with excited students.

'Are schools your main visitors here?'

'We get a lot of tourists, but increasingly more school groups. Probably because a recent report by the National Congress of American Indians found eighty-seven per cent of state history standards include no mention of Native American history after 1900, and twenty-seven states don't mention Native Americans in their K-12 curriculum at all'. Wyatt's tone was serious, it was obvious he was passionate about the topic as he continued rattling off stats like they were burned into his brain.

'However, ninety per cent of states surveyed said they are improving their Native American education curriculum, and many states claimed that Native American education is already included in their content standards. So that encourages a lot of school visits, and they make good use of the imagiNATIONS Activity Centre too, which I love, because they get to experience how Native American STEM innovations impact the modern world.'

I'm sure my eyes were hanging out of my head at how progressive the NMAI was, and how lucky New Yorkers, students and tourists alike were to be able to have free access to all this incredible knowledge.

'I love that it's free here,' I said.

'It's one of the few in the city that's free so it's very popular.'

I was getting hungry. 'And where do the staff eat lunch? Do you all go out?'

'Most of us eat it at our desks – museum wages don't pay that much. I'll show you the break room, where some of the service staff eat.'

The break room was a bland space, with cream laminated surfaces and tables.

'I think I'll eat in the park. It's such beautiful weather and a gorgeous spot on the water.'

'I'd be happy to join you, if you want company any time.'

'That'd be great, of course.'

'I need to tell you, though, in winter you'll be grateful for the heating in your office at lunchtime, trust me.'

'I'm from Canberra, so I'm used to the cold.'

'Okay, but don't say I didn't warn you.'

'And where's the best coffee?'

'Well, there's a Starbucks nearby.'

'Um . . . I don't go to Starbucks.'

'Don't say it, Guantánamo Bay?'

'Yep.'

'Me too. I'll show you the best coffee at lunchtime.' He held the door open for me as we entered another corridor. Wyatt was cool, had the coffee knowledge, the politics and he was chivalrous, leaving the likes of Hunter for dead. I wished I could send him to Australia to run some workshops with Aussie men, including Adam.

'What about after work? Is there somewhere people go for drinks?'

'We sometimes go to the White Horse Tavern for lunch or after openings, or maybe if we've just had a really, really bad day and want to debrief. I can show you where that is as well. It's not far from here.'

'You're so kind, thanks. I was really nervous about coming to New York, but everyone is incredibly helpful and hospitable.'

'Lauren, I think you'll find that most people react to you in a positive way because you give off a pleasant vibe. Keep that up and you'll be fine.'

'How was your first day, Lauren?' Maria asked me on day two.

'Excellent, but I'm still trying to absorb everything.'

'Don't wear her out in the first week, Wyatt.' They both laughed. 'Now, we need to lock in some events. Lauren, you'll be working on these too, as part of your broader role at the NMAI over the next twelve months. Okay?'

'Okay.'

'We've got the art market at the end of August, and there's storybook readings every Saturday at noon – so put that in your schedule. If you can come to one a month that would be great.'

'Of course. I'll come to this week's session.'

'I'd also like you both to come to Washington with me in March for a special screening of *Buffy Sainte-Marie: Carry It On*.'

'Washington, DC? And Buffy Sainte-Marie?' I couldn't believe my ears.

'Yes. Lauren, you need to know up-front that the NMAI in Washington is regarded as the mothership, although this building was the original base. And our research facility is in Maryland. I go there every month to attend the collections committee, where we decide on loans, donations and acquisitions. You should come with me to one of those meetings also, and you'll have a small travel budget to go to conferences and meetings out of town too. So let me know if there's something in particular you're interested in attending.'

'I've got a calendar of conferences and symposiums you can look through,' Wyatt offered.

'Thanks.' I was completely overwhelmed by the opportunities I was being given, and finally truly grateful to Emma and Libby for forcing me to take up the fellowship.

Maria went right on with business. 'I'd like to schedule a short-film festival for April next year.'

'Oh,' I cut in. 'I don't want to get ahead of myself, but do you think that we could have some short films from Australia in that?'

'That's a great idea. Your exhibit will be opening in April, so that will be a good tie-in. Can you work with the film and audio people on that, please? Wyatt, can you take Lauren down to meet the team there?'

'Absolutely.'

'And the traditional dance social is on 18 October. Public relations will be in touch about the invitation list.' Maria spoke directly to Wyatt and then looked at me, busily taking notes. 'Don't worry about the social, Lauren, there's no work involved. You just need to show up.'

'And dance!' Wyatt added with a laugh.

'It's all good, Maria, and I'm happy to help out. Not sure about the dancing, though.'

'We'll get you in a jingle dress, never mind about that,' Wyatt joked.

'Jingle dress?' I was a little embarrassed I didn't know what it was.

Maria answered. 'It's a dress worn at powwows. They have tin pieces in the shape of cones sewn carefully on them and they make a jingling noise when you dance.'

'Right, got it. Not sure how good I'd be at jingling, but I'll give it a go.'

'Okay, that's all at the moment, I think.' Maria ruffled through some papers on her desk. 'Ah, that's right, Wyatt, I need you to take Lauren to the community centre to meet everyone. They're eager for an Aboriginal Australian exhibition and I mentioned we had Lauren on board and now they're excited. Sorry, Lauren, you know being the only First Nations Australian around, everyone's going to want a piece of you.'

'Don't be sorry, it's the same back home. And we'll do the same to you when you come to Australia. I mean, if the fellowship ever becomes reciprocal.' I didn't want to commit the NAG to anything on my first week at work.

'Great idea, I *definitely* think we need a fellowship down under.' Wyatt was impressed with that idea.

'Also, Lauren, here's a list of some galleries around Chelsea that represent Native artists. It might be worth your while checking them out sometime. Just so you have an idea what the private galleries are doing and are into.' Maria handed me the paper. 'Emma told me you were a workaholic, in a good way, of course. And so is Wyatt.'

'Hey, I love my job is all.' Wyatt was defensive.

'He's one of a short list of highly esteemed Native curators in New York.'

As Wyatt and I walked back to our office I read the list Maria gave me.

'I know the galleries in the area well, Lauren. I can take you there if you like.'

'Great!' I said, arriving at my desk and thinking about the next twelve months, full of interesting events, people and work. Doing all this with Wyatt was going to be fun.

On Saturday I went to the Chelsea markets with Kirsten and Vikki, stocked up on fruit and veggies and then, while the girls grabbed a table at Day Drinks for coffee, I raced into Amy's and bought a delish assortment of cupcakes. I would take some in for Wyatt and whomever else was working that day. After coffee I made my way down to the museum. When I got there, Cherokee storyteller Gayle Ross was enthralling the kids with the tale of how the turtle's back was cracked one day when some wolves decided to teach him a lesson for bragging about being a great hunter. The crowd of about thirty-five, including Wyatt, were hanging on her every word.

'Do you organise this as well? I didn't realise storytelling fell into curatorial duties.'

'Yeah, curator means "dogsbody", you know that. Nah, I'm here because I wanted to bring my friend Julian and his daughter Cindi. I thought they'd like it. Cindi's the one in the pink dress in front.' I saw a cute girl with pink ribbons listening intently.

'And this is my buddy Julian.' Julian looked about six foot two, had thick black hair, deep blue eyes and muscles pushing through his tight grey T-shirt. He didn't look like your typical dad at story time at a museum. The other dads looked far more conservative and had dad bods. My gaydar was going off, and I wondered how Julian and Wyatt new each other.

'Julian, this is my colleague, Lauren Lucas. She's from Canberra, Australia.'

'I love Australia,' Julian declared.

'You've been there?'

'Two years ago – Sydney, Mel*bourne*, Bris*bayne* and Uluru.' My god, he'd *actually* been to Australia *and* he knew to say Uluru. Not one of those Americans who got

Austria confused with Australia or who thought it was too far away or referred to our sacred site as Ayers Rock.

'I love the Ossie accent, it's wild.'

'I love how you fellas say Bris*bayne* and Mel*bourne*. It sounds funny.'

There was clapping as the storytelling session ended.

'Looks like it's over. It was nice meeting you, albeit briefly, Julian.' I extended my hand.

'Maybe we could have a coffee and share stories about Australia. I never got to Canberra but I'd like to go one day and check out the National Museum there – looks pretty awesome.'

'Oh, it is.'

'Can I get your number from Wyatt and call you sometime for a coffee?'

'Okay, sure.' Coffee with Julian and talking about home a bit would be nice. I could brag about what Canberra had to offer.

My mobile rang about three hours later when I was back home, having a cup of tea with Vikki and Kirsten.

'Hi, Lauren, it's Julian, Wyatt's buddy.'

I was taken by surprise that he rang so soon.

'I'd like to take you to brunch tomorrow in SoHo, if you're free.'

'Um, yes, I'm free. Brunch would be cool.'

'Okay, I'll meet you at Balthazar, say eleven?'

'Eleven it is. I'll google it and see you there.'

'You realise that's a date, don't you?' Vikki said with a sly grin on her face as I put the phone down.

'It's not a date, it's brunch.'

'Brunch date, Balthazar. He's got style,' Kirsten said. 'We like him already.'

'You girls are crazy. He's got a daughter, and I'm fairly sure he's gay.'

'Was he wearing a ring on either hand?' Vikki asked.

'I didn't look. I'm sure Wyatt wouldn't have passed on my number if it was anything sinister or if he was married. He just wants to talk about Canberra.'

'Oh god, as if that isn't a lie. Who on the planet wants to talk about Canberra?' Kirsten shook her head, laughing.

'Well I do, thank you very much.' I took a bite out of one of the decadent cupcakes I'd bought that morning.

'What are you going to wear?'

'Why? If he's gay he's not going to care what I'm wearing.'

'Are you kidding? He'll be more critical than if he were straight,' Vikki said emphatically.

'And if he's *not* gay, then you'll still be hot. It's good to have all bases covered,' Kirsten said, catching crumbs in her hands from the cupcake she was devouring.

'I'm wearing jeans.'

'Casual, good idea. Don't want to make too much effort too soon, give it the take-it-or-leave-it approach.' Vikki spoke like a woman who knew her dating fashion requirements.

'It *is* the take-it-or-leave-it approach. Now stop it.'

'She's here one week and she's got a date.' Kirsten sounded envious.

'Stop it.'

'Jeans, that's good, and a cute top,' Vikki said.

'And ballet flats, perfect.' Kirsten added.

'You girls are totally mad.'

I woke the next day looking forward to brunch at the fancy French cafe, Balthazar. I found my way to Spring Street in SoHo and was seated in one of the maroon booths before Julian arrived. A waiter brought me a glass of water and I ordered a bowl of cappuccino. I'd never had a bowl of coffee before, but I had come to expect the unexpected and to be shocked by nothing in New York City.

My mouth watered reading the breakfast menu. I didn't know there were so many ways you could order eggs. Even though I could've had Eggs Benedict or Eggs Norwegian, Eggs Florentine, or Eggs en Cocotte, I knew straight away that I had to have a Soft-Boiled Organic Egg with 'soldiers'. A breakfast tribute to my childhood in Goulburn.

I watched two men across the room devouring a seafood platter, though it was still early morning, then looked to my left and recognised the Australian author Lily Brett, Libby's favourite author. She had soft, wavy, brown shoulder-length hair and matt red lips with a warm face. I wanted to meet her and pulled my camera out automatically. I went straight over, no shame at all.

'Excuse me, are you Lily Brett?'

'I am,' she said.

'I hate to interrupt but I loved *You Gotta Have Balls* and my friend adores you and would kill me if I didn't get an autograph or a photo.'

'That's very sweet, of course.'

I asked a waiter to take the pic of Lily and me together, as I tried not to smother her by getting too close. People were starting to watch now and I was embarrassed that I had drawn attention to both of us.

'Thank you, thank you. My friend will be very impressed.'

Lily smiled and I went back to my table just as Julian walked in the door. He threw me a wave, swaggering over. He wore a pair of jeans and a white T-shirt that showed off his tiny waist and broad shoulders. He was built like Adam, only taller.

'Good morning, Lauren. You look beautiful,' he said, sliding into the booth on the other side of the table. I looked down at my cute top and jeans, and thought to myself that I did indeed look beautiful.

When the waiter took our order I asked for my eggs with soldiers.

'That sounds interesting, I'll have the same,' Julian said. The waiter took the order and walked away.

'So, Julian, what do you do when you're not eating eggs?'

'I'm a personal trainer. I run boot camps in Central Park and Washington Square Park, and I train in gyms as well.'

'Your little girl Cindi, she's a cutey.'

'She looks like her mom.'

'Is she with her mums' – I slipped up, assuming he must have donated sperm to a lesbian couple or something – 'I mean, with her *mom* right now?'

'No, she's with her grandparents. Her mother, my wife, died four years ago, cancer.'

'Your wife,' I said, surprised, and then checked myself. 'Oh, that's terrible. I'm so sorry to hear it, that's awful.'

'It's hard on Cindi, because she never got to know how wonderful her mom was. But she spends Sundays with either my folks or Jenny's folks, so she's surrounded by love all the time.'

'So the trip to Australia, you took Cindi with you?'

'No, I was emotionally exhausted and depressed. I took the trip to learn how to breathe properly again after Jen died. It was hard and sudden.'

'I'm sorry, you probably don't want to talk about it.'

'No – I want to talk about it, it was a long time before I could. And it's my history. We are what our past has made us. I'm good now. Healthy, fit, getting back into life and dating again, I have to.'

Julian didn't seem to take a breath. He was telling me more than he really needed to, exposing himself, like guests do on American talk shows, à la *Maury*, or worse, *Springer*. The kind of shows that would never work in Australia because we're far more conservative. Julian was still talking as the waiter delivered our food to the table.

'I want someone in my life. I feel like I haven't lived for a long time. And this is nice, this . . .'

'Brunch?' I shot in quickly.

'Yes, I guess. My friends called it a date.'

'That's funny, so did mine. I like New York for that, you can have a coffee and a runny egg with soldiers' – we both smiled – 'and it's called a date. It sounds nice but it can still just mean we are friends.'

'Truth is, Lauren' – Julian paused and put a soldier back on his plate – 'I'm looking to settle down again. I'm not cut out for the singles scene, or massive amounts of dating. I don't roll like that. Most of my friends are single and out partying, but I can't do that with a six-year-old. I don't want to anymore anyway. I like the healthy life.'

'Me too. I didn't even drink much until I came to Manhattan and people started siphoning cocktails down my throat. I've drunk more in a week than I would in six months back home.'

Julian laughed.

I felt compelled to explain my usual workout routine because Julian was a trainer. 'No, seriously, I'm at the gym most days, when I can, but I've been working really long days since I started at the museum. I'll fall into a routine soon enough.'

'You just need discipline and focus – you look like you work out. Athletic legs, toned arms. The routine will come back quick enough, but you have to live as well, and New York is the place for that.'

The waiter returned and topped our water glasses up. Julian put both hands around his glass, looking at it momentarily, and then glanced up at me.

'I know we've just met, but I like you, Lauren. You're cute, especially in those specs, and I didn't need Wyatt to tell me you're smart and sexy. I figured that out pretty much straight away.' I frowned; we were just on a brunch date.

'I'm looking for a relationship,' he blurted out.

What had happened to the obligation-free New York date? Someone had been lying to me.

'What about you?' Julian looked desperately into my eyes.

'I'm not looking for a relationship at all. I just wanted to have brunch with you, talk about Canberra, that's all. I thought that's all this was.'

'I'm sorry . . . it's just that you won't last a week single here, Lauren. Trust me.'

'I'm not single, really. I've still got someone in my heart and head 24/7 and hope to be reunited with him soon.'

'Well. At least we sorted that out quickly. I don't want to go on six or seven dates and then realise the woman is on a different path to me. It's happened before with women I've been involved with.

'I let them get close to me and we're intimate and then weeks later they're gone because they don't actually want a relationship. So now I just lay it out on the table straight up. When you've got a child you can't let yourself get emotionally attached to someone every few weeks. I can't let Cindi see a stream of girlfriends come and go.' Julian was sincere and clearly a good catch for anyone wanting what he wanted.

'Well, it sounds like you're miles in front of the average guy, with or without kids, just by knowing what you want and how to get it. I reckon you could give women some tips too.'

As we walked down to the corner of Spring Street it was an awkward goodbye. I had been so foolish. Kirsten was right, who wanted to sit in New York on a Sunday and talk about Canberra?

'Perhaps we could be friends. Work out together?' Julian said earnestly.

'Perhaps. Either way, take care, might see you at the museum sometime.'

I walked off, unsure whether trying to be friends was a good idea or not. I messaged Libby when I got home:

> Hi there tidda! I had my first 'date' today even though I didn't think it was a date. I thought it was just 'brunch' and dressed down to prove it. It's flattering to get a date with someone you've only known a few hours and, boy, the Yanks seriously don't waste any time. But he's not the one. Hot though. Full of muscles. He'd look good in one of your firey calendars! He wants to be friends, but I don't know. Any man that's going to talk about relationships on the first date could be a little stalker-like, don't you reckon? Always up for your wisdom, sis, so message me back!

She sent me back a clip from YouTube. It was the scene from *When Harry Met Sally* where Billy Crystal's character is explaining to Meg Ryan that it's impossible for men and women to be 'just friends' because the man is always thinking about having sex with the woman. I didn't want Julian thinking about having sex with me – I wanted Adam to.

On Monday, Wyatt stuck his head around the partition between our workstations.

'How was brunch with Julian?'

'At least you didn't call it a date, like everyone else did.'

'Sorry, should I not have given you his number? He said you agreed to coffee.'

'No, it's fine, I did. But I thought that's all it was, coffee and chatting about Canberra. I'm not here to date really, Wyatt. Don't get me wrong, Julian is lovely, a really nice, smart guy, but he's looking for a relationship, and I'm not interested in a relationship right now. I want to focus on my work here, just like you really.'

'Julian is a good guy, Lauren, but really, men – and I mean *all* men – will say whatever it takes to get near a pretty woman. You'll learn this in New York.'

'Are you saying that none of them are sincere, then?'

'Not at all, I'm just saying that if they want to pursue you, they will.'

Wyatt went back to his computer and I looked at my own screen. I felt my 'Love needs faith' pendant and silently wished and hoped that things could actually pan out for

Adam and me. If I did have faith, I'd have to focus on the possibilities and not get distracted by the other options blossoming around me. If nothing else, it was better the devil I knew.

15

Managing the Manhattan life

The next few weeks were intense at work: coordinating with staff across the museum, meeting artists, getting lost in corridors that all led to new places and learning to navigate my way around the city. I was busy, and grateful for all the distractions from thinking about Adam.

I started planning my own exhibition – going through the work of some of my favourite artists and national treasures. I wanted to showcase the diversity of our styles. I also had to consider how well the works would sit within the NMAI space. I pulled together some ideas for Wyatt and Maria to consider, including Blak Dounglas's Archibald Prize winning portrait of Karla Dickens in the Lismore Floods (Emma had already done the groundwork to make it happen). His signature flatbottom clouds and graphic design-styled canvas depicting another First Nations artist would highlight two extraordinary talents in one painting. It would sit well in contrast with jewellery designed by Darrell Sibosado from the Bard people of Lombadina. Sibosado's mother-of-pearl and silver pendants had gained international interest for their fashionability in city centres.

I wanted to take a different approach with this exhibition, showcasing illustrators while promoting other artforms, so I put put images from Samantha Campbell's portfolio of children's books published by Magabala. I also included some of Julie Dowling's self-portraits, which would add commentary on identity and consider issues around Aboriginal people with fair skin.

These were on top of the artists we were including in the urban exhibition back home. I wanted to combine some of those artists with some new ones here to promote as many as possible.

I also began working with a community centre nearby. It was a social services agency that also had an unofficial gallery and performing arts program with exhibitions, workshops and social events.

Together we planned to exhibit some Qandamooka weavers from Queensland who had been running workshops nationally for years. Aunty Sonja Carmichael and her daughter Leecee worked across mediums and were well respected fibre artists, while daughter and sister Freja, had curated the *Weaving the Way* exhibition at the University of Queensland Art Museum, and we were keen to adapt it for a New York audience.

I was finally settling into Manhattan too. I did the

Saturday morning markets with the girls, felt less lost on the subway, and was being braver about travelling alone later at night.

I also learned to carry change in my pockets for buskers and beggars. Sometimes I stopped to say hello and to listen to local buskers, who added colour and atmosphere to an already thriving city.

I finally established an exercise routine at the gym, taking to the treadmill at a local sports club most mornings, sweating and panting and staring out the windows at a fancy bakery directly across the road. I upped the incline as I thought about their layer cakes and cheesecakes and French toast. I salivated and perspired thinking about their tiramisu, hamentaschen, apple danish, almond horns, and fruit tarts. But I was strong and only indulged in a fresh orange juice and deep inhalation of the scent of pastries after the gym. I remained amused by those who went in and ordered eggwhites on their toast.

At the end of the month a group of Native curators visited from Canada to talk to Maria about touring exhibitions between the various museums there and the NMAI. I was asked to give a brief presentation on the NAG – our history, mandate, current exhibitions, acquisitions policies and so on. I was proud to talk about the gallery and the role we played in maintaining Aboriginal culture in Australia, and now showcasing it to the world. There were plenty of questions about artists, mediums and markets, and Wyatt was there and seemed to be completely engaged in everything I said. I felt even more proud, knowing he could easily pass on all the information to others as part of his work from now on if need be. And that was the whole point of the fellowship – the exchange of information and ideas.

After a long but inspiring day we all went to the White Horse Tavern after work to unwind. I felt right at home when I saw a bottle of Australian Yellow Tail Merlot sitting on the bar. Not the best wine we have, but Australian nonetheless. The White Horse, although an Irish Bar, had an eclectic interior design, or lack of design, with US flags, Irish shamrocks, four-leaf clovers, hockey sticks, baseball caps and the odd sailor's hat. There were high-backed wooden stools at the long bar and booths to sit in. Christmas lights hung above the bar like they had been there for years. It was another comfortable bar, like Easy's, but with much burlier men – builders and labourers and tradesmen of all kinds, but also men in suits.

'Gee, it's busy,' I said to Wyatt as we propped ourselves at the bar.

'It's always busy on Thursday and Friday nights. The music'll start soon.'

'So this is your local?'

'Not really, but we come here after work sometimes. It's close, down to earth, the crowd is pretty mixed, chilled. By the way, Lauren, I loved your presentation today. It really made me want to go to Oz.'

'You should, it's a beautiful country, and you'd go mad with all the galleries and museums.'

'They have critters there, though, don't they?'

'Critics?'

'Critt*ers* – you know, spiders and snakes.' Wyatt squirmed in his seat and I thought, here he is, the fabulous gallery guy, frightened of bugs and reptiles. Wyatt really wasn't a blokey bloke at all.

'Oh, the sharks will get you before the red-backs or pythons.' I couldn't help myself – foreigners were always worried about shark attacks. 'Seriously, we have poisonous snakes in Australia like the taipan and the red-bellied black and the death adder, but the likelihood of getting bitten is small, especially in the city.'

Wyatt didn't answer, just kept looking at me, and I was concerned I'd freaked him out unnecessarily.

'Are you okay?' I asked.

'You have really beautiful eyes,' he said. I remembered I'd left my glasses on my desk at work.

'Oh, they look better after every beer. Drink up.'

'This is my first beer.' He picked up his glass and took a sip. 'But now, ma'am, I think we're all heading to the Fraunces Tavern for something to eat. You in?' Wyatt asked.

'Yes, sounds good, I'm starving.'

We headed out into the New York dusk and went to the Fraunces Tavern around the corner. We sat near the windows. The bar had dim lighting and the wooden chairs and tables somehow matched the American flags and rifles on the walls and the tiny kerosene lamps on the window ledge. Everyone was chatting about art and New York and trans-American and trans-Atlantic projects, and I was truly happy with my lot.

16

Macy's madness

I wasn't surprised to learn that Kirsten was a Leo, and on 2 August we celebrated her thirtieth.

'Happy birthday to you . . . happy birthday to you . . .' Vikki and I had a birthday breakfast prepared when she finally got out of bed at ten.

'Stop it – I don't even want to think about it.'

'C'mon, let's celebrate,' Vikki said. 'We're starting at Macy's, you need birthday lingerie to wear tonight for the birthday bonk.'

'Don't be ridiculous. Turning thirty is bad enough without you reminding me I haven't had sex in months.'

'It's time, then.' Vikki poured coffee into Kirsten's favourite black-spotted mug.

'I think I need some birthday underwear as well,' I said. I realised it was also some months since the last time I'd had sex.

'When's your birthday?'

'April. But it's good to be prepared.'

'Seven months ahead, that's some preparation, but I think we can go shopping again before then, love. Don't want any of those Bridget Jones moments and grandma pants getting in the way, right?' Vikki said with a completely straight face.

I ate my Vegemite toast as Kirsten opened her presents. Her phone beeped the whole time. Flowers arrived at the door from friends at work and the coffee table was covered in cards that had been sent from home.

'Wow, I love it.' I'd bought her a squash blossom necklace in turquoise and coral from the NMAI shop. 'This is my lucky birthday necklace! How does it look?'

'Deadly, sis – the coral really suits you. I should've gotten myself one.'

Vikki handed her gift over next, beautifully wrapped and ribboned.

'Oh my god, an autographed photo of Robert De Niro. I can't believe it. But you *never* ask for autographs. It's too *uncool*.'

'Yes, it is, but I was prepared to be uncool and risk my professional standing for your birthday. Just this once.'

'Wait!' I reached into the fridge. 'It's good you slept in, gave me time to get down to the markets and grab what every girl needs on her birthday.' I opened a box of cupcakes that had Kirsten's face as icing, just like the Kate ones I had the first day at Chelsea Markets. 'Tadaaaahhhh.'

'No way, how did you manage that?'

'They like my accent, apparently.'

'This is the best birthday ever! Let's shop.'

We walked the nine blocks to Macy's, grabbing a coffee from one of the 'best coffee in New York' outlets. There were endless sales along the way so we ducked in and out of shops. I bought a red satin scrunchie for my hair, Kirsten bought herself a patent purple handbag and Vikki grabbed a pair of pale pink slides.

When we hit the corner of West 34th Street and Broadway I saw the famous red and white Macy's sign. The world's largest department store, Macy's occupied almost the entire block bounded by 7th Avenue on the west, Broadway on the east, 34th Street on the south and 35th Street on the north. It was bigger than the main shopping strip in Goulburn, and I loved it.

Inside, the store was spacious, reminding me of David Jones back home. The ceiling on the ground floor was high, and the space was bright white, well lit. You could see why Macy's New York was the flagship store and I wondered what the other 800-plus stores across America looked like. Surely, none of them could've been as big as this one.

They had *everything* here, from lingerie to luggage, cameras to cakes. I watched the escalators packed with shoppers and tourists of all ages filing up and down from floor to floor.

'You know what?'

'What?' both girls asked.

'I think there are more people in here than in my little town back home.'

'That's so funny.'

'This store is larger than the entire perimeter of Goulburn. I think I've fallen in love again.'

'Ladies lingerie is up, let's go.' Vikki led the way up the escalators.

'Oh my god, there must be three thousand pairs of knickers here, and look at all the bras.' I loved lingerie, but it had always been wasted on Adam. I spent a fortune on knickers that only ever stayed on five minutes with him. At least here I could buy something and enjoy wearing it. We all grabbed a big pile and headed for the change rooms.

'I'm coming back as a man in my next life,' Kirsten said from her cubicle.

'Why?' Vikki laughed back.

'I actually hate shopping for bras and swimsuits. It's too much work. Men have no idea.'

I bought a red bra, a multicoloured striped bra and a black bra with matching knickers.

'I don't know why I bother,' Kirsten said, handing over her selection to the cashier. 'It's not like anyone's going to see them.'

'Jesus, you can be negative sometimes,' Vikki said. 'Firstly, the lingerie should be about making *you* feel even more beautiful, whether anyone else sees it or not. And secondly, you are so going to meet someone tonight. It's your birthday, this is Manhattan, and you're wearing Elle Macpherson intimates, so be ready to be intimate!!'

'Anyone hungry?' I asked.

Kirsten spun around quickly. 'Oh my god, I'm starving. It must have been all that exercise trying on bras! There's a lift just there,' she said, pointing to the wall.

'You mean elevator,' Vikki said grinning.

'I mean there's an *elevator*, yes. I'm still learning the lingo too,' Kirsten said to me, rolling her eyes. 'I've slipped into my Aussie-speak again since you arrived.'

We got in the elevator and were greeted by a chirpy operator, something we didn't have back home. He closed the doors and we started our descent down to the food hall, but before we reached the floor I started feeling dry-mouthed and my heart was palpitating. Then I was breathless.

'Are you all right?' Kirsten asked, grabbing my arm.

'I can't breathe that well, I feel too closed in.' I started to feel faint, but I didn't know why. I wasn't stressed or anxious; it must have been the confined space.

'Are you claustrophobic?' a guy behind me asked as I fell back slightly. 'Oops,' he said, holding me up.

'We need to get out,' Kirsten said urgently to the lift operator.

The girls and the guy holding me all got out together. 'Does she need resuscitating?' the guy asked.

'Nice try,' Vikki commented sarcastically.

'What do you mean?'

'Her eyes are open and she's breathing, buddy, so no, she doesn't need mouth-to-mouth.'

'Okay, I was just trying to help.'

'Resuscitation is usually done when someone has *stopped* breathing,' the lift operator said, hanging halfway out the door.

'Here's a chair.' Kirsten appeared from nowhere with a piece of furniture. I was burning with embarrassment at causing a scene yet again, remembering my flight over.

'I'm fine, please, don't fuss.'

'Nice trick, hon, we need to get you in more elevators,' Vikki whispered to me, as the guy and the lift operator stepped back into the lift and the doors closed.

'What?'

'Guys holding onto you tight and wanting to give you mouth-to-mouth when you're still breathing. Why didn't I think of that? I should get one of the actors on set to teach me how to act claustrophobic.'

'You're mad!' Kirsten declared.

'Can we just get some food and water?' I pleaded.

'There's pizza and pretzels and some other fast food on the next floor,' Vikki suggested.

'I'm turning into a pretzel. I need a sandwich or salad,' I pleaded again.

'Let's just take the escalator to the food hall.'

We sat eating salads, knowing we'd probably eat too many calories later that night. The girls politely didn't mention the incident in the elevator but I was concerned about it happening again. I wondered what Mum might suggest and then remembered Dad telling me to buy something from Macy's for Mum. On the way out of the food hall we passed a Macy's souvenir section and I went crazy, getting Mum a make-up purse, T-shirt, shopping bag, snow globe and cute key ring. I knew she'd love all of them and she could have her own Macy's experience at home.

As we headed out of the store, we all looked at the elevator and then the escalator and without saying a word walked towards the moving stairs.

I spent the afternoon resting – the lift incident in Macy's had exhausted me. I would have to avoid enclosed spaces and crowds wherever possible in New York, but it was going to be much harder in the city of eight million than it was back in Canberra. I could avoid lifts in some instances, but what about going up the Empire State building? I decided to get online and search out some ways to manage the anxiety and claustrophobia, but first I had to catch up on messaging the girls and sending postcards to the family. The Aunts liked to receive cards to put on their fridges, and I had managed to get hold of a whole collection focusing on African Americans in politics, with portraits of Barack Obama and Martin Luther King Jr, and I even found cards with images of flyers from the First Annual Convention of the People of Colour in 1831. They'd be the talk of the bingo hall back home in Goulburn.

I messaged Libby and Bec and caught them up on work, my new local pub that happened to be an Aussie bar and the shopping we'd done. I attached photos of Macy's from every angle so they could get some idea of the size. I also sent some pics of me and the girls at home in Chelsea. Bec would've loved the layout of our apartment because she always wanted to rearrange furniture back home to maximise space.

I wrapped Mum's pressie and wrote on a postcard with a huge apple on it. I knew it would generate a few laughs back in Goulburn and that Dad would even see the funny side, eventually. He'd softened a lot by the time I'd left. Nick got a Michael Jordan card, Max got Yankee Stadium and Emma got one of the George Gustav Heye Center, which housed the NMAI. As I put stamps on the cards I felt an overwhelming pang of homesickness and started to cry. I wanted to call home but knew ringing them in tears would only stress Mum and Dad out, and I didn't want them to worry. I opened Spotify and lay down on the bed listening to the hauntingly beautiful lyrics of the late Gurrumul Yunupingu. There would never be another voice the same. I dozed off, grateful that I was going out to party for Kirsten's birthday.

All dressed in our birthday underwear and slinky dresses, we headed to Kirsten's favourite Cuban bar and restaurant to meet her friends from her work. Our group took up most of the venue, which seated about sixty. There was a massive ornate ceiling fan with a gorilla hanging off it, paintings on the wall of Cuban dancers and landscapes of Havana. Waiters wearing blue shirts and black pants carried plates of food as they bustled through the crowds of people standing at the bar.

'These are for you, party girl.' Vikki handed Kirsten a plate of fried oysters. 'Little aphrodisiac to help your birthday bonk along the way.'

'You're mad, but thanks.'

'And you, try this.' Vikki stuck a straw in my mouth. 'It's a Havana Sunset.'

'Nice.'

'It's mine, though,' she said. 'Yours is on its way. I ordered you an Old Havana – thought you might like the mix of rum, triple sec and peach nectar, the fruit juice being healthy and all.' Vikki winked cheekily at me.

'Sounds yum, thanks.' We both turned back around to the bar while Kirsten took her plate of oysters to share with a guy who looked like he just might get a glimpse of her Macy's purchase.

Everyone seemed to be yelling at each other over the background music. I stood at the bar and the barman put my Old Havana in front of me. I turned to watch Kirsten laughing with her friends while Vikki chatted to a guy on her left. I stopped a waiter passing by and asked, 'What is this music?'

'It is from Puerto Rico. We have music from Cuba and Puerto Rico, but they are often referred to as *dos alas del mismo pájaro.*' He whispered into my ear and put one hand on the small of my back.

'*Dos alas del mismo pájaro,*' I repeated in my Australian accent.

'It means two wings of the same bird, because Cuba and Puerto Rico shared the same history under Spanish colonial rule.'

'Really? That's interesting.' I sipped on my drink as he walked off to serve another customer.

Vikki grabbed me by the arm and whispered in my ear, 'Remember the hierarchy, Lauren.'

'What?'

'Don't flirt with waiters.' Vikki was giving me an order.

'What? I wasn't flirting. I was talking. I'm not allowed to talk to anyone any more?'

'He was whispering in your ear, that's flirting.'

'It's loud in here – no-one can hear anything. He wasn't flirting.'

'*I'm* not whispering in your ear, and *nor* do I have my hand on your back. Trust me, he was flirting.'

'You're being ridiculous.'

We looked over to Kirsten and could see the guy pushing hair out of her face.

'Now, that's flirting!' I said.

'He may just get an audience with her birthday knickers,' Vikki said, sipping long on her cocktail and winking at me at the same time.

17

Navajo Nate is naughty but nice

'I'm excited,' I said to Wyatt as we watched the artists setting up their stalls. It was the first Saturday in October and the art market was due to open at 10 am. The markets were one of the flagships of the NMAI, providing locals the opportunity to meet Native artists from across the Americas, while giving creators the opportunity to showcase their arts and crafts.

'I'm just hoping it all goes smoothly,' Wyatt said, scanning the Diker Pavilion. I looked too as Choctaw, Navajo, Cree and San Felipe Pueblo artists, among others, started to lay out their finest works – both traditional and contemporary. There were paintings and prints, sculptures, traditional beadwork, baskets and my favourite, jewellery.

'Well, here come the visitors already, right on ten, so I think that's a good sign for a successful day.' I was about to walk off when Wyatt gently took my arm.

'I just want to thank you for all your help these past few days,' he said.

'Oh, don't thank me. It was great for me to speak to the artists, even if it was just confirming their space allocations and so on. Now I can meet them and it will be easier to talk.'

'No, really, it was a relief to be able to give you that list of calls to make. I get a bit anxious about checking and double-checking details so I was relieved to be able just to give you the task and know it was done.' Wyatt smiled a thank you and I could see the same anxiety in his eyes that I often felt. We worked well as a team, having the same notions of how things *should* be done. His phone rang.

'I've gotta take this. You go have some fun!'

He didn't have to tell me twice. I walked to the nearest stall and tried on a silver and turquoise bracelet and knew immediately I had to have it.

'That's yours,' the artist stallholder said.

'It feels perfect.'

'I must have made it for you.'

'I'm Lauren Lucas, from the Wiradyuri Aboriginal nation in Australia. I'm working here for a year.'

'I know, I read about you in the magazine. I'm Nate, I'm Navajo.' Nate was over six foot tall and tanned with dark brown eyes and jet-black hair to his shoulders. He wore thin titanium-framed glasses and he had a cute dimple to the left of his mouth.

'I'd like to take this, and can I have these, too?' I picked up two almost identical chokers that I could give to Libby and Emma for Christmas.

'I tell you what, the cuff is yours, from me, a welcome to Turtle Island, or North America as people call it today. You should wear it now, and I'll wrap the chokers for you.'

'No, I can't, really.'

'This is our way.'

It was our way as well, to give a gift to a visitor, and to argue would be rude.

'Just make sure the clasp is done up properly,' Nate said, and turned my wrist over, holding my hand gently in his own. He startled.

'Are you all right?' I asked, not sure what he was doing.

'Didn't you feel that?'

'Feel what?'

'I felt something – maybe an electric shock.'

I giggled like a schoolgirl. Nate was flirting with me. This was New York City and I shouldn't have been surprised – men here really were more forward than back home.

A child came and grabbed Nate by his shirt. 'Hey mister, how much for this?' She held a little doll dressed in full regalia.

'Lauren, we should talk,' Nate whispered as I pulled my wrist from his grasp.

'I've got to check out the other stalls,' I said as I walked off.

At the end of the market day Wyatt and I went with many of the stallholders to the White Horse Tavern for a drink, and Nate never left my side.

'I have tickets to a show next Saturday, on Broadway – it's something I like to do whenever I get to New York.

Would you like to come? It's got rave reviews.' He handed me a flyer to *The Piano Lesson*.

'Yes, I've heard about it. Everyone's saying it's incredible.

'I was going to take my cousin who I'm staying with, but he's got to go out of town now. So there's a spare ticket if you'd like to come with me.'

I really wanted to see the play, so said, 'Sure, I'd love to.'

'What's going on?' Wyatt asked, sitting down next to me and looking at the flyer in my hand.

'Lauren's going on a date with me,' Nate told him.

'We're just going to see a play, that's all,' and I handed Wyatt the piece of paper.

'I've seen it, it's great. You'll enjoy it,' he said, then turned to Nate. 'And you take care of our sister here all right, or you'll have me to answer to.'

'What? You playing big brother, are you?'

'Someone needs to keep an eye out for the innocents from down under.' Wyatt threw me a grin.

'Thank you for the theatre excursion, Nate, and thank you for the protection, Wyatt – I feel well taken care of.'

We all left the bar at the same time and Nate gave me an awkward kiss on the cheek. Every day that week he texted me. He knew that I was too busy during the day to talk and I guessed that perhaps Wyatt had told him I wasn't really looking for anything while in New York. But I remembered Wyatt's words. 'If a man wants to pursue you, he will.' I couldn't help feeling flattered.

'Wyatt?' I asked around the desk partition.

'Lauren?' He smiled.

'Can I ask you for some manly advice?'

He came cruising around on his chair and I told him about the texts and Nate's persistence.

'Well, what do you want from this situation? He's only here a week.'

'To be honest, I don't want to be excited about seeing him on Saturday because I feel guilty about Adam, but it's really hard not to be impressed by a good-looking artist who makes jewellery and goes to the theatre and is, let's face it, pretty hot.' I expected Wyatt to agree with me on all those fronts but he didn't.

'I guess I look at him differently to you, like a colleague, and a cousin of sorts too. He's a nice guy, but I thought you weren't interested in dating here?'

'I'm not – it's just that I never thought I'd be interested in anyone other than Adam. Maybe I'm just lonely.'

'In New York you can go on a date and there's no obligation.'

'You're right, I'll just go and enjoy the play. Thanks for listening.'

I held out my jar of M&Ms for him to take a handful. I always had something sweet on my desk.

I was nervous as I emerged from the subway and walked north to West 47th Street. I was learning how to find my way around the city now, but at night it was still daunting.

I was looking forward to seeing *The Piano Lesson* because it had received the Pulitzer Prize for Drama when it was originally performed in 1987, and this version could only be improved by the likes of Samuel L. Jackson! I stood outside the Barrymore waiting for Nate to arrive. I really hadn't learned to be fashionably late. Back home I was always early because I was so desperate to break down myths about Aboriginal people being on 'Koori Time'. I took a moment to look at all the other theatregoers, and then saw Nate sauntering towards me looking very cool in black jeans, a T-shirt and jacket. He was clean-shaven and smelled good as he leaned in and gave me a peck on the cheek.

We were completely spellbound during the play, and afterwards Nate took me to to his favourite French restaurant, Manny's Bistro in the Upper West Side. We were greeted by the owner Manny as we entered, and made to feel at home immediately. I loved the New York welcoming married with the elegance and classic French style of the dimly lit bistro. As we settled into the burgundy velvet banquette, I felt truly international as I ordered the Soupe à l'Oignon and the Margret de Canard, because I literally never ate duck back home.

'I love this place, Nate.'

'It's my favourite New York restaurant. Manny always takes care of me, Naomi behind the bar makes the best cocktail in Manhattan, and there's an eclectic mix of people, from all over the city and the world.'

'Is that an actor?' I motioned my head to a familiar face sitting at the bar.

Nate laughed. 'Yes, Tony Danza.'

'My mum will flip, she loved him in *The Good Cop*.'

I stopped myself from suggesting I should get a selfie, but I was truly impressed with the entire night. Nate knew how to entertain himself in New York.

When dinner arrived Nate started to dissect the play.

'I can relate to the dysfunctionalism of that family,' he said. 'We've had suicides from depression and drug abuse.'

'I've had similar things in my extended family, too. Right now, though, my brother's in jail and that causes no end of worry. I felt bad about leaving Australia while Nick is still inside, but he'll be out soon.'

'It's funny that the things Indigenous people have in common are often the negatives – don't you think?' Nate said.

'Some of them are, but that play showed that *every* family is pretty much dysfunctional, there are just different levels of it.'

'Yeah, you're right, and in some ways it made *my* family look normal.'

We both laughed.

'Whatever *normal* is,' I said.

I could feel sleep taking hold before I even finished eating. On the last mouthful I looked at my watch.

'I'm sorry Nate but I am shattered. I really need to head off.'

'I'll see you home, Lauren,' Nate said. Was he being chivalrous or inviting himself back to my place?

I was nervous and excited and pleased all at the same time. But I had no intention of sleeping with him. We came out of the subway on my corner, still talking about the play, and Nate walked me home and up my five flights of stairs. Knowing that Kirsten was away, and suspecting Vikki wouldn't be home either, I didn't really want to invite him in.

'I think we need to say goodnight here, Nate.'

'You do?' he said, surprised, putting one arm against the door and one on my waist.

'Um, yes, my roommate is probably asleep and has to get up early for a film shoot—' Without letting me say anything else, he kissed me, so slowly and gently I couldn't help but melt. I pulled him close and kissed him back as he pushed me up against the door. I moaned and he held me tighter and then a door slammed down the hall, breaking the moment. What was I doing? I still had feelings for Adam, this was a bad idea. It would only cause me more confusion, and mess with Nate at the same time. A river of guilt ran through me as Nate leaned in to kiss me again.

'I'm sorry,' I whispered, 'but you can't stay. I don't have one-night stands, Nate, this isn't my style.' I didn't want to lead him on at all.

'Whatever you want, Lauren,' he said, and then kissed me again. I pushed him away immediately, feeling like I had betrayed my true self.

'Good night, Nate.'

'Good night, Lauren.' He smiled and walked back downstairs. When he was two flights down I went into the apartment and collapsed onto my bed. I looked at my laptop and hesitated before I logged on, but I couldn't help myself. I just had to know what Adam was up to.

He'd posted a story featuring a video of him on the field, and 'Start Me Up' by the Rolling Stones playing. I imagined Adam moving around his house like Mick Jagger, trying to impress one of the bimbos from his page. I was sure he wouldn't be feeling any rushes of guilt about me. I shut the laptop and looked at my mobile, wondering if I should text Nate. But while I regretted sending Nate away, I still wasn't the booty-call kind of girl. I went to sleep remembering words of wisdom Bec had shared with me one night: 'Never regret NOT doing it.'

18

I want to suck your blood

Nate called me the following week to say he was staying in town a while longer – some international buyers wanted to meet him about his work. The memory of his kiss was still close to the surface but I didn't want to pursue something with someone who didn't live in New York, didn't live in Canberra and who was also technically a professional connection of mine and Wyatt's. I couldn't have Wyatt or Maria thinking I was running around with visiting artists, so I declined Nate's offers for dinner and drinks.

Time was moving quickly anyway, and I loved living in Chelsea, working at Bowling Green and exploring Manhattan generally. I was going to the gym regularly and felt healthy, I'd almost mastered the subway, and because the girls were so busy with work, even on weekends, Wyatt and I had started hanging out. We'd explored all the galleries around Chelsea and had a few bagels along the way. Later, he took me to a Yankees game and I had so much fun taking photos for Max back home. He also introduced me to Union Square and its Saturday morning 'Greenmarket', which sold locally grown produce to New Yorkers and had the best organic goats' cheese *ever*.

Wyatt and I commuted to work together more often than not, talking about what was planned for the day ahead, and then debriefing on the way home. I tried to ask a couple of times whether he was seeing anyone or not, but he always said he was 'between dates' and never elaborated.

It was starting to get cold as we headed towards the end of October. I was thinking of spring in Canberra as autumn arrived in New York City. I'd started wearing tights and the fashions were changing in the shops. The cooler weather didn't bother me, although it was colder when I went out of a night. It certainly didn't affect my excitement about the Thunderbird American Indian Dancers and Singers Community Social on Saturday night. I was looking forward to meeting some of the local community members and hearing some deadly music. I hadn't helped organise it, so I needed a quick briefing on the way there.

When the buzzer went from downstairs, I knew it was Wyatt.

'Hello there, come up if you're good-looking.' It was what Bec and I used to say when we buzzed people into our apartment back in Manuka. Vicki and Kirsten were eagerly awaiting Wyatt, keen to check him out.

'Not sure if I fulfil your entry requirements, but I'm here anyway,' Wyatt said cheekily. He knew he was good-looking.

'Girls?' I turned to my housemates. 'Does he pass?'

They both gave the thumbs up and walked over to be introduced properly. I could see the naughty glint in both women's eyes. They didn't even try to hide the fact they were looking him up and down. He looked good in his suede jacket, jeans and boots. He was always casually sophisticated. And he smelled good too.

'Did you girls want to come to the social? It's open to the public,' Wyatt said.

'Oh, I've already got plans. We've got plans, haven't we?' Kirsten said to Vikki. She was clearly trying to ensure Wyatt and I had time alone together. As if it mattered.

'That's a pity, there'll be lots of guys there who would've loved to meet you, I'm sure.'

Both girls looked disappointed. Just then Wyatt's phone rang. Wyatt's phone was never on silent, and I must've rolled my eyes out of habit.

'Sorry, it's work.' He excused himself and stepped back out into the hall while I grabbed my bag and coat.

'He's hot,' Vikki said.

'And so lovely,' Kirsten added. 'If you're not going there, Lauren, then I might try.'

I laughed. 'He's gay,' I whispered.

'Oh!' they both mouthed in response and nodded knowingly.

'Figures,' Vikki added.

The girls waved us down the stairs and we headed to the station on 23rd Street.

'So what's the plan for tonight then?' I asked.

'About 5.30 pm we'll meet with the Hopi-Winnebago choreographer Louis Mofsie, who directs the troupe of singers and dancers, before they set up and get organised. At 6 pm, all the families will come along and have a great night of moving and shaking Native style.'

'Sounds awesome!' I said.

'Yeah, too deadly, as your mob say.'

'Wow, deadly and mob, you've picked up the lingo all right.'

'And the drumming group Heyna Second Sons are too solid.' We both laughed at Wyatt's attempts at Koori slang.

By seven o'clock the pavilion was in full swing. It was fun seeing the local community and all the people who had travelled from far and wide fill the space. Wyatt was moving about the room like he was the main man. Kids were dancing and playing, elders were seated and being tended to like royalty and people were dancing all different styles of traditional dance. I wanted to have a go myself, but Wyatt came over with Nate in tow.

'Look who I found,' Wyatt said, surprised.

Nate stood there in a ribbon shirt and blue jeans that looked fancy enough for a powwow with a smile right across his face.

'Couldn't miss a good dance, and the chance to see my favourite Aboriginal Australian,' he said with hope in his voice.

'This is great, isn't it?'

'Sure is. Your first social?' Nate asked.

'Most of the things I'm doing in New York are firsts.'

'I'm going to leave you two to catch up, I've got some guests to see to.' Wyatt walked off.

'It's good to see you, Lauren. I've been thinking about you a lot,' Nate said, looking straight into my eyes. I couldn't hold his gaze – it was penetrating and a little overwhelming, and his mouth was so inviting that in a more private setting I could easily have kissed him again.

'Wyatt's a great guy,' I said, looking at my friend on the dance floor. He could move like the professional dancers who travelled from powwow to powwow performing in competitions. I wondered if he'd been to the workshops the museum ran.

'He is, and very good at his job, but let's talk about you. What are you doing for Halloween?' Nate asked, smiling and wide-eyed.

'I was going to see what my roommates were doing, but Vikki works in film and is hardly ever home, and Kirsten works really long days at the UN, so it's unlikely they'll be around. I haven't given it much thought, really.'

Nate started rubbing his hands together. 'Great, then I think it would be the perfect New York experience for you to go to the parade in the West Village with me. It's on every year and it's awesome.'

It sounded awesome but I didn't want it to be anything serious. I was sure of that.

'Nate, can we just be clear that I'm not interested in dating while in New York?' I hoped I didn't sound ungrateful, because I knew both Kirsten and Vikki and Bec and even Libby would've jumped at the invitation, *hoping* it was a date.

'I always get dressed up in a costume, Lauren – and trust me, it's not the way I would ever take a woman out on a date.' He laughed and I breathed a sigh of relief and gratitude at the hospitality of my Native brothers, just taking care of me.

'Well then, I'd *love* to do that,' I said.

'Cool, I'll text you the address and see you on the 28th then.'

I borrowed a witch costume from Vikki, who had an array of items to choose from thanks to working in film. I'd never done Halloween before. It wasn't something that I had grown up with. Only once did someone buzz our door in Canberra, and we'd had to give the child dressed up as Spiderman a whole packet of Tim Tams. As it turned out, neither Vikki or Kirsten were working so I asked them if they wanted to come with me, as it wasn't a date, but they were both too tired and had stocked up on trick-or-treat delights themselves: packets of chips and dozens of candy bars.

'I just hope all of that is gone by the time I get home!' I said as I walked out the door, knowing the consequences to my waistline if anything was lying around the apartment late at night.

Nate and I started early evening, watching the Village Halloween Parade that went for about a mile. It was like

Mardi Gras crossed with street performers and backpackers, puppeteers and pet-lovers. I loved it and took so many photos I was worried my phone was going to run out of storage. Nate was a vampire for the night and looked like he was having a great time, clapping as every character walked past. There were very traditional costumes, lots of zombies and ninjas and ghosts, while some others were dressed up as Barbie and Buzz Lightyear. I couldn't imagine a Halloween parade like this ever hitting Northbourne Avenue in Canberra.

After a couple of hours of intense entertainment and energy we both felt exhausted.

'I'm beat and I've got to get this wig off, my head's itchy,' Nate said, scratching his hairline. 'Let's go back to my place, we can order some delivery.'

'Cool,' I said. I was still buzzing from the colour and sound of the parade. 'Nate, do you think it's odd that even Native Americans have adopted Halloween? I mean if it's from Ireland anyway?'

'I think there's lots of odd things that have happened with colonisation, and now both our nations have a whole new set of traditions we embrace.'

'True – we never had cricket before whitefellas arrived.'

There were orange and black streamers in the doorway and jack-o'-lanterns in the window of Nate's cousin's brownstone.

'I just need to get changed, and then I'll order some Chinese, that okay with you?' Nate asked.

'Perfect.' I took off my witch's hat with attached wig and Nate took off his plastic Dracula hair and we simultaneously scratched our heads. We both laughed and then there was an awkward moment of silence. He walked towards me and said in a Dracula accent, 'I want to suck your blood,' and started to kiss my neck. I closed my eyes and let him push me gently against the fridge in the tiny kitchen.

I wanted to kiss Nate, but I knew I wasn't going to have sex with him and I hated to lead him on. All too quickly, Nate's hands were in the back of my knickers and he was trying to get them down. I pushed him away.

'I'm sorry, Nate, I told you I didn't want to have a date. I just wanted to enjoy Halloween and Chinese, and I like hanging out with you, really, I do. But you and I aren't going to happen.'

Nate looked disappointed and confused, and slumped back against the kitchen sink. 'I'm sorry, I didn't mean to disrespect you, really. It's just you looked so lovely there, and I thought maybe you wanted to play as well.'

'Even if I did it would be a bit too fast for me, and I don't have one-night stands, I told you that already.'

'But technically, this is, or would've been, our second date. And I'd like to see you again, so not really a one-nighter.' He grinned. 'Anyway, there's lots of ways to play, we don't have to do them all in one night. We could have many nights.' He raised his eyebrows as if to say, *Don't you agree?*

I laughed, embarrassed, but there was nothing I could be but honest. 'I'm afraid I've lost my playfulness, or perhaps I just left it back in Canberra.'

'Lauren, you are so amazing. I can't believe an Australian man hasn't married you already.'

'Nate, we should really keep this professional, especially if we're going to be exhibiting your work soon.'

'Fair enough,' he said, pushing out his bottom lip like a child. 'I'll order us some food, shall I?' And he took out his phone and started scrolling.

The Chinese came in the cardboard boxes I'd only ever seen on the television, not like the plastic containers we used back home. We sat on Nate's couch, both of us trying to ignore the chemistry between us as we ate our beef with broccoli and General Tso's chicken. Every time Nate looked longer than necessary into my eyes, I asked a question about the proposal to exhibit and sell his beautiful jewellery internationally.

It was hard not to be attracted to him, as he spoke with passion about his work and his community, and asked me lots of questions about Aboriginal arts back home. It was wonderful to have someone be truly interested in my work and mind and not just sex. Adam and I never sat for hours talking that way. He was always trying to get into my knickers the minute I got in the door – and when we did talk it was only ever about him.

19

Lights, camera, action

Come November, I started to overhear people talking about their plans for Thanksgiving. Needless to say, I did not feel good about the holiday – the pilgrims were colonisers, and one friendly dinner didn't erase a whole genocide – and it reminded me too much of Australia Day back home. I did like the idea of giving thanks though, so I went souvenir shopping in Chinatown where I ♥ NY paraphernalia was everywhere: T-shirts, mugs, wall clocks, greeting cards, journals, fridge magnets, stickers and badges. I bought Statue of Liberty aprons for the aunties, plastic New York taxis and firetrucks and a couple of tiny T-shirts saying 'Someone in New York Loves Me' for the young cousins, and a Barack Obama calendar for Nick in jail so he could count his days down with some sense of inspiration. I sent Dad an I ♥ NY T-shirt and sticker for his truck, and for Libby and Bec I bought Big Apple flavoured condoms, stealing a couple of them for myself in case I needed them in the future.

The weekend of Thanksgiving, Wyatt was out of town visiting family, and Kirsten was showing a friend of her brother's around the city with a hectic schedule of galleries that I'd already done, so I opted out of the invitation to join them. But I jumped at the chance to join Vikki on a location scout downtown. I'd never done a 'scout' before and I finally got an understanding of how important and interesting her job was.

'We're shooting a drama about money, revenge, infidelity and murder.'

'Sounds familiar,' I laughed. 'Who's in it?'

'Denzel Washington, Will Smith and Keanu Reeves.'

'Oh my god! Your job is a perve fest.'

'Yes, I guess it is,' Vikki said seriously, and then smiled.

'Can you ask for autographs?'

'No, that would be uncool, like taking photos. I've only done it a couple of times, like for Kirsten's birthday.'

'So, what exactly do you do? I really have no idea – I just go to the movies once they're made.'

'Come along today and you'll see,' she said.

We went to a number of restaurants downtown looking for the perfect setting for the exchange of cash and drugs. Vikki knew the managers at some venues and was introducing herself for the first time at others. At the final venue in Little Italy, Vikki stopped the minute we walked in and declared, 'This is it. The size, the shape of the room, the decor. It's perfect for what we need.'

We both stood and looked around the recently renovated space. There were high tables with stools along one wall and above them were colourful wall-lights in different shades of reds and pinks. Along another wall there were black and white portraits of people in various poses: on a step, riding a bus, waving from a ship. The other walls were lined shoulder-height and upwards with wine. There were chandelier-like pendant lights hanging through the space, except above the bar, which was long and white and had one long light above it with what looked like hundreds of light globes. There was a line of funky high-backed white leather stools along the bar. Tables were set for the evening with wine goblets and white linen tablecloths. I loved the place immediately because it was so cool.

Just as I turned around from the bar, I saw what I assumed was the manager emerge from a door at the back of the restaurant. He was more than six foot tall – American men were all so tall – wearing a white shirt and a pair of low-waisted, straight-leg Armani jeans. He looked cool, and sexy. His smile took my breath away.

'Hello there, Ms V. Long time no see.'

'Cash Brannigan! I wasn't sure if you were still here. I spoke to Allen – he just said drop in.'

'I'm still here. I'll die downtown. It's my home.' He kissed Vikki on both cheeks and turned to me. 'Hello, I'm Cash Brannigan.' He shook my hand and I felt a rush of electricity.

'Hi, I'm Lauren Lucas,' I said.

Cash smiled. 'Lauren Lucas, from Australia.'

'Yes. How did you know that?'

'I recognise that accent. And you're a Blackfellow, aren't you?'

'How did you know *that*?

'I've been down under, spent some time in Darwin and Perth. I could just tell. Where's your mob from?'

Vikki was walking around the venue looking at the ceiling and the fittings, taking photos from every angle, and gauging, I thought, the size of the space. She was on the phone at the same time.

'I'm a Lucas, Wiradyuri, born in Goulburn, but we're all over central New South Wales. I live in Canberra now, it's just down the road from Goulburn.'

'Goal*borne*,' Cash said, the way Americans said Mel*borne*. I liked it. I liked listening to him talk. I didn't care what he said.

'Where are you from? I know you said you'll die here, but where were you born?'

'I was born here too, at St Barnabas Hospital in the Bronx, to be exact. I've travelled a lot, but I always come back here to New York. It's where I feel most at home. D'ya know what I mean?'

'I understand completely. I love New York, but I miss my country and my mob too much to move anywhere forever, either.'

Just then Vikki walked back to us, notepad in hand.

'This is perfect. I'll email over the dates, contracts, insurance information and so on and we'll sort it out asap if we can,' she said, all business-like.

Cash started writing something on a yellow notepad.

'I'm having a Fucksgiving party at my place on Tuesday, for people who don't want to celebrate the invasion, and any stray foreigners I meet are always invited – you girls should drop by if you don't have plans. I'll put on some food and drinks. My signature cranberry martini is truly something to be thankful for.'

'We'll be there,' Vikki said.

'Here's the address, on Broadway in Tribeca.' He handed me the piece of paper with the address and his number.

'Thanks,' I said shyly, suddenly unnerved by this handsome, confident Black man who lived on Broadway in Tribeca, an up-market and glamorous part of town, or so I had read in one of my numerous travel guides.

'See you both then.' He kissed Vikki on the cheek and then me.

As we walked out of the bar at dusk I heard the sound of sirens and watched one, two, three, then six fire trucks pull up at a high-rise building with smoke billowing out of what I guessed was maybe the fifteenth floor. Libby had asked me to get a photo of some firemen and to date I hadn't managed it, so I didn't want to miss the opportunity.

'Would it be really bad to ask one of the firemen for a photo?' I said softly to Vikki. It was a ridiculous question, considering they were busy putting a fire out.

'Just walk past them slowly, then turn around and I'll click. I see fans do it with movie stars all the time.'

'It's not for me, it's for Libby.'

'*Sure* it is! I really don't care, they're cute anyway. Go.'

'But they're working.' I looked up at the smoke, then at the trucks and at the police cars that had arrived. I looked up at the smoke again. 'I can't. This is stupid.' I just took a photo of them in action and hoped that would suffice until the next opportunity.

Thanksgiving Day arrived and there was a buzz in the street as people rushed around, but all I could think about was the darker history surrounding the holiday. My mind also kept wandering back to Cash, and how much I wanted to see him again. I'd developed a small crush from just one brief meeting and spent hours choosing the right dress to wear to his place – a cerise-coloured woollen dress to the knee, which looked great with black boots and coat.

Vikki and I arrived at his place in the evening and saw about thirty people gathered there, eating and drinking. The beer and wine flowed and there was a feeling of camaraderie in the air. Vikki and I sat on a comfy white leather lounge chatting and choosing songs on Spotify. Cash was busy playing host, but he made a point of checking on me regularly, ensuring I was comfortable and telling me to make myself at home. When I went into the kitchen to get another cranberry martini, he came up behind me and said, 'It's great you could make it. I hope we can have some time later to talk about Australia some more.'

Unlike Julian, wanting to 'talk about Canberra' as a code for a date, at least this time Cash and I were both on the same page. I didn't care if that 'talk' was code for getting to know each other better – I really liked him. He was smart and hot and had class. I was quite happy to hang out in his stylish apartment. Everything was white and sleek, except for a couple of artworks on the wall and a sculpture in one corner. I heard him telling another guest the sculpture was by a Bolivian artist working in Brooklyn and that it was of a marsupial based on the merging of a platypus and an echidna. He smiled at me when he said it, knowing the Australian connection. In the kitchen was a glass fridge that held the best wines, while the main fridge was full of food for entertaining as well as healthy living, with fruits and vegetables and every condiment imaginable. I looked at the fridge, then across the room to Cash, and I saw a worldly man with good taste and good health. He was a catch.

I texted Adam in a moment of weakness – our song was playing:

> I'm listening to *Hold My Hand* – remember our Lady Gaga song?

He texted back:

> Haha nice.

He didn't even ask where I was, or what I was doing. Just as I was beginning to feel sorry for myself, Cash turned the music down and the room hushed. He asked everyone to take a moment to decide who or what they would most like to say 'fuck you' to this Fucksgiving Day.

'COVID!' said a girl with long braids. 'The pigs,' said a guy standing over by the speaker system. 'Trump!' 'My boss!' 'Landlords', 'Vladimir Putin', 'Trans-fucking-phobia!' Everyone was getting passionate, laughing and talking about all the problems in the world. It felt really empowering. When it was finally my turn, I realised I was a little tipsy from all the cranberry martinis.

'I just want to say what an awesome holiday this is. For me, it's a tie between Peter Dutton, Elon Musk, Anti-Vaxers . . . and my ex-boyfriend.' Everybody laughed and cheered, although I don't think many of them knew who Dutton was. Afterwards, the crowd began to thin as Cash's guests headed out on the town – all his friends seemed to have exciting lives to go and live. Vikki disappeared too because she had an early shoot. She texted me from the cab:

Have fun with Cash – he's a good one!

As more guests left, I started to get nervous about being alone with Cash, so I busied myself cleaning up the kitchen, stacking the dishwasher, putting empty bottles in one corner of the kitchen and placing cushions back on the lounge.

When I was the only guest left, Cash came into the kitchen and fussed around the sink, pretending to clean what I had already cleaned. We talked about some of the issues that had been brought up by the Fucksgiving share session, and I was impressed by how politically aware and switched on Cash was. The air was electric with excitement and relief and sexual tension. I turned to rinse a dishcloth and Cash stood behind me, put his arms around my waist and kissed the back of my neck. I closed my eyes and moaned softly.

He whispered in my ear, 'You know what? I may hate what this holiday represents, but I'm thankful that you came tonight.'

'I'm thankful you wanted me to come,' I whispered back.

He turned me around gently and kissed my neck. I wanted Cash right then. It felt right, he felt right. His hands moved down my body and then pushed my dress over my head, revealing my black silk slip and bra.

'And now I want you to come again,' he said, dropping to his knees.

I was grateful I'd cleaned the long white kitchen bench as he lifted me onto it, quickly shoving a tea towel under my head. Fucksgiving sex was only going to be hot if we were both comfortable. He kissed my ankles slowly, teasingly, and I wriggled impatiently, wanting his mouth to work its way up my thighs at a much faster pace. It had been months since I'd had sex and I didn't mind if it was over quickly.

'Cash,' I whispered, worried about safe sex. He knew what I was thinking and pulled out a Big Apple flavoured condom. 'You read my mind,' I said.

Afterwards we lay on the heated kitchen tiles wrapped in tablecloths. I stared at the city lights coming through the window and I didn't feel guilty at all. I allowed myself to celebrate the moment with someone who made me feel good. Someone who was worlds apart from Adam Fuller. I could feel myself letting go, finally.

'We need to eat,' Cash said jumping up, wrapping a tablecloth around his waist and offering a hand to help me up.

I tried to be as ladylike as possible as I got up from the floor with little to cover me, unsure of what the next move would or should be. What happened in one-night stands? Adam always rolled over and started snoring after sex.

'You don't want to sleep?' I asked.

'It's only 10.30. How fast can you get dressed? I have the perfect place for food.' Cash was on the phone immediately making a booking. 'We'll be there in half an hour.'

'Wow, this really is the city that never sleeps, isn't it?' I liked that Cash was capable of organising a table that late.

'It's great for me, running the bar and still being able to have a social life separate to work. And Buddakan is one of my favourite places, I know you'll love it.'

The fact Cash even wanted to go out impressed me. Adam only ever wanted to order Thai takeaway.

'So where's the restaurant?' I asked, as we climbed into an Uber.

'It's in the Meatpacking District,' Cash answered. 'The whole district's open twenty-four hours and it covers twenty square blocks. Actually it goes nearly all the way to the Chelsea Markets.'

'It's right near Chelsea then, where I live.'

'Yes, love it there, it's arty, with writers, designers, architects and luxury boutiques and great restaurants and bars. It's one of my favourite parts of the city,' Cash said as the Uber pulled up to the curb.

We walked into the restaurant and we were seated in the bar area for a few minutes. 'Why don't you order a drink. I need to use the restroom.'

I ordered a Vigor – montelobos mezcal, milagro SBR silver tequila, coconut, campari, and pineapple. I looked at the crowd of business people, couples, and two girls enjoying a drink at the bar. It was dimly lit and busy with chatter. It looked like people were waiting for tables but no-one seemed to worry because it was the place to be and the luscious smells of spices of the Far East wafted through the restaurant.

The barman gave me my drink and I liked the service, friendly but not sugary sweet. Cash returned, pleased we would be seated shortly.

'Apart from my own restaurant, this is the best service I've had in New York,' he told me.

'Really?'

'There-but-not-there-waiters, not in your face. And it's the perfect place to be on a cold night.' Cash put his arm around my waist and ordered himself a beer.

I was still glowing from the sex, and every sense was piqued. I could even smell the earthy hops aroma of Cash's beer on the low table.

'You look beautiful, Lauren, and you look like you belong in Manhattan.'

'Well, this certainly isn't Manuka or Goulburn.'

The hostess came and ushered us to our table. 'Is there anything in particular that takes your fancy, Lauren?' Cash asked.

'It all looks good to me. Can you order?'

Cash ordered us both kumquat mojitos and a twelve-course tasting menu and then we started to discuss politics.

'Do you think there's any chance Trump will actually get indicted?' I asked.

'I sure hope so, but you never know with that slippery sucker.' He shook his head.

'I'm so disgusted at the level of amateurishness of the Republicans and their dirty campaigns. I'm so glad Sarah Palin lost to Mary Pelota, she's—' Cash was looking for the right word, and I knew he didn't want to swear.

'She's like our own Pauline Hanson back home – also a redneck – but at least Hanson doesn't wield a rifle!' It was good to know that Cash and I could talk politics, but he also gave me theatre reviews and football tips, and the snow forecast for the next twenty-four hours. As the first course arrived I believed I was on the best date of my life.

Three weeks later and I was officially 'dating' Cash. Not the famous obligation-free New York-style dating, but proper dating. I went to his bar after work. Sometimes he cooked for me at his place, and sometimes he took me out.

I started to see what I had been missing out on with Adam, how a relationship should work, unfold, develop.

I was making plans on the phone with Cash when I finally had a chance to tell Wyatt about him. We were friends and I was finally excited and wanted to share my happiness. Seeing as I'd told Wyatt previously that I wasn't looking for a relationship in New York, I felt slightly strange about telling him about Cash and hadn't mentioned it. It was now the right time.

'So,' I said wheeling my chair around to his side of the partition. 'I really like Cash.'

'I guessed that, you've been smiling big the last week. He's a good guy, right?'

'He's a good guy, and I like being around him. He's funny, and clever.'

'Ah, but is he organised, like you?'

'He is! *And* he's interested in my work and Aboriginal politics, art and culture. He's perfect. You'll meet him later, he's coming in to check out the exhibition, but mainly to see me. He just likes being around me, apparently.'

'Of course he does, why wouldn't he? Deadly Aboriginal woman. That's what you are.'

'It's really nice not to have to do much work – I did all the work with Adam. But as you once told me, if a man wants to see you, he will make it happen. Cash makes things happen. I like that.'

'He's a lucky guy.' Wyatt was looking at his computer screen again. 'Sorry, I've got to get this email off to Maria asap.'

Cash came in for lunch and went through the museum before coming up and meeting Wyatt briefly. As soon as I'd seen him out of the building I raced back to see what Wyatt thought. But he was very restrained, only commenting, 'Cash appears to be a genuine guy.'

I didn't know whether that was a good thing or a bad thing, but I didn't want to push it. I had to remember we were colleagues and I was a guest at the NMAI.

The opening night of the Quandamooka Weavers at the community centre had arrived finally, and so had the UN's Permanent Indigenous Forum members. Kirsten had been working fourteen-hour days and we'd hardly seen each other. She was bringing the members to the opening, though, and we'd planned to go out for dinner afterwards. Cash came along too and mingled effortlessly before I introduced him to the artist.

Aunty Sonia, Freja and Leecee were all smiles and joy as they spoke generously to those who were there to celebrate their exhibition.

I introduced Cash to the three women just as the speeches were about to begin, then he slid to the back of the room.

After the speeches were done and the crowd thinned out, the artists said they were jet-lagged and went back to their hotel uptown to crash. Cash and I went to a local Irish pub because we were desperately hungry.

Vikki said she'd pop by later, but when we arrived I found her sulking in a corner.

'What's wrong?'

'My ex-boyfriend is working behind the bar,' she said, and took a sip of her drink. 'He was a complete jerk to me, cheated on me and *apparently* he's still with the woman.'

I'd never seen Vikki so upset. I didn't even recall her mentioning an ex-boyfriend who had cheated on her. She always seemed so strong, as if she didn't care about men that much. It suddenly dawned on me that dating three men at a time was actually a protective mechanism for her.

'He's the reason I don't want to let anyone else get close to me again, not for a long time. I just don't understand why people cheat. He could've just broken up with me if he wanted out. I gave him an out, he didn't take it. Instead he was fucking her and fucking me over at the same time.'

Cash came towards us with a bottle of champagne and some menus.

'You ladies look like you need some perking up, and can I suggest you both eat something, please?'

'You don't have to tell me twice to eat. Show me the desserts!' I joked, trying to cheer Vikki up and taking the menu from him.

'He's a keeper, Lauren,' Vikki whispered in my ear as Cash poured the bubbly. 'You're very lucky.'

'I like him, we're friends and we're having fun. But I'm definitely going home next year as planned.'

20

Beware the black ice

December brought with it below-zero temperatures and snowfall. One day, the snow lifted and Cash took me for a stroll through Brooklyn Park and taught me how to make snow angels by lying straight out and scissoring my legs and arms, like doing jumping jacks lying down. We took photos of each other and watched kids ice-skating. I had fun and the sun shone strongly. But as we walked over the Brooklyn Bridge into the city the temperature dropped rapidly and I could feel the icy wind tear through me. Everyone in New York looked miserable now, not like in summer, when I'd first arrived. It was a little like the Canberra winter that I didn't miss.

I was wearing so many layers I could hardly move. Underwear, thermal vest, skivvy, jumper – or 'sweater' as Vikki had pointed out – a coat, hat, scarf, gloves and boots. It was impossible to feel sexy with so many layers on. I always felt bulky. I didn't want to buy one of the down coats that every second woman had on, but I had no choice. My Canberra coat just wasn't doing the job.

'Just a tip, the really long down coats you see people wear, they're called "drug dealer coats" because the dealers who stand on the corner all night wear them to stay warm,' Vikki advised as I headed to Bloomingdale's and headed straight for the sale rack. I bought a three-quarter-length black coat with a faux-fur lined hood. I felt a bit glamorous and much warmer walking out into the frosty weather.

The weather became increasingly unbearable, especially when the heating went out in our building. Sometimes it lasted a few hours, sometimes a few days, depending on what needed to be fixed. On the odd occasion when the pipes froze, there'd be no hot water either. One night I went to bed looking like a cat-burglar about to take a catnap: black socks, leggings, skivvy, Koori Radio beanie and my Qantas eye mask. It was a rough night's sleep. When the heating finally came back on it made so much noise – spluttering, hissing, banging and farting – that the radiator sounded like it was going to blow up.

'Stay with me,' Cash offered when I complained about the first frozen and sleepless night.

I stayed with him for two nights because of the heating, but it wasn't something I wanted to do too often. I didn't want to lunge into anything serious, knowing I'd be going back to Australia in July anyway.

I was really sick with a bad flu by the second week of December, but grateful it wasn't COVID. I didn't know how the whole of New York wasn't ill, considering that people generally spent their nights in stifling apartment blocks with central heating and then headed out into the freezing blizzard. In and out, in and out, to the point that my body just couldn't take it any longer. And then, just as Wyatt and Maria had convinced me to go home to bed, I sprained my ankle.

It was my own fault. I didn't want to be like everyone else, staring at the ground looking miserable. I always walked facing the day, facing the world. But I didn't listen to Vikki, who warned me constantly to 'watch out for the black ice'. I should've been watching the footpath, making sure I didn't slip and slide in the slush, but I didn't. My left foot slid on black ice and I almost did the splits, twisting my right ankle. I can't imagine what it must have looked like from front on or behind me. My leg started to throb immediately and then I started to cry.

'Are you okay, ma'am?' A security guard came out of CVS pharmacy on 8th Avenue and grabbed my elbow. I was weeping like a child, my nose still running from my cold, I had a temperature, and now I was embarrassed with a sprained ankle.

'I'm not sure,' I sobbed.

'Let me help you up.'

'I didn't see the ice.'

'Black ice, it's got three people today already.'

'Good. At least I don't look like the *only* fool.'

'You're a pretty fool. I also had to help up a 250-pound man, so you're a pleasure.' He was trying to make me feel better. 'Where are you going?'

'Just up to 25th.'

'Charlie . . . Charlie,' he called in towards the shop entrance. Charlie came to the door. 'I'm going to walk this lady to 25th, she's hurt her ankle.'

'All right, man. Don't be long.'

'Really, I'll be fine,' I said, putting my foot down and then cringing with the pain. He walked me all the way to my door and I buzzed Vikki to come down.

'Hon, are you all right? I *told* you about the black ice. It's a killer.'

'I know.' I wept all the way upstairs.

'Let's get you into bed, where you need to STAY for the next couple of days.'

I felt miserable, and couldn't be around anyone. Cash took the following afternoon off and came over with a bag of food to keep me nourished for the week, knowing that I would be stuck in bed. He insisted we stream *The West Wing*, since I hadn't seen it.

'Tonight, Ms Lucas, we have my world-famous cure-all chicken soup that is sure to make you feel better from top to sprained ankle and then toe!'

Cash sat at my bedside and ate the chicken soup with me as we watched the series. I was enjoying all the attention he was giving me.

'I bought some chest rub that will help you breathe when you sleep. Shall I?' He pulled the jar out of his bag.

'Oh all right,' I said, giving in. He gently worked the rub into my back first and then my chest.

'I suppose you want me to do you too?' I asked with an attempted laugh.

'No, sugar, tonight it's all about you.' Wow, *all about me*, that was a first. Cash slid into bed next to me for an hour before he had to go to the restaurant at six. I told him to stay away for the rest of the week because I didn't want him to get sick. As he left he handed me a menu.

'I know you like butter chicken, so if you have a craving, call this restaurant. They deliver and I have a tab there, order whatever you like. It will make me happy if I can't see you that at least I know you're eating properly.' Cash was the perfect friend, considerate lover *and* nurse.

When he left, I zoomed Libby, because it had been weeks since we'd talked properly and she was arriving to visit in only eight days. With the laptop resting on a pillow and a cup of tea next to the bed, I sniffled over the ether.

'Miss you guys so much,' I said through a semi-blocked nose.

'Not half as much as we miss you. And what's wrong with you? You look awful.'

'Thanks a million. I'm sick, bad flu, and sprained my ankle.'

'Poor thing! You'd dry out quickly back here, it's stifling. I just put some washing on the line and it dried in about an hour! Are you okay?'

'I'll be fine, Cash has just been here, made me chicken soup and everything.'

'He sounds like a good guy.'

'He is, and so attentive it almost feels abnormal. Well, abnormal for me. He fusses, and thinks ahead, and we don't argue and he's not running around with other women.'

'Now don't be putting him on a pedestal straight away, tidda, okay?' I could see the restraint in Libby's face, no doubt worrying I'd fall for Cash and end up being hurt again.

'Oh no, my days of doing that are definitely over, and it's not like I'm in love with him or going to fall in love with him, because what would be the point? I'm going home in July.'

'Well, then, I'm glad to hear you'll have someone to take care of you until I get there in EIGHT DAYS!' she screamed. 'I am soooooo excited, look!' She panned her laptop around her bedroom and showed me her half-filled suitcase and travel books and brochures. 'I'm going to be well prepared.'

'I can see that,' I laughed, 'but leave some room for shopping, okay?'

'Oh, I'll buy another case and fill that up.'

'Attagirl, I'll have to send some gifts home with you, too.'

'All good, tidda, but I'll have to get to work now, 9 am meeting. See you soon. We're going to have so much fun. I'm still working on my list of things to do, I'll send it to you.'

'Can't wait,' I sneezed and coughed.

'Get better all right? Bye.'

'Bye, love to everyone there.'

Libby logged off first. I didn't want to break the connection, I felt homesick for Canberra. For my friends and my family. I didn't want to call Mum and Dad because I knew I'd cry and that would only upset them.

In a moment of extreme weakness I went onto Instagram and checked Adam's feed. Nothing had changed at his end, but for some reason I felt the need to message him. I wanted him to know I was sick.

> Hey there, just wanted to say hello from Chelsea. Am laid up in bed with a cold and a sprained ankle but doing fine. Libby arrives in eight days so we'll have some fun. What news do you bear?

I assumed that when he read that I was sick he'd message me back with at least some words of comfort and good wishes. But by the time I went back to work a week later I still hadn't heard from him, and I felt like an idiot, again.

21

I'm dreaming of a white Christmas

'This is like production line packing,' I joked as I watched the girls organise their luggage in the middle of the apartment. Vikki was meeting her family in Hawaii for Christmas and Kirsten was going home to Australia. Coincidentally they were leaving La Guardia within thirty minutes of each other, and so were sharing an Uber to the airport.

'I'm sorry I won't get a chance to meet Libby – she sounds wonderful,' Kirsten said sincerely.

'She is. I still can't believe you'll be missing her by just days. She would love you both,' I said, handing her a small gift – a pair of earrings from the NMAI. 'It's just something for you from me, not to be opened until Christmas morning.'

'Aww gee, wait there.' And she took off into her bedroom.

'And the same rules apply to you, Ms Vikki,' I said, handing her a gift-wrapped bracelet, also from the museum shop.

'Then the same rules for you too!' She handed me a small gift bag with a massive red bow, and, not to be outdone, Kirsten returned from her room with the same bag and bigger green bow. Because we were all working right up until that day, we hadn't had time to organise a Christmas dinner together, but none of us were fussed. The girls were looking forward to seeing their families and I was excited about seeing Libby and hearing about home.

When they were finally out the door I made a cup of tea and sat down in my room, looking at the gifts I needed to wrap for Libby to take home to the family: a collection of Yankees paraphernalia for Max, and Knicks paraphernalia for Nick. I got Mum a gorgeous handbag on sale in SoHo and Dad the boxed set of *New York: A Documentary Film*, a fourteen-hour series on New York's history, covering 400 years. I didn't watch it myself but I thought that it might him help understand the attraction of the city. And I could never convince him to sign up to Netflix so he still used his DVD player for films. It was something that Mum and he could do together as well. After I'd finished wrapping I sat there and felt lonely, counting down the hours to Libby's arrival. I don't think I could've managed being away for Christmas without someone from home to celebrate with. The ringing phone snapped me out of my daydreaming.

'Hello, beautiful.' I was grateful to hear Cash's voice down the line.

'Hey yourself, what's happening? Are you working?'

'I'm here, keeping the public happy, just checking in on you.'

'I'm fine. Vikki and Kirsten have gone, I've wrapped all the pressies for my family, and I'm just going to tidy up ready for Libby.'

'So, am I going to see you at *all* over the Christmas break?' I could hear a whine in Cash's voice.

'I hope so, but Libs is only here until January 6 and we have so much to catch up on.'

'And I just get the flick then, do I?' I could tell he was annoyed.

'Libby is an important part of my life.'

'And *I'm* not?' He sounded cranky.

'Now you're being irrational. I think I better go.'

'I'm sorry, it's just that I miss you the days I don't see you.'

'Okay, but I'm not one of those women who dump their girlfriends the minute they meet a man. I never want to be one of those women. You don't get that about me. And Libby is like a sister to me, family.'

'I'm sorry. I'll let you go and call later.' I could hear the apology in his voice but the last thing I needed was a bloke being jealous of me going out with friends. I couldn't even get Adam to worry about other men.

I got off the phone, vacuumed and dusted the apartment, put the rubbish out, rummaged through the fridge considering what I'd have for dinner, and then checked my phone. Libby had messaged me her own 'Libby in New York – To Do List' and I went through it, thinking about the best days to do what when she arrived:

- Saks Off 5th
- Bloomingdale's and Macy's

- Ground Zero Memorial
- Empire State Building
- Central Park: skating, Carousel
- 5th Avenue
- Times Square
- Statue of Liberty/Ellis Island
- Museum of Modern Art
- More shopping, bars, firemen

I was taking two weeks off in one hit, while other staff had to go back to work straight after Christmas. They generally saved their holidays for summer, just like back home. I was on my last day before break and was still working hard, as was Wyatt.

'Last day for me,' I bragged from my desk.

'That's not fair.' Wyatt mocked, sulking over our desk partition. 'Why do you get two weeks' Christmas leave while we only get one?'

'Fair, schmair . . .' I passed a wrapped Christmas present to him, the hardcover edition of Gurrumul Yunupingu's biography.

He handed a gift back, obviously a book, and we both laughed. 'Snap,' I said. I opened mine and gasped with joy; it was a picture book by Buffy Saint-Marie and Cree-Metis artist Julie Flett titled *Still This Love Goes On*.

'It's a picture book but the message is about missing loved ones, and the promise of seeing each other again. I thought it was apt.'

'It really is, Wyatt.' I said, as I flicked through the pages and read the song words to the title of the book.

'And I thought you might be able to get it signed when we go to D.C.'

'That would be INCREDIBLE! Thank you so much.' I gave him a hug.

'So, what have you got planned other than time with your friend Libby?' Wyatt asked.

'Oh, I'm pretty sure Libby will be most of my holidays. We'll do a Christmas lunch and then complete her long to-do list.' I waved the printed list in the air.

'No Cash? I mean, I assume you've been seeing him a lot recently because we hardly hang out anymore.' Wyatt sounded disappointed.

'I'm sorry we haven't been doing much together. Life really is hectic in New York, isn't it?' Wyatt just looked at me, silent, and I felt compelled to offer more. 'Cash is struggling with Libs coming for two weeks, but he'll have to manage.'

'Indeed.'

'And what are your plans?'

'Oh, we do the family thing, you know, cousins and cousins of cousins and kids everywhere and too much food.'

'Sounds like back home! Do you wanna hang out with Libs and me maybe after Christmas? I'd love you to meet her, and anyway, she works with me, so you should. You could write it off as work.'

'I like your style, Lauren, count me in.'

At 5.30 pm it was dark and I was ready to leave. Wyatt was still at his desk. He really was a workaholic.

'I'm off now, so give me a hug,' I said as I put my coat on.

Wyatt jumped up and hugged me.

'I'm going to miss ya,' I said, 'but I'll be in touch about catching up, okay?'

'You better. Now go so I can try and get out of here by seven.'

'Merry Christmas.'

'Merry Christmas.'

♡

I took an Uber to meet Libby at the airport. We screamed down the arrivals area, and a couple standing nearby laughed at us.

'Get your gloves and scarf on, love, or you'll freeze outside. It's like minus five.'

'Righty-o.' She dove into her handbag and pulled out black leather gloves and a red scarf.

'Um, you dropped something, ma'am,' the driver said.

We all looked to the ground and there was a pair of red knickers sitting near the wheel of the trolley.

'Well, doesn't hurt to advertise, I guess,' Libby said, with only a hint of embarrassment.

We were hardly up the stairs at the apartment before Libby was talking about Macy's. She insisted on going straight away. No sleep, just a shower and a coffee and off we went.

We walked along 7th Avenue.

'That's the Museum at FIT.' I pointed to our left and saw Libby frown. 'Sorry, FIT is the Fashion Institute of Technology.'

'Has it got a gift shop?' Libby asked, stopping to look at a mannequin in the window.

'Come on, we'll never get to Macy's if we stop at every shop along the way.' I linked arms with Libby and set a steady pace for us, chatting and trying to keep warm. 'Madison Square Garden is just up ahead on the left, next block,' I said as we approached West 30th, 'and Penn Station is right there too.'

'Gees, you're a real local aren't you?'

'I guess I am.'

We turned right into 34th and I upped our pace. 'Come on, next block is your shopping heaven, Libs.'

We were almost running when we finally arrived at Macy's and we went straight to get Libby's ten per cent discount visitor's card and store map and started the exploration.

'This place is amazing!'

'I know, the whole of Centro Goulburn could fit on one floor, and you should see their bra section, there's every single kind of push-up bra in the world here.'

'Those of us who are well-endowed don't need assistance to produce cleavage and thank goodness, because shopping for bras is just too time-consuming an activity.' I knew then that Libby and Kirsten were probably twins separated at birth.

Later, we stopped for a break and had a pretzel and a coffee. I noticed someone staring at us.

'Did I tell you men stare at me – well, at all women – a lot here?' I said, leaning over the table to Libby.

'Really, where? Which men?' Libby asked with interest.

'Well, there's one, over there.' And I nodded to a guy who kept staring at me. But it was an odd stare, not a flirtatious stare.

'Oh my god, he *is* staring.'

'Yes, but he's probably thinking I look like a woollen blimp.'

'He hasn't taken his eyes off you. Seriously, is this normal? Maybe he likes your pink hat.'

'Well, he ain't getting it!' I said as a busboy came to wipe the table and take our rubbish.

'Hello ladies, are you having a good day?'

'Great day,' Libby said.

'The great day suits you,' he said as he looked her up and down and walked off.

'Did he just flirt with me?'

'I think so. It's normal here,' I said as another guy in jeans and a grey coat approached our table.

'Do you mind if I join you?'

'Actually, yes, we're having a meeting,' I said abruptly, and he walked off.

'What was that? Are you telling me people can pick up in a department store in New York?'

'Apparently. Just keep watching – thirty seconds of eye contact is all it takes for a come-on.'

On the way back to Chelsea we stood on the subway platform and chatted excitedly about all the things we were going to do.

'Do you need someone to show you around?' a guy behind us asked.

'Oh, I'm pretty much a guide now, but thank you,' I said politely.

'Do you think I could just have your number, then?'

'I live south of the equator,' I said.

'She lives here, for now anyway,' Libby butted in, and I glared at her.

Our train arrived and we got in. Libby was straining to look out the window at the guy we left behind.

'Are you mad? He was gorgeous!'

'I've told you about Cash, so I'm not really seeing anyone else. We're spending a lot of time together. Actually, he's pretty unhappy that I punted him for the time you're here.'

'You didn't have to do that.'

'Yes, I did! Anyway, you and Bec were right, there are so many choices here. As you just saw, I don't have to settle for Cash Brannigan even if he is the sexiest man on the planet.' I showed her a photo of Cash on my phone.

'Is it *really* that good here?'

'Libs, I have had five years' of self-esteem work in the last five months. Men here actually *like* women, even if they like football too.'

Libby was like a tourist-robot the first forty-eight hours she was in New York, not sleeping much at all but guzzling coffee to stay awake and keep on the go. In the first two days we did Macy's, the Chelsea Hotel bar (because Libby was a massive Dylan fan), the Chelsea Market, had dinner in Chinatown one night and ordered in pizza the other. I was exhausted and already feeling toxic when we sat down to breakfast on Christmas Eve and Libby pulled out her list.

'Right! Well, today I want to walk the perimeter of and then through Central Park,' she said, looking intently at her map spread out on the kitchen table.

Although I needed the exercise, it was, after all, Christmas Eve and I wanted to put the tree up and take it easy. Plus, it was cold and snowing.

'Are you serious? It's like six kilometres all the way around, or maybe it's six miles. And it's about four degrees, and it's Christmas Eve. Can't we just take it easy today? I don't think you've even had enough sleep. I'm not going to have to deal with you being all shitty by two o'clock this afternoon, am I?'

'I'm not the one sounding shitty,' she said, still staring at the map.

'Fine, let's walk around the park then.' Working with Libby and having her planning every minute of my day were two very different things.

We started our walk at the north-east corner of the park. 'We must be freaking mad,' I said, trying to get a pace up to warm up. 'We'd NEVER do this back home.'

'We're in New York, darling, we *must* do this.' My hands were numb even through my gloves.

After fifteen minutes I saw a corner deli. 'I'm going in there for a coffee and some food. You can keep walking if you like,' I said. Libby could sense I was almost over it.

'Okay, I guess we can take a break from the schedule.'

We walked down some iron steps into a little Turkish deli.

'Welcome to New York,' the owner said, true to the hospitality New Yorkers were famous for. He fussed about what we might want to eat, and what we might prefer to drink with our hot spinach and eggplant dish. I just wanted to sit down and rest my feet and thaw out.

When we were done, Libby got up from the table before I had a chance to get my wallet out.

'I've got it,' she said, counting out and handing over notes.

'Did you leave a tip?' I whispered on the way out.

'Yes, but . . .'

We walked outside and snowflakes fell gently onto us as we climbed back up the stairs.

'But what?'

'I really don't like tipping. I mean, what's all that about?'

'That was good service, he was a good guy, and tipping is normal here. It's expected.'

'Oh, I know it's *expected*, and yes he was a nice guy, but we've had so much sugary and insincere service since I got here. I'm just over it.'

'Lots of people rely on their tips to survive, especially in hospitality.'

'I know, and that's the problem. I feel like I'm subsidising the American wage system. And it's not like our dollar is strong either. I love New York, I'm excited to be here, and to see you, tidda.' She linked arms with mine. 'But the tipping scenario is the one thing I hate. In Australia you tip for good service, not just for *being* served.'

I didn't want to admit it, but Libby was right. I had to tip the woman who washed my hair, then the one who cut my hair, and if someone else coloured it I was supposed to tip her too. I'd even seen people chased out of restaurants for not paying the expected twenty per cent tip. It was obscene, but Americans didn't seem to think so.

'I'm just saying that I think everyone should get paid decent wages and hourly rates and let the consumer choose whether they think the service was worthy of a tip or not. The next tip I'm going to give them is "Get a union"!'

'Let's check out the skating rink in the park,' I said, anxious to stop the tipping debate.

'We need to head south,' she said, looking at her map. 'We just keep heading down 5th Avenue, so, at least that's one side of the park done. Good idea, tidda.'

We watched families, and teenagers and couples holding hands.

'This is really romantic, isn't it, Loz? Have you tried skating yet? With Cash Pash Man perhaps?'

'No, we haven't, but he's very romantic, so I'm sure we will.' I had thought about doing it with Adam, when I first arrived and saw a brochure at the hotel. But standing there with Libby I realised that Adam probably wouldn't have liked it. He never wanted to do anything romantic.

'Central Park Zoo is in that direction,' Libby pointed. 'Let's go!' she said, like an excited child.

'Oh cute,' I said, bending down to take a pic of a nearby squirrel, just waiting as if posing for the camera. Did I have to tip that little creature too?

Libby grabbed my arm.

'Come on, remember when we watched *Madagascar*, you loved it.'

'It was a movie, Libs. I'm cold.'

'I know, but you've got six more months here. I don't, so I have to go now.'

I had no argument.

'This is nothing like the movie *Madagascar*,' I said as we entered the zoo.

'Well, for a start that movie was an animation, and these are real animals,' Libby said, dragging me by the arm. 'Don't be such a misery guts.'

'But look, there's no-one here, because it's freezing. See, even the freaking polar bear is hiding.' I pointed to a huge white bear poking halfway out of a cave.

'Haha, he's face down with his butt out.'

'I don't blame him. I feel like doing the same.'

'What? Lie face down with your arse in the air? Go on, then.' Libby was being facetious.

'You know what I mean.'

'Ooh, the penguins are sooo cute, though. I could watch them for hours.'

'We'll have frostbite by then.'

We walked through the park far more slowly than I wanted to. I was grateful to find a cafe where we sat, ate hotdogs and drank hot chocolate. On full stomachs again, we watched the sea lions put on a show for us, and the snow monkey sitting on a rock picking things out of his fur and eating them.

Towards the end of the day we stopped in front of the red panda enclosure. 'Where are they?' Libby said, disappointed she couldn't see them.

'They've found somewhere warmer to be, and that's what I'm going to do too. Let's go, the sun's going down.'

I wanted to go to my Aussie pub that night, to see Matt and the gang and get an idea of what might be happening back home in the football world. I hadn't had a chance to check Instagram since Libby arrived, but seeing her had made me think of Adam.

'I am NOT going to an Australian pub in New York. You know my rules, Loz.'

'The owner's now a mate of mine, and he knows heaps of Kooris back home. I want to give him a Christmas present, please. What if I take you to the Monarch Roof Top for a cocktail first, a bit of glam with a stunning view?'

'I'll take that glam cocktail view offer, but after that I can't say.' Libs was Libs and I loved her for it.

We both wore red cocktail dresses to look Christmassy and then piled on the coats and scarves. I liked the penthouse cocktail bar. People were dressed up either from working in town or ready for a night out. The space was fun, with animal print couches, and a stunning view over Herald Square, including Macy's, and the cocktail list was off the charts fabulous. We both had a Let's Get Lit Mojito and we were buzzing within minutes.

'See, this is New York, tidda, this is why we're here. These are the memories I need to take home. Cheers.' Libby clinked her glass to mine.

'You want a photo with your drink?'

'Not yet, there's some cute men in suits over there, might look a bit touristy if I do that.' She raised her glass to them. 'I think we should have another.'

'You do remember it's all free-pour here? One drink is like three of ours.'

'It's Christmas, Loz, let's be merry.'

'Let's be merry indeed.'

My phone rang – it was Cash.

'And hello there,' I said, already feeling merry.

'Where are you, gorgeous?'

'Monarch Rooftop with Libby. It's the best. We'll head to the Aussie pub tonight – I'm a little homesick.'

'We're not going,' Libby tried to say into the phone before heading to the bar.

'Libs isn't that keen.'

Cash laughed down the line.

'Are you going to be there for a while? Should I come and meet you? It's quiet here, Allen can manage without me.'

'Cash, I'd love to see you but I really need to just hang with Libby tonight if that's all right. I haven't seen her for six months, and she's my bestie, I told you that.' Having said it out loud, I felt bad for being so short-tempered with her earlier that day.

'I know, it's just I miss you. I've got your Christmas present too. When can I give it to you? Do you know I blew off my own family to see you?'

'Don't make me feel guilty. I didn't ask you to do that.'

'I know you didn't, I wanted to. I have to work early on the 26th, so couldn't really leave town anyway.'

I felt guilty even though it wasn't my fault. 'Why don't you come over tomorrow? Libby and I are cooking lunch. Why don't you join us?'

'Really?'

'Really. Now I've got to go. I'll see you tomorrow.' I hung up as Libby came back with an unexpected bottle of champagne. The night was going to be very messy, I just knew it.

When we were both sufficiently lubricated I suggested it was time to go to another bar.

'Can we have the bill, please?' Libby asked the barman.

'We settle the tab, or get the check here, sis.'

'You've learned a whole new language here, haven't you?'

'Your tab has already been settled,' the barman said as we both pulled out our credit cards.

'It can't have been,' I said, adamantly.

He read from a piece of paper. 'A Mr Cash Brannigan called and said he'd cover whatever you ladies had.'

'Seems like the Cash man is cashed up. He's a keeper, tidda. You have to bring him home with you.'

'You know money's never been my motive,' I said. I felt a bit weird about Cash doing that. I'd always liked paying my own way. I was hoping that he hadn't called ahead and spoken to Matt as well.

We got in an Uber and I didn't tell Libby where we were going. She was busy sending text messages to Australia because it was already Christmas Day at home. To the driver's delight, she sang 'Start spreading the news . . .' down the phone to her sister back home.

Only after we walked into the bar and I said hello to Matt did Libby realise that we had arrived at the pub.

'Merry Christmas, Loz, great to see you.' He gave me a bear hug.

'This is my wonderful friend Libby. She's from Canberra also, but originally from Moree.'

'Ah, the Moree Boomerangs.'

'You know them?'

'Yeah, know the Cutmores and the Wrights, sorry' – Matt grabbed his phone – 'I'll be back. Sit down, I'll send over two Ozmos.'

Libby propped herself on a bar stool. 'He's deadly, eh?'

'I told you.'

'And what's an Ozmo?' she asked.

'It's an Australian cosmo, of course.'

We sat holding court at the bar. Hunter appeared to have been punted.

'Hey, you sound strange for a New Yorker,' Libby said to the new barman.

'That's because I'm from Melbourne.'

'I'm from Canberra via Moree,' Libby said proudly.

The barman pushed our drinks towards us. 'From Matt, Merry Christmas.' He winked at Libby and walked off.

Libby grabbed me. 'He is so hot. He's equivalent to about five guys in Canberra. I think I want to kiss him. I want him to kiss my ankles.'

'Well, you've changed your tune about men, but, good, go for it.'

'But what about my track record?' She took a long sip of her orange drink. 'Are you sure he's not gay?'

'Matt . . . pst, come here.' Matt walked over to us. 'Is the new barman gay?' I whispered.

'No,' he whispered back.

'Does he have an unhealthy relationship with his mother?' Libby whispered.

'Highly unlikely, his mother died some years ago,' Matt whispered to Libby.

'Good.'

'What?' I was shocked.

'I mean good he's no Hamlet, not good his mother died. You know what I mean.'

'Last question, Matt.' Libby leaned in and grabbed Matt's shirt. 'Is he likely to drag me to New York's equivalent of Fyshwick?'

'That I can't tell you, but hell, it's New York, might just be fun to find out.'

'You're right. I'm in New York and what happens on tour stays on tour.'

'She knows the drill, Loz,' Matt said to me, and then turned to Libby. 'You can come here any time.'

'I like it here,' Libby said, turning around to the bar again as she looked for the barman.

'Any footy news from home, Matt?'

'Off season, Loz, you'd know that. Is Full-of-himself coming over for Christmas?'

'No, we're not together anymore.'

'That's good, I mean, not good – you know what I mean.'

'I know what you mean.' And I took a sip of my drink. It really was good that I wasn't with Adam anymore. My whole life was better. I was sleeping the best I had in years and seeing a thoughtful, generous, attentive man who I could also have a real conversation with. I'd always have a soft spot for Adam because he was my first love, and I didn't really want to settle down with Cash, but I had truly moved on. I was living the life that Libby and Bec had said I could have in New York. I now believed I could have that real love – reciprocal, respectful love – one day. I touched my 'Love needs faith' pendant and toasted myself that I was finally in control.

22

Christmas celebration brings love revelation

'Oh my god,' I heard Libby shriek from the lounge room.

'What?' I said, shuffling out as fast as I could.

'It's snowing on Christmas morning. It's so beautiful, I love it.'

She had her face crushed against the glass like a child.

'Yeah, bit different from the dry heat of Canberra's summer, eh?'

'This is so magical! Let's go outside, come on, go get dressed.' Libby was back into organisation mode, but I didn't mind. It was the perfect white Christmas morning.

On the street we bundled snow together, attempting to make our first snowman.

'I think it should remain genderless, let's just make a snowperson,' Libby said, taking the exercise far more seriously than me.

'Say New York cheesecake,' I directed as I pointed my phone at Libby and our snowperson, who was wearing an old National Aboriginal Sporting Chance Academy beanie, a Sydney Swans scarf, a traditional carrot for nose, Oreo biscuits for eyes and a mouth made of red snakes, left over from Halloween.

As I put my phone back in my pocket I felt something hit me hard on the arm; it was a snowball and the fight had begun.

'You will so pay for that, Libs!' I threw one back in retaliation, hitting her on the knee.

'Your aim is about as good as your ability to drink,' she said, winding her arm up like she was going to bowl a cricket ball to me. I opted for the baseball pitch and we both threw at the same time, cracking each other in the chest, and fell about laughing. The next thing we knew there were snowballs coming from everywhere and kids appeared laughing and having fun.

'That's for talking funny,' one child in a red jacket said, throwing a small snowball at me.

'Ah, yes, I probably do. You better throw another one at my friend too.' The children all laughed as Libby and I pretended to be wounded, falling about for their Christmas pleasure.

After only a few minutes Libby and I had had enough and we bid the children farewell and headed back upstairs.

We sat down with coffees and looked at the carefully wrapped presents sitting under our small Christmas tree. It was all we could manage after walking up the stairs.

'Well, everyone will be in bed at my place now,' I said, 'or close to it. Mum said they were having a barbecue and all the rels would drop by during the day. Dad splashed out and got some seafood and Mum was making a massive pavlova. God, I'd kill for a pav today.'

'Let's make one,' Libby said. 'We've got everything in the fridge – eggs, cream, strawberries.'

'I think I've got a tin of passionfruit somewhere in the cupboard. What a great idea.' I was already looking forward to the pav but the idea was making me feel homesick and Libby could tell straight away.

'Don't worry, tidda, you'll be back home soon enough. In the meantime, I have some pressies for you from Emma, Bec and your family.' And she went to the tree and piled them together.

I unwrapped everything slowly, savouring every bow and piece of curling ribbon. Emma had sent me a coat pin made by an Aboriginal jewellery designer in Brisbane and Bec had sent a photo-frame with pink crystals around the edges. Mum and Dad had sent me some money to take to the factory outlets in New Jersey that Libby had googled and told them about, and Max had sent me a pair of fluffy slippers in the shape of frogs that were the kind of thing kids would wear but in an adult's size. I loved them and put them on straight away.

'Take a photo of me to send back, will you?' I handed Libby the camera.

We then swapped our own gifts. I gave Libby the choker I'd bought from Nate and the Greek palmette velvet scarf that I bought at the Met when I'd first arrived. She loved it, and true to form started explaining to me, 'Did you know that the palmette is one of the most frequently used motifs in classical art of all media and periods?'

'Really? You don't say?' I said cheekily.

'Well, there'll be plenty back home that don't know,' she said, tying the scarf around her neck. 'Now open yours.'

She handed me an awkward-shaped present that looked to have been difficult to wrap. I ripped the paper off to find a stylish chocolate brown suede handbag that I knew would go with everything. 'This is absolutely perfect. I love it. Bus Depot Markets?'

'Bus Depot Markets,' she confirmed. 'But wait, there's more.'

Libby got up and went to the fridge, rummaged around for a minute and came back with something in a plastic bag. Inside it was a package wrapped in Christmas paper.

'Oh my god? How did you manage this?' It was four packets of Mersey Valley cheese which I had flippantly mentioned I missed in a message to her. 'I can't believe you got it here and into the fridge without me knowing. My life in New York is now complete.' We had chunky toast with vegemite and sliced cheese done under the griller and wondered what our families back home would be doing.

With our snowperson, breakfast and pressies out of the way, we moved into the kitchen and started cooking up a storm. Together we prepared roast turkey with all the trimmings, including Libby's 'sensational stuffing' and our

New York-style deconstructed pavlova for dessert. The one thing I hadn't left behind in Canberra was my appetite.

Cash arrived at 1 pm with Christmas pudding and wine and chocolates.

'Merry Christmas, beautiful,' he said as I opened the door. He put his bag on the ground and hugged and kissed me passionately before he realised Libby was sitting at the dining table.

'Sorry, I didn't see you there,' he said, slightly embarrassed.

'Don't be sorry.' She stood up as Cash made his way around the table to her. 'I'm Libby or Libs,' she said, turning her cheek for Cash to kiss it.

'Welcome to New York. I believe you've already been painting the town red, black and yellow.'

'Wow, you've got our colours down pat! And yes, we've been shaking up the city a little, but we've got a long way to go.'

'Well, I look forward to hearing all about your planned adventures, but I need to put some things in the kitchen first,' he said as he picked his parcels up off the floor. 'Do you need me to do anything, Lauren? Carve the turkey perhaps?'

'I'd love you to do that for us. To be honest, I have no idea where to start with a turkey. We usually have seafood or a barbie for Christmas.'

'Consider it done,' he said as he walked off.

'Oh my god,' Libby said, dragging me to her, 'he is wonderful, lovely, gorgeous! Keep him please, I'm telling you! You can keep this one, okay?'

I laughed, pulling myself out of her grip. 'He is lovely. I like him, a lot.'

'What's not to like?' Libby said, peering into the kitchen as Cash was getting the turkey out of the oven.

'I better go see he's all right.'

In the kitchen Cash had it all organised, which impressed me. I'd never really been much of a cook, and admired anyone who was. I poured a glass of wine and stood next to him.

'I have to tell you something,' he said, taking the glass from my hand, putting it on the kitchen sink and taking my face in his hands. 'I love you. I've missed you these past days and I realised that I was in love with the most wonderful woman on the planet. I woke up this morning feeling blessed that I was spending Christmas Day with you.' And then he kissed me before I had the chance to say anything.

'It's a dry argument out here,' Libby sang out, breaking our kiss.

'That means her glass is empty,' I said to Cash, who looked confused.

'You go top it up, I'll bring the turkey out.' He pecked my lips, handed me the bottle and I went into the dining room, still overwhelmed by the preceding revelations.

We stuffed ourselves stupid with lunch and pavlova and the Christmas pudding and chocolates that Cash insisted we also try. It was all delicious and I hated to admit to myself that while I missed my family, it was one of the loveliest Christmas Days I'd ever had.

'I have a little something for my two favourite Aussie women,' Cash said, putting gifts on the table.

'Something for you, Libby,' he said, handing her a bottle of champagne.

'My fave! thank you, thank you, thank you! This is going straight in the fridge,' she said, as she walked out to the kitchen.

'And this is for you, gorgeous girl.' He handed me an eggshell blue bag and my heart skipped a beat. Tiffany & Co. Inside was a bottle of their latest perfume, which I sprayed myself with instantly, and tickets to Crowded House at the Beacon Theatre.

'Wow, this is too much, but thank you.' I kissed him on the mouth.

'I'm hoping you might take me with you. I thought a little Aussie–Kiwi night out might be fun.'

I checked the date, knowing it would be awkward if Libby was still around, but it wasn't till May, perfect.

'Of course.'

I gave Cash a book on Native cooking from the museum gift store, and a range of organic teas from Kirsten's favourite shop at Chelsea market.

'This is great,' he said, flicking through the pages. 'I can cook up a storm for you, and drink tea while I do it.' He leaned in and kissed me on the mouth and held me for a few too many seconds, given Libby was in the room.

'Okay, Mr Cash Pash, we have company.' I smiled in Libby's direction.

'Don't mind me, I'm finding it all surreal. And I'm a

little jealous,' she said, pushing her bottom lip out. 'In the nicest possible way, of course.'

That night when Cash had left and Libby and I sat holding our full stomachs and staring at the television, I told her about Cash's kitchen revelation.

'Cash said he loved me today and I couldn't say it back.'

'Why not?'

'Because I don't love him. I like him, a lot, but it's not love, not yet. I don't know if I can love someone else, just yet, or ever.' I could see Libby starting to get her 'intervention look' on her face.

'It's not because of Chubby Neck, is it? Please tell me you're over him.'

'I'm over him,' I said quietly. 'I'm just not ready to love someone again, and anyway I'm going back to Australia in July and Cash is completely bound to his restaurant here. He'd never leave New York.'

'I think you're mad. He's perfect. Smart, hot, entrepreneurial, cashed up and kind. And he is a man who *can* and *wants to* give you everything that Full-of-himself couldn't, especially commitment.'

'I know, but I have to want to have *everything* with him and right now I don't think I do. I wish I did.'

I almost wished I hadn't mentioned it to Libby at all.

'And that's my office, the Palace.' I pointed out the Smithsonian to Libby as we came out of the subway at Bowling Green the next day.

'That looks much cooler than Old Parliament House, eh?'

'It is. There's really interesting history and the spaces are great. Much more modern than ours.'

I went through the usual flirtation with security and Libby thought it was hilarious. I gave her a tour of the museum and we walked through the exhibitions and programs that were running, also stopping at the gift store as tradition dictated. She bought five pairs of earrings that had been designed by Native artists across America. Afterwards we walked the back corridors to my office and I could see the same confusion on Libby's face that was on mine the first day I landed at the museum.

'Yes, before you ask, I do get lost sometimes,' I said truthfully. 'But I eventually find myself here, with Wyatt, nearly always already working – and here he is!'

Wyatt jumped up to greet us.

'Hey there, Lauren! You just couldn't stay away, could you?'

'No, I missed you too much.' I gave him a peck on the cheek. 'This is my friend Libby and I really wanted you two to meet.'

'I've heard a lot about you, Libby, so great to see you in the flesh.' He shook Libby's hand.

'Likewise, and thanks for taking care of my tidda here. We're all missing her terribly, but really, really jealous of her as well.'

'I bet you are, on both counts.'

'I've given Libs a tour already but I wondered if you had time for a quick coffee before we head to see Lady Liberty?'

'Always time for coffee, Lauren, you know that.'

We went to a small coffee shop near the museum and Libby grilled Wyatt about the artists, local galleries, sponsors and so forth. I knew she'd be feeding it all back to Emma on her return. Wyatt asked as many questions as he answered, though, and I loved it that my old and new besties, both of them colleagues, got on so well. It could only bode well for future partnerships.

'Okay, you two – one of us is officially on holidays, so let's wrap it up or we'll miss the ferry,' I said, getting up and moving to the counter to pay.

'Wyatt – I'm interested in how you use the term Native here. Back home that's a negative term, like "primitive" and "barbaric". It's considered offensive,' Libby said.

'Really? I guess for me it just means First Peoples.'

'I think it's good to have embraced it. We generally go by Aboriginal or Indigenous when others want to lump us together, and otherwise by nations and clans.' I could hear Libby from the counter.

'Well, I'd prefer Native to some of the alternatives from our past.' Wyatt stood up and handed Libby her jacket. 'Like red men or redskin, or god forbid, injun! Now *that* is offensive,' Wyatt continued, ushering Libby towards me.

'We better go, Libs,' I said, putting my gloves on.

'It was deadly to meet you, Wyatt,' Libby said.

'Awesome to meet you, too.'

Wyatt turned left out of the coffee shop and we turned right and ran all the way to Battery Park to board the ferry, meeting up with lots of other international tourists just like Libby and me.

'Wyatt is such a nice guy, and cluey about the arts, eh?'

'Yes, he really is, and he's on the ball about work.'

'So why aren't you interested in him? You've almost got the same CV, you get on better than any couple I know, and you'd look great together.'

'What are you going on about?'

'Don't tell me you haven't noticed how funny he is, and of course he's Indigenous, so there's a whole lot of stuff you wouldn't have to explain about life and culture. Actually, maybe *I* should date him?'

'He's gay for starters and even if he weren't . . . you know I don't mix business with pleasure.'

I felt strange at the thought of Libby dating him.

'Really? He's gay? I didn't get that vibe at all,' Libby said.

'Aren't you the one that said a straight man will make a pass at you almost immediately?'

'Oh yes,' and she looked me up and down, 'he *definitely* would've made a pass at you for sure by now if he were straight. You're looking good, Lauren. New York really suits you.'

'Thank you for the compliment.'

'Well, all I can say is that it's a shame for us if Wyatt's gay, but not for the guys of New York,' Libby said as we boarded the ferry and scanned the lower deck for a seat.

'Anyway, I'm with Cash,' I said, almost as an afterthought, but Libby wasn't listening anymore. Cash loved me, and that's what I had wanted all along. I just wished I could feel happier about it, and that I could love him back. My plans for going home were probably keeping my feelings under control and that wasn't necessarily a bad thing.

'Why don't they get a room,' Libby groaned about a couple making out in front of everyone on the boat. 'God, that turns my stomach.'

'What? Public shows of affection? I think it's nice. Cash likes to pash in public.'

'Oh god, the public pash, aren't you too old for that?'

'No, I missed out on it back home so I don't mind catching up a bit here.'

'Oh my god,' Libby cringed.

'What now?'

'Look at those souvenirs.' She pointed to the foam Miss Liberty crowns and glasses and caps. 'They're so tacky, but I have to have one. You want one?'

'Not my style,' I said, running my hands over my furry pink hat.

'You've gone all Manhattan snobby on us, haven't you? Loz the lover of the Big Merino would've got something for sure.' Libby tried one of the crowns on.

'I just think it's a waste of money. I'd rather save it up for going out.'

Libby spent the entire boat ride taking photos of everything but I just wanted to sit back and soak it all in – the water, the view, the meaning of Miss Liberty – and

I wondered if in fact I had become snobby since moving to Manhattan.

The Hudson was a long way from Lake George at home, and I thought back to the drive between Goulburn and Canberra, feeling homesick, interrupted only when Libby nudged me for a photo of her with the statue in the background.

We arrived on the island and queued up to get to the statue.

'The security guard is cute,' Libby said, smiling hugely at him as we got to the first check point. He was too busy telling people they couldn't take food or water or backpacks into the area to notice her smile – and then he focused on her bag.

'Ma'am, where are you from?' he asked Libby.

'Australia. Canberra, to be exact,' she said, smiling as if he was coming on to her.

'Well, those bags might be fashionable in Australia, but it's the size of a mail sack. Perhaps you put kangaroos in there, but it's too big to take inside. You'll have to put it in a locker.'

'What? It's not *that* big.' Libby grasped her tote from the gallery defensively.

'Ma'am, the truth is I could fit my cousin Lenny in there. Good luck trying to get it through the next round of security.'

'I'd be happy to put Lenny in here and take him back with me,' Libby flirted, and the guard just smiled and waved her through.

We continued on to the main security screening, which was noisy with families and couples, school groups and teenagers out for the day, all of us queuing together in a marquee. Libby's bag went in unchallenged. Once in the building we were greeted by a guide who introduced himself as Sid.

'Good morning, ladies, where are you from?' Sid asked.

'Canberra, Australia,' we said in unison.

'I've never heard of Canberra – I mainly meet people who come from Mel*bourne*, and I tell them to get a life and move to Sydney. They have that fabulous Mardi Gras there. Do you want me to take a photo of you together?'

'Thanks,' we both said and then began the tour proper.

'I think Sid would really like Sydney,' Libs said as we walked through the museum.

We had to decide if we wanted to take the lift or the stairs to the Lady. As I was on a fitness kick, the stairs were my preferred option, but Libby wanted to take the lift. We were just about to have an argument when Libby started talking to Rick, a park ranger. Rick wanted us to hang out with him for the day. I dragged Libby away.

'Why did you do that? We could've hung out!'

'God, it is so painfully obvious you've been without male company for eighteen months. Let's burn off that frustration by climbing the 186 steps up to the woman herself.'

'Yes, Rick said the stairs were a better idea than the lift, so let's do that.'

We climbed the stairs but not into the eyes of Lady Liberty, rather to her base. Both Libby and I were annoyed.

'What? You don't actually get to go UP the statue? What's the point?' Libby said at the top of her voice.

'Oh, I didn't know, I thought you could get into the eyeballs, like we used to do in the Big Merino.'

We left the statue and boarded the boat to Ellis Island and Libby was excited. I was still a tourist, of course, but New York was so intense and tiring I'd become exhausted from work and the cold. The tourist adrenaline is not something you can maintain for months on end.

The Ellis Island Immigration Processing Center was interesting, and it really made us think about the way in which migrants and especially refugees today were processed back home, and the shame we felt at Australia being the only developed nation to have a policy of mandatory detention for refugees arriving over its borders.

We missed the ferry back so went back in to have a coffee while we waited for the next one. I wanted to have a Diet Coke and salad because I had been eating more than I usually did back in Canberra, but I caved in and had chocolate fudge and a hot chocolate.

'I really should watch my waistline,' Libby said, as she dug her teeth into the fudge before we left the counter.

'What for, girl? You're looking good,' the barista said, taking all of Libby in with his eyes. She loved it. I laughed. It was the sort of thing I had become used to in New York.

'I'm moving here,' Libby said as she looked back towards the fella, still grinning. 'I can't believe the men here. They're so forward. And not Fyshwick forward either. I love it.'

'Yeah, it's pretty special. I told you. But then, didn't you tell me first? You know, the Manhattan Movie weekend we had. I'm really only here because of you and Bec.'

23

The Empire State Building = rift, not romance

We stood in the crowd at Times Square and counted down – 10, 9, 8, 7, 6, 5, 4, 3, 2, 1! New Year's Eve rang out across New York, only fourteen hours behind Sydney and Canberra. Cash kissed me.

It was the moment I had been waiting for – not the kiss, but the famous New Year's Eve Ball descending from the flagpole atop number one Times Square. And I wasn't the only one excited about it – there were a million other revellers there as well, just waiting for the clock to strike midnight. I'd seen it on telly back home, and nothing in Goulburn or Canberra came close to this tradition. I took photo after photo for Mum and the aunties to enjoy when I got back.

'It's a work of art,' I said to Cash.

'What is?'

'The beautiful ball, with all those Waterford Crystals. Over two thousand of them, and look at all the colours.'

'That kaleidoscope effect is awesome, isn't it?' Even

Cash was overwhelmed, perhaps a little too much. 'Happy New Year,' he said, kissing me again, and I held the kiss as long as I could, but then it got too hot and heavy and we were, after all, in a public place, and even on New Year's Eve you had to contain yourself.

The cheering and singing continued and I was glad for the crowd and the noise as it confused the moment and gave me space to think, and at least not speak too much. Cash didn't seem too concerned, just happy to be there with me. My phone was vibrating with messages.

Libby had gone to our Aussie pub so she could be with the guy we only referred to as 'The Barman' at midnight. She'd done a huge about-face on the Australian pubs overseas issue. And her manfast was finally over. Eighteen months was a long time to go without sex, especially in Canberra, where winter left you cold without someone to cuddle up to whereas New Year's in New York made loving mandatory. Vikki and Kirsten were still away, so Cash was glad to have me to himself for the night.

At 1 am we went back to his restaurant and stayed until dawn with his staff and some of his regular customers. As the sun was rising Libby sent me a text with a photo of her in the cabin of an NYFD truck with firies on either side of her. She looked content and I was glad I could just tick the photo request off my 'To Do' list.

Over the next week Libby and I stuck to her schedule. We visited the Museum of Modern Art, otherwise known as MoMA, and then we spent a sobering few hours at the 9/11 memorial and museum. We went shopping at Bloomingdale's, and then, as we sat in Easy's on the afternoon of Libby's last night in New York, she went through her list. It had more and more items added to it every day, and by now it looked like the New York subway map.

'Oh my god, we forgot to go up the Empire State Building. Let's do that at sunset,' Libby said, looking at her watch, 'and then go out for dinner. It'd be the perfect end to the perfect holiday.'

'Oh, um, I don't know,' is all I could say, but I didn't know why.

'Have you done it already?' Libby asked. 'It's okay if you have, but can't you do it again? I told you I wanted to do it before you even left Canberra. I'll shout.'

'I haven't done it, but Vikki said Top of the Rock is better, we should go there. And you will not shout!'

'Top of the Rock? Shit, what's wrong with you? That's not the Empire State Building. What about Cary Grant and Tom Hanks and *Sleepless in Seattle*? I thought *you* were meant to be the romantic.'

'You knocked any notion of romance I had right out of me with your freaking intervention.'

'Ah, so this is about Adam, is it? That'd be right. Six months later, thousands of miles away and you're still letting him ruin your life.'

'It's not about him, and he's not ruining my life. I'm claustrophobic. I'm frightened of the lift and being in it all that time.'

'What? You've been in lifts. I've been in lifts *with you.* You did Black Mountain Tower.' Libby had an accusatory tone in her voice.

'The Empire State Building is taller, and are you calling me a liar?'

'Don't worry, I'll go by myself.' She got up and walked out of the bar, and before I had a chance to catch her I saw her jumping in a cab.

I felt terrible. We had never had a fight, and we were in New York and it was wrong. I should have gone after her. She was my best friend. But I just couldn't do it. I had my ideas about the Empire State Building, and if I wasn't going to do it with Adam then I didn't want to do it at all. And I certainly wasn't going to do it today without warning and risk being embarrassingly sick. I went back home and hoped she'd call soon.

For twenty-five minutes I walked around the lounge room fuming that she'd run off, and not sure what to do. I was worried. I loved Libby, and she was my dearest friend. I texted her but she didn't text me back. I put my coat on again and went uptown, not knowing exactly what I would do. When I got to the building I still couldn't go up, so I just waited and watched people queuing for their tickets. A security guard approached me.

'Ma'am, you'll have to either move forward or leave. We can't have people loitering.'

'I'm sorry, I'm just nervous about the lift. I don't think I can do it. My friend is up there, but I just can't do it.' I still didn't really know why, but blamed the claustrophobia anyway.

'That's okay, ma'am, it happens a lot, but you can't stand there any longer, I'm sorry.'

'I understand, but where would a woman go next if she were stood up here? I mean, if she went to the top and was disappointed, you know, if a friend didn't go with her?'

'Oh, there are plenty of bars around here, but are you looking for somewhere special, fancy?' He looked at me for agreement.

'Yes, I want something nice.'

'Then definitely head to the Campbell Apartment at Grand Central Station. They do good martinis.'

'Thank you,' I said, hurrying out the door. I legged it to Grand Central and found the cocktail bar, where I got a seat and texted Libby immediately.

> I'm so sorry. Please come to Campbell Apartment bar at Grand Central. I have a martini waiting for you. I'm sorry. Xxxx

And then I just waited and waited and waited for what felt like hours, but was only forty minutes. Then my phone beeped with a message from Libby.

> Getting an Uber now. X

I breathed a sigh of relief, drank Libby's martini, and ordered another round.

I started to cry the minute she sat down.

'I'm so sorry, I should've gone with you. Can you ever forgive me?'

'It's fine, Lauren. Turns out you were right anyway, this time.'

'What?'

'It was a major let down, really. There was no magic up there, or romance, not that I was looking for that. I was interested in the history, but it was just really bland. And it was so cold, Jesus, I nearly froze to death.'

'Here, this'll warm you up.' I moved the martini towards her, and she sipped.

'I'm surprised there's no bar in the building. It's the perfect place to have one, what with all those broken hearts who've been stood up. They could go to the same bar and just hook up with each other.'

'Sounds like a great marketing idea.'

'And it was so bloody cramped. There was no room for Cary Grant's ghost, let alone the real Tom Hanks. I should've listened to you.'

'I should've been honest with you ages ago about the claustrophobia – I managed to keep it hidden in Canberra because none of the buildings are that tall, and there's no lifts at the NAG. I had an incident on the plane coming over, and another at Macy's, so I try and avoid them whereas altogether now.'

'I'm sorry I doubted you, but I had no idea you were a claustrophobic freak,' Libby said jokingly.

'And I had no idea you were such a bloody schedule freak!' I said laughing, pretending to tear up the now tattered list.

'Here's cheers to freaky friends,' I said, and we toasted the night away.

24

MLK to BLM

It was Martin Luther King Jr Day and the city was quiet. I still felt a little lost with Libby gone. I took the day off work, as did most of New York, turning it into a long weekend. I hadn't seen Cash since New Year's Eve, and I'd pulled back a little since his revelation at Christmas. He knew something was wrong. He hadn't told me he loved me again – I think he understood that I didn't feel the same. But he still wanted to see me.

We made plans to celebrate MLK Jr Day by going to Miss Mamie's Spoonbread restaurant and then up to the Schomburg Center for Research in Black Culture in Harlem. I loved Miss Mamie's the minute I walked in. There were yellow walls with red lamp shades and wicker chairs, and the Four Tops singing in the background. Families, couples and groups of uni students sat eating all the food the restaurant was famous for. The smell of southern fried chicken lingered in the air and made my stomach ache for some.

'Can you order for me please, Cash?' I said. 'I want to eat whatever you think I should try from the menu, you being the food connoisseur and all.'

'Right, happy to help out. This is one of my favourite places. I recommend the collard greens, southern fried chicken, black eyed peas, cornbread and candied yams.' Cash seemed glad of the small duty.

'Am I going to be able to eat all that?'

'I'll eat whatever you can't.'

'Hah, with a sixpack like that' – I patted his taut stomach – 'you can afford to. But I can see me having to move into the gym after this meal.'

As I took the last bite of chicken, wishing that I could fit in dessert, I relaxed back into my chair and moaned contentment.

'I told you it was good,' Cash said, getting up to pay the bill.

After lunch we headed up to Harlem, and the Schomburg Center. Walking through Harlem was amazing, all Blackfellas, hustle and bustle, stalls lining both sides of the road, and plenty of shopping, but Cash was focused on our destination.

'Come on, Lauren, keep up,' Cash joked, making me feel like I was a six-year-old trying to walk next to a grown-up. He put his arm around my shoulder and marched me along 125th Street, keeping me warm at the same time.

'Excuse me,' a man said as he accidentally bumped into me crossing the road. People were even friendlier in Harlem than on the subway. Perhaps it was because it wasn't so cold up there. Harlem seemed to have missed out on the harsh winds that almost froze me down in Chelsea.

At the Schomburg, Cash and I slowly went through the history of Black politics and politicians in America. There was rolling footage of Obama's victory speech and a shrine dedicated to him. But it was the memorial created in honour of George Floyd that moved us both to tears. Cash stood behind me with his arms around my belly and we both cried as we stood watching a montage of footage from the international Black Lives Matter movement triggered by the gutwrenching murder of Mr Floyd in Minneapolis in June 2020.

We separated and I walked through the exhibit checking out everything from the National Convention of Colored Citizens in 1872 to heartbreaking images of lynchings in 1935.

We reunited downstairs, then held hands and walked quietly through the photographic exhibition 'Obama: the Historic Campaign and Victory'. I realised that what Cash and I shared was an understanding and respect as people of colour, who have remained essentially voiceless in mainstream politics. But it didn't necessarily mean I had to be in love with him.

As we left, I saw Cash put a $100 bill in the donations box without fuss or fanfare and I admired his generosity and commitment to change.

Cash and I shared the most amazing afternoon at the Apollo's annual MLK celebration. We listened to passionate activists speaking about King's legacy and what activism means today, and then we were treated to music by the Harlem Chamber Players and the Dream Launchers choir.

The next day at work I totally ear-bashed Wyatt about it all.

'It was just so moving and inspiring. I'm so in awe of the whole history of Black activism here,' I said, and Wyatt and I just hugged with the emotion of it all.

'So, it's fair to say you're getting deep into American history and politics,' he said, slowly letting go.

'I just keep thinking about how much has been achieved, and how much further there is to go. And then I think about home – one day we might have a Black president of the Republic of Australia.'

'That would be awesome.'

'Don't you dream about a Native president?'

'I think it's really possible now, and there's blogs everywhere and groups on Facebook already making lists of who people think might work. Haven't seen my own name up there yet, though.'

'Haha, would you like me to go into one of the forums and write it for you?'

'Yes, please! But first, can you answer the two dozen emails I pawned off to you while you were out celebrating?'

Australia Week had been timed to coincide with 'Australia Day'. It was a day of contention as far as I was concerned. While the date marked the arrival of the First Fleet and white settlers, for Aboriginal Australians it marked the beginning of invasion, colonisation and attempted genocide. At home I always went to Sydney to celebrate at the annual Yabun Festival with Koori musicians and arts and crafts from around New South Wales, but this time I chose to go along to the 'Australia Day' events on 26 January in New York, to see how the celebrations played out in my current home.

Kirsten and I went to the Aussie pub but only because we both felt like roo and pav. By the time we got there much of the crowd was blind drunk.

The bar was packed and jumping to good old Australian classics by Midnight Oil, AC/DC, and Jimmy Barnes. When Goanna came on singing 'Solid Rock' Kirsten and I finally found the lungs to sing.

We stood at the bar but it was so loud it was difficult to talk. 'Let's sit in the restaurant,' I yelled at Kirsten. 'I need pavlova.'

Kirsten rarely had to wait for a table in any of the Australian establishments in New York.

'You do realise, by removing ourselves from that rowdy party we'd be accused of being un-Australian and unpatriotic today don't you?' she told me as we sat down.

'Good. If being patriotic means I have to wear a green and gold headband reading "Made in Australia", then I am un-Australian. But at least I've got fashion sense.'

'I should've worn a rugby union sweatshirt,' Kirsten said sarcastically.

'And an Australian flag tied around your neck à la Pauline Hanson,' I added.

'The flag should be flown on flagpoles, not bogans.'

'Sounds like a slogan to me!'

I saw a tiny Aboriginal flag near the coat rack and went and took it off the wall. I stuck it in a glass on our table. 'There. That's better. I feel like I've made a native title claim on this place.'

'I gave that to Matt, you can't keep it,' Kirsten said, just as a guy wearing an Australian flag singlet came crashing into our table. He looked at us and yelled, 'Aussie Aussie Aussie, oi oi oi.'

Kirsten pushed him away and then we just sat there quietly for a while. I ate my pavlova and watched the Australian Open on the telly on one wall, while Kirsten watched *Crocodile Dundee* on the wall behind me.

A girl sat down next to us with an Australian flag made into a bandeau top.

Kirsten leaned over the table to me and said, 'Love, I think we need to come up with some elegant patriotic wear, in the red, black and yellow.'

'I'll toast that,' I said, raising my glass.

I put a spoonful of pav in my mouth and before I'd swallowed Cash was sitting next to me.

'Happy Invasion Day,' he said, planting a kiss on my cheek.

'This is a surprise,' I said, wiping cream from the corner of my mouth.

'I knew you'd be here and I wanted to see you.'

'I just spotted someone I know.' And Kirsten was off.

'We need to talk.' Cash took my hand.

Back at Cash's apartment, the Ozmos had kicked in. I felt sexy and desirable. Sex with Cash was effortless and he always made sure I was pleased before he was. He was considerate in so many ways.

'I have something for you,' he said, walking back into the room with a glass of juice after we'd made love.

'Yum, juice, just what every girl wants.' I laughed.

'Very funny – it's juice . . . and this.' He handed me a small velvet pouch. In it was a key.

'What's this for?'

'It's commonly known as a key. It opens doors.'

'Who's being funny now?'

'You have the key to my heart already. This one is to my door. I want you to move in.'

'What?' I sat up fully in bed. 'But it's too soon – we've only known each other a couple of months. And I'm not staying in New York, I go home in July.' I could see his disappointment. 'I'm sorry, that came out all wrong.' I touched his face.

'I want to be with you.' He took me by both arms and stared into my eyes. 'I'd be happy for you to move in here. With my shifts at the restaurant we probably wouldn't see much more of each other anyway, but I want to take care of you.'

He wanted to take care of me. It echoed in my head.

The perfect man was offering me all the love and affection and practical things any girl in her right mind could want and yet my mouth was moving faster than I could think. 'It's just that it's too soon for me, and by the time it's not too soon, I'll be going back to Canberra, to my mob, to my family. It's where I belong.'

Cash stood up in his boxers and shook his head.

'But I don't want to lose you. I don't know how you're single in Australia, but I know that I'll lose you if I don't make a real commitment to you, if not now, then soon.'

'I won't be staying here, Cash, I already know that. Australia is my home and I could never move anywhere for a man. My grandfather used to say that a man should love the woman enough to follow her anywhere, but a woman should never follow a man anywhere.'

'I'm not asking you to follow me anywhere.' He was getting annoyed. 'You're already here. I know you love it here, and I'm making it easier for you to stay. We could have a great life together. I know you know it. You just need some time, is that what you want?'

'You make out as if I don't know what I want. It's not true. I know I want to go home, I don't need time to think about that. Australia is my home, that's where I belong.' I felt like Cash wasn't hearing me, that he didn't want to hear me, but I was being completely honest with him. I realised sitting there how many times Adam must have said things that I too had failed to hear.

Cash sat back down on the bed and held my hand. 'And this is where *I* belong, here in New York. This is *my* home. And I want to stay in *my* home too. It's just that I want *my* home to be *your* home. *Mi casa es su casa*.' He smiled weakly.

'I'm sorry,' I said and leaned in and hugged the perfect guy, knowing it was the last time we would be together.

25

The heart has its reasons, which reason knows nothing of . . .

Cash called and texted me every day for the following week and even though I missed him terribly – our regular chats, his affection, our friendship – I told him there was no point in seeing each other again, the future was clear. I was sad, but much stronger than I was when breaking up with Adam. I could now recognise when something just wasn't going to work. I was grateful for the minor epiphany. I also knew now what a true and loving companion could be like and how a healthy relationship *should* look, thanks to Cash.

Libby had emailed me three times that week about work and gossip, but I hadn't responded to the personal ones. I didn't want to talk about it. I just wanted to get on with the rest of my life, for the rest of the time I had in New York. I dropped her a quick message later to let her know what was going on:

Hi Libs – it's still freeeeezing here, but my big jacket is doing its job. Sorry I've been slack, have been busy, but also need to tell you Cash and I broke up. I don't love him and I'm going home in six months anyways. We'll be friends. There's really nothing to talk about and I'm FINE – really – I AM. And busy preparing for a lecture I have to give, so no time to mope around anyway. So don't worry. Miss you xoxo

She messaged back:

I knew something was up, but I won't worry, I could see you had life under control for yourself over there. Cash was a catch, but I get that he's not right for you. Send him to me, and I'm sure Bec wouldn't mind him either! 😃 Seriously, let me know if you want to talk, and we can Zoom, else just keep living the life I wish I had, and eat some New York cheesecake – but I'm sure you've already done that this week! Luv ya heaps xx

It was true that I didn't have too much time to dwell on Cash as there were only two weeks before I had to give the lecture on Aboriginal art at the progressive NYU New School in Greenwich Village. I did a quick web search to determine what my student audience might be like and found that most of the programs at the uni were in design, liberal arts, the performing arts, and social and political science. The institution itself aimed to create a place where global peace and justice were more than theoretical ideals, so I was keen to speak there and help achieve their mission through my lecture.

My excitement was tempered by anxiety, though. Wyatt said my lecture would build up our relationship with the university, and Emma had emailed me some notes on artists I should include. I just hoped I didn't have a panic attack on the day.

I wanted to give an inspiring lecture but I wanted to be practical too, pointing the students in the right direction if they wanted to find books on Aboriginal art after the lecture. So I went to the New York Public Library to see what they had on their shelves.

I had a spring in my step walking from home along 7th Avenue in the direction of the library. I wore my pink hat and a matching pink scarf Mum had sent from home. The sun was shining and although it was cold, at least people in the street were smiling again. The snow had melted on the sidewalk for the time being but I still looked for black ice.

I turned at 40th Street and headed towards 5th Avenue. I stopped at Bryant Park and watched people ice-skating. One guy kept eyeballing me each time he went past; was it a particular pick-up gesture in New York? I wasn't quite sure, so I walked off.

I took photos of the world-renowned marble lion statues out the front of the library – Patience and Fortitude. The pair were as important to the city landscape as the library itself and I was happy to take more photos for an Italian couple who wanted to be snapped with them.

I walked up the stairs into the huge foyer, looking at the monstrous white columns that framed it, and recalled the scene from *Sex and the City* when Carrie first arrived at the wedding that never happened.

Once inside it was like other galleries and museums, where volunteers greeted me with maps, knowledge and smiles. I first went to the Bill Blass Public Catalog Room and marvelled at the sheer grandiosity of it all. I felt like I was in a modern day sacred site. It was so quiet. I sat in an old wooden carved chair on tiled floors that added to the cold feeling of the space. A guy sat opposite me at a computer at a long wooden desk, with four computers either side. I looked up and admired the ornate ceilings.

I searched the library catalogue for Australian Aborigines, Aboriginal Australians and Aboriginal artists to see what was available there. I found Michael Riley's *Sights Unseen* edited by Brenda L Croft. There were other titles, but this was the most appropriate for the students, I thought. It had essays by renowned Indigenous and non-Indigenous Australian contributors and some of the country's top art experts. I also searched American Indian art, Inuit art, Indians of North America and 'Eskimos' of Alaska – offensive and outdated terminology but still in catalogues and I could speak to changing language as well. There were thousands of entries.

I went to the reading room to finish my research and develop a resource guide for the students. The room felt highbrow and intellectual. It was what I would call a traditional library, very different to my old library back in

Goulburn, and even different to the National Library in Canberra. I felt smarter just walking through it. The space made me want to read and learn more, and although I was there to research, I felt the tourist wave come over me. I wanted to take photos but I didn't.

I scanned the reading room and saw people who were studying. There were men in suits and students in college sweatshirts. And there was no talking at all, and definitely no talking to yourself, at the New York Library. I had to snap myself out of daydreaming and get stuck into my lecture plan. I wrote a structure that I could use also to deliver a paper at the NMAI if Emma ever wanted me to.

Lecture structure:

1. Intro self – acknowledge traditional owners of New York
2. Intro to First Nations Australia – history of defining Indigenous Australians, basic demographics – stats on where we live (rural/remote), where we're employed, etc.
3. The diversity of First Nations Australian visual arts by form:
   - photography
   - linocuts
   - painting
   - sculpture
   - installation art

I was getting inspired as I typed quickly on my laptop.

4. Main themes to discuss
   - identity/representation
   - politics
   - history

My only concern as I punched the keys was that I would run out of time with all the information, ideas and artists I wanted to inspire the students with. Back at the NMAI I showed Wyatt the plan.

'It's good, Lauren. Actually, it's great. There's so much here that will give the students a foundation and understanding not only of the art scene, but the social and political too,' he said, concentrating on the page as he spoke.

'Thanks, your opinion means the world to me. Is there anything else I should add?'

'It's not essential, but it would be helpful to the students if you did some comparisons along the way, with the demographics and the like, what's similar and what's different in terms of population sizes, but also the most popular artforms for each nation. For example, I know rock art is significant in some parts of your country, but many might not know that the Monte Alegre culture rock paintings at Caverna da Pedra Pintada are believed to be some of the oldest paintings in the Americas. I'm sure many of the students will be surprised to learn that.'

'Wow, well yes, they will be, because I was.' My head was spinning at this new knowledge, and I was typing fast.

'Ok, so I've got quite a bit of writing to do now. I'll get on to it right away. Thank you.'

I'd get Wyatt to check everything when I finished my draft.

The day arrived and I was excited about giving the lecture. NYU sounded flash, but Vikki told me the New School was like UTS in Sydney, basically a concrete slab. I didn't care. The students were friendly in the way only New Yorkers could be, and they were genuinely interested in art from the oldest surviving culture in the world. After a general introduction I gave my lecture, focusing on the regions I had been fortunate enough to visit and artists whose work I had exhibited, including material from the East Kimberley, the Tiwi Islands and major cities like Sydney and Brisbane.

I was intrigued by some of the questions from the students: Is Australia a racist country? How did I think art empowered Aboriginal people? Can anyone do dot painting? Is Aboriginal history taught in schools? I loved all the questions, and I got to explain that there is no such thing as Aboriginal history, that everything post-invasion was Australian history. And just as Captain Cook did not discover Australia, Christopher Columbus did not discover the Americas. You cannot discover a country that already has people in it. I loved watching the lightbulbs in student minds go on.

The clock struck 4 pm and students started packing up folders and bags and moving out of the room. I couldn't believe how quickly the time went.

'Hi, my name's Dason.' A student introduced himself to me while I unplugged my laptop. 'I really enjoyed your lecture, and I'll definitely check out the books and websites you recommended. I wondered if I might buy you a coffee and talk a little about my PhD? I'm thinking of incorporating a discussion of art.'

I looked at my watch.

'There's a group of us going,' he added.

'Sure, just let me call the office.'

I told Wyatt I was going to do some follow up with the students and headed to Caffé Reggio in MacDougal Street with Dason and the group. I knew Bec and Libby would be jealous of me hanging out with the cool people in the 'cool street'.

Dason and I chatted on the phone a few days later. He seemed to have developed a crush on me over the coffee and chat, but I wasn't interested. And not just because he was a student. On Valentine's Day two weeks later, a massive bouquet of flowers arrived at the NMAI. Both Wyatt and I were at our desks when security called.

'Wow, I've got flowers downstairs,' I said, rushing out the office door.

'Lucky you.'

I walked back hidden behind a massive bouquet of roses, busting to read the card in private.

'Gees, that's some Valentine.'

'I know, aren't they beautiful?' I sat down and took the card from the small gold envelope.

The heart has its reasons which reason knows nothing of. —Pascal.

I sighed out loud.

'Is that a good sigh?' Wyatt asked.

'I'm not quite sure who they're from.'

'Your man in Australia, perhaps?'

'Highly unlikely.'

Even though I had sent Adam a card, just because I wanted to send *someone, anyone*, a card, I was fairly sure the flowers were from Cash. He was the romantic one with money to spare. I sent him a text to say thank you for the flowers, but there was no response.

26

DC delights

'You should check out the exhibitions in our public area,' Kirsten said, as we ate dinner in our apartment, the first meal we'd had together for weeks. 'Joyce Dallal's work "Descent" is there. There's like a thousand paper airplanes with the text of the third and fourth Geneva Conventions about the victims of war written on each one. It's very powerful and clever.'

'Sounds awesome,' I said, and then realised, 'God, I've gone all American, haven't I?'

'Yes, you have, but with an Australian accent, so that's all right.'

I went to the exhibit a couple of days later at the UN, and Kirsten was right. It was innovative, but my attention was stolen by an exhibit called 'Stories of Survival and Remembrance: A Call to Action for Genocide Prevention', which spoke of the genocide in Rwanda against the Tutsi, the genocide in Cambodia, and atrocity crimes in

Bosnia. I'd never heard the term before, but learned that the UN defined atrocity crimes as those that included genocide, crime against humanity and war crimes. Each story told through the experiences of survivors hit my heart hard. I spent the rest of the afternoon trying to come to grips with the harsh realities experienced in some countries that the *whole* world should be talking about. Furious about.

I felt sorry for the stain that Nazi Germany had left on its own nation and the world. I wanted to learn more, and with such a large Jewish community in New York, I had to, so the following weekend I went to the Jewish Museum near Central Park.

As I walked the building I was surprised how few people were there. I wondered if it was because of what was happening in Gaza at the time, and what kind of references to Palestine I might find.

I learned about the seven-branched candelabrum, and the four fundamental themes of Jewish history and identity – Covenant, Exodus, Law, Land. I discovered that Israelites became Jews in 586 BC with the Babylonian conquest of Judah. I saw a whole range of Hanukkah lamps – one even had a kangaroo and emus – and I tried to remember if there was a visible Jewish community in Canberra. There surely wasn't one in Goulburn.

A talk, dark and very handsome guy walked past me wearing a black roll neck sweater. I wondered if he was Jewish. Did he have any comments on Gaza? Would he marry out? I had a lot of questions, but no-one to ask.

I always hated being expected to be the walking talking Aboriginal encyclopedia back home.

I wept as I looked at the 'Art of Holocaust' exhibit. An installation of dead bodies made out of plaster lay on the ground.

'Don't worry, miss, a lot of people cry when they look at this space,' a security guard said, holding out a box of tissues.

I felt for the Jewish people, but wondered why the warfare and genocide in Australia related to Aboriginal people had never been termed a holocaust.

With holocaust sadness still in my heart I was glad to be going to Washington at the end of the week with Maria and Wyatt to see the advanced screening of *Buffy Sainte-Marie: Carry It On*.

We flew to DC on Thursday for the showing that night. Wyatt explained on the way that the DC museum was seen by many as the flagship because it was considered the first National Museum for American Indians, even though the New York venue had opened first.

'See, the DC site is on the National Mall with all the major cultural venues – the Washington Monument, the National Museum of Natural History, the United States Capitol – so it means it has a higher profile through association. But of course we believe our site is better,' he joked.

'Of course we do,' I agreed.

It was just falling dusk when we arrived at the National Mall near the NMAI. I had to stop and imagine what it must have been like to be there for Barack Obama's inauguration. I closed my eyes and I could feel the vibrations of millions of people all cheering. It would've been mind-blowing.

'Are you okay?' Wyatt asked, looking concerned.

'I'm good, just thinking. This place is amazing. I'm sorry, but I now understand why everyone thinks the DC site is the flagship, there's so much wonderful energy here.'

'We can argue about this later – we've got twenty minutes to get in there and be seen and then seated.'

We headed towards the building and I admired it immediately, with its curvilinear design evoking natural rock formations shaped by wind and water over thousands of years. I was excited as we headed in, trying to read the flyer about the documentary and remember who all the key players were.

I stood outside the Rasmuson Theater on the first floor and was energised by the size of the crowd. Wyatt and Maria introduced me to the world-renowned singer-songwriter, who was also a deadly muso, composer and visual artist. My mouth was so dry with nerves I could barely speak. And there was no way I was getting my book out to be signed. I mumbled something incoherent and was manoeuvred in close for a group photo, and then the legend was being moved on to meet and inspire another group of people. I didn't have time to digest the moment as Maria and Wyatt were introducing me to people every step

I took. It was great to make the connections in relation to Aboriginal actors back home and celebrate being part of the international Indigenous community.

We watched the screening of *Buffy Sainte-Marie: Carry It On*, which was an inspiring in-depth look at the artist's activist life and her journey as a musician, including footage of her on stage but also interviews with her, her bandmates and peers. I felt incredibly privileged to be in that space and inspired by the important educational role Buffy Sainte-Marie was playing not just in North America, but globally.

The next morning we had meetings with the team in Washington, and then Maria flew back to New York. Wyatt and I had organised to do some sightseeing and head back late Saturday afternoon, the day of my birthday.

'What do you want to do first?' Wyatt asked.

'I'm easy, what about you?'

'I'm easy too.' There was a stark difference between the chilled Wyatt and the scheduled Libby. It was so simple to hang out with my NYC mate.

'Don't laugh,' Wyatt said, 'but I wouldn't mind checking out the Cherry Blossom Festival in the National Building Museum.'

'The what festival?'

'I read about it on the plane. It's an annual event that features three thousand cherry blossom trees that the city of Tokyo gave to DC. I thought it might be fun. There's events all across town, and at the National Building Museum there's music, ballet, cherry blossoms, a floating Japanese tea room, and we can even plant some seedlings.'

'Sounds all right, I guess.'

'*And* there's a gift store!' Wyatt said, grabbing both my arms and trying to shake some excitement into me, but he didn't need to.

'Sold, lead the way.'

We spent the afternoon just strolling around the festival, then we had a green tea and some sushi. In the gift store I wavered over two different prints. One had a black background with red cherry blossoms and one had a gold background. I couldn't decide which one I liked best.

'Which one do you like?' I held the prints up to Wyatt.

'The one with the black background would look best in your apartment, I think.' Wyatt's curatorial eye was always working.

'You're right, and it'd look great back at my place back in Manuka, too.' And so I bought it, looking forward to showing the girls when I got back.

That night Wyatt had booked us a table at the Lafayette, which overlooked Lafayette Square and the White House. I'm sure it was one of the fanciest restaurants in the city, with Tom Vogt playing the piano to entertain us.

'Do you know that Lena Horne called this guy her "favourite pianist in Washington"?' Wyatt said.

'I can see why, I love all the jazz and show tunes he's been playing. This is so much fun, really. Thanks for hanging out with me.'

'What? I should be thanking you. I've been to DC before but it's never been this awesome. And none of my friends would come to this restaurant, so thank *you.* I'm told they do sensational desserts here.' Wyatt winked and smiled.

'You certainly know the way to a woman's heart is through her sweet tooth.'

'So I've heard.'

I ordered the 'decadent' chocolate truffle cake and Wyatt ordered the Grand Marnier soufflé and we shared.

'You like sweets too, then?'

'My one and only vice.'

'Really?'

'Well, the only one I'll admit to.'

After we'd finished our desserts and tea Wyatt put a tiny box on the table.

'What is it?'

'It's for you.'

'Why?'

'I heard it's your birthday tomorrow, so I thought we could start celebrating early. Anyway, I couldn't wait to give it to you.'

'Wow, an early birthday present. I love birthdays.'

'So do I. Open it.'

I opened it to find tiny cherry blossom earrings.

'They're gorgeous, I love them.' I took out my silver hoops and put the blossoms on straight away.

'I saw them in the store today, and met the artist. She's from Virginia, and she was really nice, so I thought I could make you both happy by buying them. I aim to please.'

'They're the perfect memento from DC and will go with my print. I can stand next to it at home and be a piece of installation art as well.'

'They look beautiful on, Lauren.'

'Thank you.' I leaned across the table and kissed Wyatt on the cheek.

I felt like I was finally having that elusive obligation-free date I'd been waiting for. If only he wasn't gay!

Wyatt insisted on sharing an Uber from the airport and then carrying my bag upstairs. Only when I opened the door did I realise why.

'Surprise!' the mob sang out as I walked in and turned the lights on.

'What the . . .?'

'We thought we should have a little soiree in honour of your birthday, sis, so happy birthday,' Kirsten said, wearing a party hat and lei and handing me a present.

'Hey,' I squealed when I saw Matt. 'And you fibber, you said you had to get back to your kids!' I accused Maria.

Maria shrugged her shoulders, looking for forgiveness. 'It's not a complete lie – I feel a bit like you're one of my kids.'

Vikki pulled out a chair and motioned me towards it. 'Sit, we have a feast prepared – Kirsten and I were at the markets super early today, and we got the best of everything.' She poured me some wine as cooking smells wafted through the apartment.

They were all in foil hats and leis and I couldn't help laughing. 'I need a photo of this, really, no-one back home will believe this mad hatter's birthday party. I can't believe it.' I set my phone up on the bookcase, set the automatic timer, and ran around next to Wyatt.

'Everyone say . . . New York cheesecake . . .'

'New York cheesecake!' we all squealed and laughed. 'This is so awesome,' I said.

'So awesome you're talking like us now,' Maria said.

'I'm cool with that,' I replied, holding my glass up. 'Here's to awesomeness.'

Vikki and Kirsten brought out two massive bowls of pasta, one seafood and one chicken pesto, homemade garlic bread, a huge green salad and more wine. There was no room on the table at all, as we all squashed round sitting on odd chairs, including an office chair that had come from the NMAI especially for the night. I laughed when I saw it.

Maria grabbed the sides of her seat. 'Well, Kirsten said if I wanted to sit, I'd have to bring my own chair. I like sitting, so I did.'

'I think I will be the first human being to have a carb explosion but this is the best seafood pasta I have *ever* had,' I said, my stomach swelling with each mouthful. 'I can't eat another thing.'

'Nothing?' Kirsten asked with a sly smile.

'Absolutely nothing.'

'Not even a piece of key lime pie? Not even a sliver of New York cheesecake? Not even a crumb of chocolate mud cake with raspberry coulis?'

'Why would you do that to me now? You know I always read the dessert menu first.'

Just as I finished saying that the lights went out and a huge chocolate cake with ribbons of chocolate curls on top appeared, its candles breaking the darkness, and then the singing started. I reached for my phone and hoped the flash would capture the cake, the hats and the merriment.

'Happy birthday to you, happy birthday to you . . .' and they all sang along in tune while I got choked up.

'We all just wanted to wish you the deadliest New York birthday you could have, Lauren, so happy happy birthday,' Kirsten said at the end of the song, holding her glass up to a toast. The rest of the table said, 'Happy happy birthday.'

I blew the candles out and forgot to make a wish.

'This is so Ossie,' Vikki said. 'I think we need some Stevie Wonder singing "Happy Birthday" to Americanise this party a bit. You cut the cake, hon, I'll do the music.' While I started cutting and plating, I got all teary at the thought of such friendship and kindness so far from home. Wyatt saw me wipe a tear from my cheek and winked.

He took the cake and served a piece to me. 'And now, you must eat cake. It's a birthday tradition we have here in New York, Lauren,' he said.

I lay down flat and full when everyone had left. It was one of the most loving birthdays I had ever enjoyed. I felt the earrings that Wyatt had given me and wondered what would arrive in the post later in the week from Mum and Dad. The mail had been slow but Mum said she'd sent something. I checked my phone to find lots of text messages from back home. The picture I'd posted on Instagram of us around the table with the cake had already attracted dozens of likes and comments wishing me happy birthday. I saw the icon that meant Adam had posted a new story and realised I hadn't thought about him in days. I was pleased with myself.

27

The perfect closing to opening night

April was another crazy month as we prepared for the short film festival and the opening of my exhibition. I met with the services staff about hanging the works, the media people about the promotions and material for the website, and the catering team about the food.

'I get a rush doing this,' I said to Wyatt as I put the phone down, having just spoken to an NYU professor wanting to bring some postgrad students to the opening. 'I'm excited when others get excited.' I was on a high.

'The adrenaline's pumping then, is it?' He swung around on his chair.

'Certainly is.' I handed him a sheet of paper. 'How does this running order look to you?'

He started to scan the page, but before he had a chance to comment I thrust another piece under his nose. 'And can you double-check' – I stopped myself – 'okay, I know, *triple*-check this guest list and see if there's anyone else, especially key community members that are missing?'

Wyatt smiled.

'What?' I asked accusingly.

'You remind me of me. It makes me laugh is all. We must drive other people nuts with details.'

I took the paper from him and waved it flamboyantly. 'Ah, but we get the job done, *and* we get the good jobs, so I'm happy to drive people nuts.'

I jumped up urgently. 'Shit!'

'What?' Wyatt jumped up too.

'I've gotta go, I've got a meeting at the American Museum of Natural History. I'll be back later.' And I grabbed my bag and ran out the door.

In the middle of my exhibition preparations Emma had emailed to say she wanted me to meet with the staff at the American Museum of Natural History to see what potential partnerships could be brokered, and this morning the museum was celebrating the anniversary of Henry Hudson's voyage up the Hudson River. I was glad to be part of a ceremonial welcome from the descendants of those stewards of country who were there when Hudson first sailed. The welcome pulled at my heartstrings and made me homesick, and then the drummers started playing and I was completely in awe. One particular drummer in a green ribbon shirt, baseball cap and Nike runners showed the fusion of cultures and the pride instilled in young Native men even today. My heart was beating in time with the drums, and I felt hypnotised as I walked through the exhibits of the museum, wishing we had three square blocks for our own space back in Australia. I met with their education officer to discuss a potential partnership and all the while thought about the green ribbon shirt guy, and how I could get his group to the NAG.

Back at the NMAI, Wyatt and I finalised the last-minute preparations for the exhibition opening. The artworks were being hung, media interest was gathering momentum, and the opening night party looked like it was going to be a swinging bash. I was excited.

The film festival was scheduled to happen at the same time and so we had filmmakers and reviewers floating around the museum as well. And I was working on the program with a passion, planning on including Leah Purcell's film *The Drover's Wife: The Legend of Molly Johnson* because it was a significant re-imagining of her play and the iconic Australian short story by Henry Lawson; the Noongar Daa revoiced version of the kung fu classic *Fist of Fury* would be a hit because, as the Noongar dub director Kylie Bracknell had told the media, 'Blackfellas loved Bruce Lee'; and it wasn't simply because I adored the entire cast of *The Sapphires* that I included it – but rather to acknowledge the incredible international success of the 2012 film. Because the scooping up of children and raising them in white institutions was also part of American history, it was important for me to include the late Doris Pilkington Garimara's *Rabbit-Proof Fence* on the program as well. There were so many connections between our nations, and I knew her story of the Stolen Generations would speak to local audiences as well.

The original plan was to run the Australian films concurrently with local Indigenous films, but after Maria and Wyatt had watched them all we had agreed to give the festival a purely Australian focus.

I had wanted to show the range of genres our filmmakers were working in and the variety of stories and representations they offered, and by all accounts my goals had been met. Feedback forms so far were all positive, with lots of viewers saying they had had no idea there were still Aboriginal people in Australia, and especially in the cities. The educational aspect of the program couldn't be measured fully but I was so pleased at the thought of the impact it could have.

'Lauren, we've never had such a response to international films before. This is a huge success for us. Maria is never, ever going to let you leave.' Wyatt was stroking my professional ego.

'What? They're not *my* films.'

'No, but this wouldn't have happened if it wasn't for you, if you hadn't taken up the fellowship. We all know that.'

I felt a huge sense of accomplishment, but by the time the opening night for the exhibition finally arrived, I was more nervous than I'd ever been in my life. I was just hoping I didn't have an anxiety attack and confided in Wyatt.

'Try this.' He handed me some ashwagandha. 'Works for me every time.'

People started streaming through the exhibition, taking in the artwork by Karen Mills, whose work incorporated the loop pattern of both traditional dilly bag weaving and knitting stitches which took the artist and the viewer through a spiritual journey using the medium of paint. Students huddled around the work of Judy Watson from the Waanyi language group: *a preponderance of aboriginal blood* was a 2005 series of fifteen etchings and a colophon making up the artist's book of the same title. The pages, having recently shown at the Tate Modern, represented official government documents splashed with red paint to infer blood. Everyone was talking, frowning, shaking their heads as they grasped the intention and meaning of the work. There were huge portraits by photographer Ricky Maynard from his *No More Than What You See* series, reporting on Indigenous inmates in South Australian prisons. Some of the students revelled in the late Lin Onus's work *Kaptn Koori*, on loan from the National Gallery of Victoria, and his sculpture *Fruit Bats* featuring rarrk painted fibreglass bats, hanging from an urban washing line. His traditional cross-hatching on man-made material was innovative and respected across the industry.

I tried to be incognito so I could enjoy looking at the artwork as a viewer but also because I wanted to take in everyone else absorbing the pieces. I was pleased people were reading the catalogue and using it as a reference. I stopped at one of Ricky's portraits and stared hard, thinking of Nick in Goulburn and knowing he'd be out soon.

'You okay?' Wyatt asked, standing close to me.

'Just a little homesick.'

He put his arm around me and stared at the photo too, and I knew he knew what I was thinking.

"There's some people who want to meet you, but I can put them off.'

'No, where are they?'

Wyatt led me to some of the city's top collectors, and eager agents hoping to represent some of the exhibited artists. Then I met students from various universities. There were a couple of students from the class I spoke to who came and said hello and raved about the lecture I'd given them. I was glad Maria was in earshot at the time.

Maria gave a welcome speech, I spoke briefly about the concept of the exhibition, and then Soni Moreno – a well-known singer with an incredible voice – performed. She was from the Mayan/Apache and Yaqui peoples and I was so excited to meet her.

'It's been a huge success already, Lauren, you should be proud,' Maria said as the evening drew to a close. 'There's reviewers here, so we'll get some coverage in the *New York Times* and the *Daily News* and that's pretty good for us. Well done.' She hugged me and then had to race over to farewell an elder who was about to leave.

After the opening, Maria, Wyatt and some of the visiting and local artists all went out to dinner at Alfredo's near the Rockefeller Center and I went too. I relaxed finally, but the adrenaline was still rushing, and we spent a lot of time laughing, mostly at couples sitting at tables and not talking to each other but sending text messages or talking on phones. We toasted the artists, the curators, the museum, the spring weather and the poor waiters who had to deal with our rather loud table in an otherwise quiet establishment. And we all ate too much.

'Who wants to go ice-skating?' one of the artists asked.

'Great idea,' Wyatt said, as did most others, and so we all went, except for Maria, who had to get home to her kids.

I hadn't skated since I was a teenager, when Mum and Dad took us to Sydney. I loved it then, but I was nervous wondering how my skinny Koori ankles would cope standing on thin blades.

'Are you all right?' Wyatt asked as I stood frozen with fear.

'I'm petrified of falling over and someone skating over my hands. I kind of like my fingers,' I said with a half-smile.

'You make me laugh, Lucas.' He had recently taken to calling me Lucas, and I liked it. 'Come on, you can't stand there all night.' He moved onto the ice and held out his hand.

I apprehensively reached out and took Wyatt's gloved hand and slowly we inched into the crowd. I was awkward at first but he was patient, at least for the first two laps.

'Okay, now we're starting to look like grandparents compared to the kids. That five-year-old has lapped us about twenty times already.'

'They've got youth on their side,' I said. 'You can let go now, if you like. I think I'm okay.'

'There's no way I'm going to be responsible for you coming to work on Monday with no fingers.'

I was glad he didn't let go – I wasn't feeling confident, but I was having a lot of fun. The music in the background was eighties and nineties and couples were doing routines, parents towed kids, friends just had fun. By 11 pm the group had dispersed to their respective boroughs and bars, leaving just Wyatt and me to skate with the other late-nighters. I was eventually able to get some speed up and also do some backwards gliding, with no falls at all. It was the perfect closing to the opening night.

28

Adam comes to town

In the first week of June I met with Maria regarding my future at the NMAI.

'There's only six weeks left on your contract, Lauren, and I'm already missing your great work here. The exhibition was a notable success and I've let Emma know that, of course. We've had many potential partners suddenly appear for future exhibits – including more at the community centre – and indeed, film festivals, thanks to your curating of both.'

'Thanks, Maria, your acknowledgement means a lot, but you know I was helped all along by Wyatt and other museum staff. It's the same back home.'

'Yes, I know, but you have energy and drive, and vision, and that's what made it all work in the end.'

I smiled, knowing that Maria was right about my energy and drive. It was what I liked about myself. It had landed me my great job and the fellowship.

'I've had such a wonderful experience here. The opportunity to bring our artists here and be able to curate at the Smithsonian would've been enough. But I loved working with the team here, too. Wyatt is one in a million, and I've got so many ideas to take back home. It will be very hard for me to say goodbye to everyone here.'

'Well,' Maria said, looking just like Emma sitting behind her desk back at the NAG, 'you do realise the fellowship can be extended for another twelve months. I know Wyatt would be thrilled to have you as a co-curator for longer . . . and the security guards wouldn't mind you staying either.'

'What?'

'It's a small organisation, and the woman with the funny accent is often mentioned, in a nice way, of course.'

'Of course.'

'Have you thought about extending your contract?'

'To be completely honest with you, Maria, I love it here. It's a great place to work, but I always knew I would only stay the twelve months. I miss my family and friends and the NAG. I've also been toying with the idea of setting up an Aboriginal Artists Management Agency back home – to help facilitate more international exhibitions.' I couldn't tell her that Nick was out of jail too, and I wanted to spend some time with him. It had been too long. I acknowledged to myself that I didn't actually miss Adam any more, though, and mentally applauded myself for not looking at his Instagram at all in recent weeks. I just wanted to go home, it was time.

Three days later, out of nowhere, Adam called as I sat at home, sweaty after the gym and eating a bowl of fruit salad while Kirsten ironed and we both watched telly.

'House of hotties,' I answered without looking at who was calling. I had orange stains on my singlet top and my hair was all messy, my left foot propped on the windowsill in an attempted stretch. Kirsten just shook her head as if to say I was ridiculous.

'Babycakes! How are you?'

I was stunned, and almost dropped my bowl. I put my foot down on the floor.

'Hello, Lauren? It's me, Adam.'

'I know who it is.' I moved back against the wall and slid down it. 'I'm just a bit shocked, that's all. What's wrong?'

Kirsten put the iron down and mouthed, 'Are you okay?' I just nodded.

'Nothing's wrong,' Adam said. 'I'm calling to say I'm going to be in New York next week. To see you. To see the city.'

I was still stunned. He was coming to see me? The city? Next week?

'This is a bit sudden, isn't it? I mean I haven't heard from you in months. Where have you been? Why now?' I had so many questions I didn't know where to start. I didn't even *want* to start. I was over him. I didn't want to see him.

'We can talk about it all when I get there. I'll message you my flight details. Are you still at the same address? Where is it? Chelsea?'

So he'd received my messages, he'd even read them, and *now* he could apparently manage to send me a message with his flight details, so it appeared he knew how to reply as well.

'Babycakes? Are you there?'

I no longer got weak at the name Babycakes. In fact, it annoyed me.

'I'm here. And stop calling me that. Email me your flight details. I'll find you a hotel. You can't stay here, I've got two roommates.'

'I've missed you, Loz, really.'

'I'll see you when you get here. Bye.' I couldn't bring myself to say I missed him back, not after all this time.

'It was him, wasn't it? That footyhead fella. What the hell did he want?'

'He's coming here, to see me, to see New York.'

'Are you okay with that? Do you want to see him?'

'Oh fuck, I don't know. And see, he even makes me swear. It's over, I'm over it, him.'

'It's so typical, men that is. When it suits them they get their shit together. It's good you're making him stay in a hotel, though. That's the best hint.'

I put my bowl on the table, still flustered. 'This fruit's not enough, sis, I need something harder. You wanna go to the Oz for a drink?'

'Oh, I'm so sorry, I have work emails I have to send

tonight and can't do it blurry-eyed or minded. But you go. You'll be right there.'

'Yeah, I'm a local yokel for sure by now.'

I showered and changed and went to the pub, hoping I could also get Matt's opinion. He was a straight bloke, thought like a straight bloke, and would tell me straight like a bloke.

'This is a surprise, seeing you here on a school night,' Matt joked.

'I know, I needed a drink.'

'Sounds serious. Usual?'

'Please.'

'So what's up?'

'Adam called – he's coming to New York next week. I don't know why. He said he wants to see me. You're a bloke – do you think that's true?'

'I'm sure he'll be happy to see you, of course. What bloke wouldn't?' Matt said as he poured my drink.

'But?'

'Lauren, he probably didn't tell you he's been dropped from the team. His game is off, they're losing, and everyone's blaming him.'

'And?'

'And no other club will touch him, he can't get a contract.'

'For a few lost games? That's ridiculous, he's got a good track record.'

'It's not just that, he's been in the papers again about his off-field behaviour, you don't need to know the details.

I knew he was coming – footy grapevine. A lot of players come to New York if they're in the shit back home.'

'Why here?'

'Because it's a big city perfect for hiding in until things settle down in Oz. He would've showed up here at some point.'

I was confused and annoyed. I didn't want him to come to New York. I was happy now and I had friends I wanted to myself. 'Well, I knew you first, so your loyalties should be with me, right?'

'Right.' Matt laughed. I was being ridiculous.

I drank my one Ozmo and as I got up to leave Matt gave me some pavlova to take home. I ate it in the bath. No-one would've believed me if I told them. But I wanted to think, relax, spoil myself with sugar and stare at the Empire State Building. I was in emotional turmoil. I didn't think I wanted Adam anymore. I'd stopped looking at his page. I hadn't messaged him for months. And yet just the sound of his voice had pulled my heartstrings, but why? He hadn't changed, he hadn't really missed me, and he was only coming to America because he was shamed out of Australia. Why did I even care anymore? Because he was my first real love, and my only love. But I was still determined not to let him get under my skin again.

I felt ill walking down the corridor of the hotel I'd booked Adam into at Times Square. I knew he'd want to be in the middle of everything. I wasn't even convinced he deserved to see me. I wasn't sure I wanted to see him, but I was undeniably curious. I hadn't even bothered to wear anything special, he didn't deserve that either. I was hoping the evening would be over quickly.

He opened the door and grabbed me tightly and started kissing my neck. Nothing had changed, he hadn't changed, it was always just physical with Adam. He knew my weakness, but things were different now. I'd had other men kiss my neck, other men who had wanted to be with me properly, took me to restaurants, answered my messages and called me. Other men who wanted to do things during the day, and not just at night. But there was still the same intense attraction that I had for him back in Canberra. I tried to resist.

'Wait.'

'What? Loz, come on, I've missed you. And I know you've missed me, I read all your messages and saved some of the photos.'

'Why didn't you respond, then?'

'I'm not great with words, you know that. I'm here now. We're together. We're in New York. Let's get busy.'

It had been months since I'd had sex, although I knew it had probably only been days since Adam had. But seeing him then made me want him again, at least physically, and my heart was being pulled in by him as well. I could feel myself weakening.

'I want to make love to you, Lauren,' he whispered.

'And me to you.'

I thought making love to Adam when I didn't love him any more would be different – maybe mechanical, maybe more exciting. Since coming to New York I'd felt less inhibited, and I wasn't going to let it all be about Adam now. But it was comforting to be with him again, it was familiar. And without intending or wanting it, all my feelings for him came flooding back. I left before sunrise and hoped Kirsten and Vikki hadn't noticed me staying out for the night. I was still the strong Lauren at home in Chelsea.

Adam slept the first two days away with jet lag, which was fine, because I had to make up enough hours to take some time off to hang out with him. As soon as he felt human, though, he wanted to go to Chelsea Piers to check out all the sporting spaces there. We stopped at the Empire Diner on 10th Avenue for brekky on the way.

'It's a twenty-four-hour diner, great for brekky and brunch,' I said as we walked along the street, Adam holding my hand like we were a couple, the couple I had wanted to be back in Canberra a year ago.

Inside, I sat down, desperate for some caffeine, and Adam dying for a fry-up.

'What do you call this kind of diner-style thing, Loz?'

'It's art deco,' I said, looking at the chrome stools with black patent vinyl seats and black glass-top tables. 'I like coming here cos it's off the main drag, but there's not a lot to look at.'

'You can watch all those dog walkers,' he said, and we both looked out the window at the tracksuited men and women with dogs on leashes.

'Finished?' Adam asked before I'd even put my mug down. 'I can't wait to get to the Piers, they've got hockey and a driving range and heaps of sporting stuff to do.'

'Apparently.'

Chelsea Piers was a huge sporting complex on the river. I was keen to ice-skate again but Adam wouldn't be in it. He just wanted to watch the ice-hockey and hit golf balls. So we did what he wanted, and I hit balls for the first time since leaving Canberra. I quickly got my swing back, and could tell that Adam noticed too by the way he smiled when I drove the ball to the 100-metre mark. I missed the open spaces that Canberra had for things like golf, and it was good to be doing something 'normal' with Adam again. I'd forgotten how much fun we could have together, but I wasn't the one on holidays, so the fun didn't last long.

'I have to go to work for the afternoon. You can come and hang out at the museum if you like.'

He pulled a brochure out of his back pocket.

'Loz, the only museum I want to go to is the Sports Museum of America – it's on Broadway, near a bowling green.'

'It's not a bowling green, the place is *called* Bowling Green. It's near my work, we can get the subway together.'

'Great,' he said, putting his arm around my waist. 'I really am happy to see you, babycakes.'

I glared at him.

'I mean Lauren,' he said, 'but you'll always be my babycakes.'

I couldn't help but smile. He was sweet and that's what I had always liked about him. As we sat on the subway saying nothing I was remembering the nice times we'd enjoyed back in Canberra, just the two of us in simple circumstances.

As we emerged above ground, I said, 'I'll meet you here at 5.30 pm, okay?'

'Okay,' he said and kissed me hard on the mouth.

'This place is awesome, Loz, I can see why you love it here. I had a great time at the sports museum, so much fun, and the guys there were cool. They told me about this pop-up brewery place on 5th Avenue, right near the Empire State Building. Can we go tonight?'

'Go where? The brewery or the Empire State Building?'

'We can do both, can't we? They reckon you can go up really late and there'll be less people in the line-up – that's what they call a queue here.'

'Yes, I know line-up.' I was thinking about how my dream of a romantic reunion wasn't going to happen, and especially not after two hours at a brewery. Sport and beer really were all Adam was interested in. 'Let's just go for dinner now and see how we feel after that.'

We took the subway uptown and went to the recommended brewery.

'Here's one for you, babycakes – the Goddess brew.' Adam was trying to convince me to get drunk too.

'No, I know, I bet you'd rather some New York cheesecake from that bakery across the road. I bet you've still got that sweet tooth, haven't you?' He put his hand on mine. He knew me well.

We sat there for hours as Adam tried as many beers as he could. It wasn't romantic at all.

'Does this make you happy?' I asked him.

'What?'

'Sitting in a pop-up bar just drinking.'

'I'm sitting in a bar with the most beautiful woman in New York, who is also the most talented woman I've ever met. I'm in heaven. Having the beer just means my hands are busy on the glass and not all over you.'

'You're mad.' I shook my head.

'I might be mad, but to answer your question, yes, this makes me happy.'

'Well, I'm tired, Adam, it's been a really long day,' I said, reaching for my bag.

'What about the Empire State Building? It's just there – I can see the sign to the entrance.'

'I don't think tonight's the right night for it. I might meet you up there after work later in the week.'

'Whatever you want, babycakes.'

Adam dropped into the Smithsonian after he did the Statue of Liberty tour the next day. He was wearing one of the foam crowns that I had refused to buy with Libby. He didn't care what people thought of him, which is something I had liked about him before.

'Take it off – you look like an idiot.'

'You don't like it?' He posed like a model at a photo-shoot. 'I know you want one.'

'I don't, and this is my place of work.'

'You used to have fun with me and laugh.'

'I used to do a lot of things.'

We walked the back corridors to my office.

'Hello, have you got a minute?' I asked Wyatt, who spun around immediately.

'Of course.'

'This is Wyatt, my colleague and buddy here. This is Adam.'

I motioned Adam forwards and he shook Wyatt's hand roughly, as if staking his claim over me. I wondered what Wyatt thought about it and hoped he didn't hold it against me. Seeing them next to each other was a little strange, and I realised that they were both equally handsome in different ways. Adam was cheeky and rugged and muscly, and Wyatt was earthy, well-groomed and fit.

'Lauren has talked about you quite a bit,' Wyatt said politely.

'Well, that doesn't surprise me,' Adam said, cocky.

'We're just going out for some lunch – I'll be back by two.'

'Have fun. Enjoy your time here, Adam.'

'Thanks mate, I will.' Adam put his arm around me again as we walked out.

'Is he a poof?' Adam whispered in my ear as we left the building.

'What are you mumbling about? And don't be so offensive.'

'Wyatt. Is he gay or do I have to be worried about you hanging out with him?'

'He's chivalrous and a total gentleman and he's been a real help to me here at work and just getting around New York.'

'So he's not *gay*, then?'

'What does it matter if he is or isn't?'

'Because you share a confined space together and I know what any *normal* guy like me would want to do in that space with you.'

'You're not normal!' I said, looking at him with the foam crown back on his head, but knew that there's no real normal in society anyway.

'I bet he thinks sports are boring.'

'We don't talk about sports, we talk about art and music and our work.'

'He's gay.'

'How do you figure that?'

'Look how he's dressed all tidy and clean and nice. I bet he's obsessed with clothes.'

'He's not obsessed with fashion – he just likes to look good. Professional. I have no doubt whatsoever that you spend more time in front of the mirror than he does.'

'I bet he loves to dance, doesn't he? Tell me.' And I thought back to the social, where Wyatt spent most of the night dancing, and he was good.

'You are being absolutely stupid.'

'I bet you guys hang out a lot, don't you?'

'Yes, we're mates, he's my friend. A good friend.'

'Yeah, yeah, they always have a girl-pal by their side. That makes you a fag hag.'

'You're such a jackass sometimes.'

'Now you're talking like a Yank – "jackass". I wouldn't mind jackassing your beautiful ass,' he said, grabbing me from behind.

'Stop it, we're in public.' I pushed him away.

'So you like this Wyatt better than me?'

'That's like comparing apples and oranges. Wyatt's got a masters in fine arts from NYU, he likes the theatre and art.'

'He is *so* gay.'

'And you're so ignorant and offensive. Stop it!' I stood still and looked hard at him, I could feel my temper rising and my patience waning.

'I'm sorry, I was just winding you up. He seems like a really nice guy, and I'm glad you had someone taking care of you here. You should be taken care of.'

'He's a good guy.'

'Of course he is. You have impeccable taste in friends,' he said, smiling as if to include himself in that list of friends. We walked in silence, ate some sushi in Stone Street and then sat in Battery Park watching the tourists taking photos of the statues and clapping along to the street performers.

'By the way, I have a surprise for you,' Adam said, getting something from his pocket.

'Really? I love surprises.' Jewellery? Earrings, a bracelet, a *ring* perhaps?

'Close your eyes and put your hands out.' I did as I was instructed and Adam placed two tickets in my hand.

I immediately imagined the theatre or perhaps a musical or a concert. Then I read them.

'The Knicks,' he said excitedly. 'I got us tickets to the Knicks at Madison Square Garden tonight, babycakes.'

'I don't finish work until 6.30 tonight.' I was slightly disappointed – it was more sports.

'Can you meet me there, then?'

'I'll meet you out the front of Hudson Booksellers – next to the stadium.'

'Okay, well here's your ticket, in case we get separated or lost or whatever.'

After lunch I went back to the office.

'So, is it back on with Adam? It looks like it.' Wyatt's question threw me a little.

'I'm not sure. I'm confused. I was so hurt and angry with him for cheating on me that I know I should never get back with him. But he's a nice guy, and funny, and when we're together, it's only about me. And his sports.'

'He seems like a nice guy, Lucas,' Wyatt said, ignoring the arrogant behaviour he'd seen Adam display earlier.

'He is, I guess. I decided ages ago I was over him, that we'd never be together again. That he could never be trusted again. But he seems different here. We're almost like a normal couple. He must've changed – after all, he came all this way to see me.'

'Some say a leopard doesn't change its spots, but Adam might be the one that proves them wrong.'

'Maybe.'

'Where are you?' I said into the phone, at the same time looking desperately for Adam among everyone else who had decided to meet out the front of Hudson Booksellers. It was 6.35 pm.

'I couldn't see you, so I came in.'

I hung up annoyed and made my way into the venue. I felt overwhelmed by the crowds and started to feel claustrophobic. I couldn't imagine what it might be like to have to get out during an emergency. I was trying to remember to breathe properly before I got completely anxious. I had no idea where I was supposed to go, but at every ticket check the ushers were all very helpful men.

The final usher walked me right to my seat, where Adam was sitting with a beer and a big foam finger.

'Lozzie, I was getting worried.'

'Why didn't you wait?'

'There was no point in *both* of us missing the start of the game, and I didn't know how long you would be. Here, I bought you a cap.'

'Thanks.'

I sat back and took in the view of the teams warming up on the court. Lots of stretching and ball work. There was music in the background and a buzz in the air. There wasn't a certain 'type' of basketball fan either – rather there were men in suits and men in sweats, there was a couple next to us, and three businesswomen in front. There was a whole row of men behind us with their faces painted orange and blue.

'The thing about the Gardens, Loz, is that all the seats are good here. These seats we're in are called Center Court.'

'Yes, I know, Wyatt showed me the seating plan online today. He follows the Knicks.'

'He would. Their name comes from Knickerbockers, the gayest name in sport.'

'And who are you barracking for tonight, then?'

'Yeah, but I'm straight.'

Before I had the chance to tell him off we were on our feet standing for the national anthem. The rest of the night the music swung from Jennifer Lopez's 'Let's Get Loud' to the anthem 'We Will Rock You'. With each musical interlude the crowd sang loudly. I got an adrenaline rush and couldn't stop smiling – it was loads of fun being at one of the world's most famous venues. There was so much positive energy in the air, as well as the smell of hotdogs and pretzels and peanuts.

The Knicks were pummelling the Hawks and long, lean, lanky bodies were running up and down the court; hoops were being shot from unbelievably difficult positions. There were a couple of collisions between the opposing teams and the bodies hit the wooden flooring hard. I cringed with how painful it must have been, but they were up playing again in no time.

'I want some crackerjacks or peanuts,' I told Adam.

'You wanna crack whose nuts?' He was trying to be funny. 'Do you want some fairy floss? I bet your mate Wyatt would, being a fairy and all.'

'It's called cotton candy here, and if you don't stop being an idiot about Wyatt I'm going to leave.'

'Come on, babycakes, you know I'm just kidding. He looks like a nice fella, and I'm glad you've got good friends here. But you should've worn orange and blue to be in the team colours, Loz.' Adam's attention span was short away from sport. 'Carn the Knicks!' he yelled.

'Carn the Knicks,' I echoed.

'You're sexy when you're cheering, Loz. We can have victory sex tonight, babycakes, cos the Knicks have knocked out the Hawks for sure.' I thought back to celebrating Fucksgiving with Cash and felt a pang of guilt.

We went back to Adam's hotel. Even though I'd told Vikki and Kirsten that we were trying to work it out, I hadn't taken him to meet them just in case we didn't.

Adam was full of beans and beer from the Knicks win. I was on a high too, from the rush that came with being there live. With our arms linked, everything felt good, normal, okay.

We went to his room and he was undressed before I even had my shoes off.

'Come here, babycakes.' He pulled me onto the bed.

Adam was impatient, and within minutes, so was I, so we made love frantically, thanks to the thrill of the Knicks win. And while I didn't feel like I was falling in love with him again, the sex was still better than anything we'd had in Canberra.

29

An affair to remember

Adam had finally been made an offer with a new club, the Goulburn Giants, and I could already hear Libby calling them the Goulburn Gorillas. He had to fly back to Australia for a meeting with his manager. We both knew it would make or break his career. He called me at work to tell me he'd be leaving the following day.

'That's good news, I guess,' I said down the line.

'I need to see you tonight.'

'I know. Can we do something romantic?'

'Of course, anything you want, babycakes.'

'I've watched so many movies with romantic scenes up the Empire State Building. I want us to go up together, while you're still here. I haven't been up there yet.'

'Okay, babycakes, I hear you. I'll meet you there.'

'At sunset, okay, and then we can go have dinner somewhere nice.'

When I got off the phone I realised Wyatt was at

his desk and had heard everything, but I didn't mind. There wasn't much he didn't know about me and my life these days.

'Sounds like a hot date.'

'Adam's going back to Australia tomorrow, it's his last night, and we're going up the Empire State Building. I want one of those scenes, you know, like in *Sleepless in Seattle*?'

'Yes, it's one of my favourite movies.'

'I need to go and make myself gorgeous.'

'That'll take all of five minutes.' Wyatt stood up. 'I hope it works out this time, Lucas. He's a lucky man.'

'Thank you.' I touched Wyatt's hand. 'See you in the morning.' I went home and spent two hours getting ready. Luckily the summer meant the sun went down later. Kirsten and Vikki were both home and were excited for me and the prospect of a happy ending.

'Meg Ryan had a happy ending,' Kirsten said.

'She did.' I was talking but not really focused on the conversation. 'I feel sick with nerves and I don't know about the lift.'

'Here, try this.' Vikki handed me some ashwagandha.

'Gees, you fellas are crazy about this stuff, aren't you?'

'It works, that's why.'

I should've taken it with food but I just couldn't eat. I swallowed and waited for the miracle cure. If only it were that easy.

The girls walked up to 7th Avenue with me, deep breathing along the way. It must have looked hysterical to watch from across the street. They put me in a cab and I checked and rechecked my lipstick as the driver wound his way to my final destination. I wondered if Adam was already on his way there.

Inside the building I couldn't believe the queue was so long. Everyone wanted to be there at sunset and have their own affair to remember. There was an elderly couple queuing in front of me, holding hands and smiling. They were both in jeans and wearing matching sloppy-joes with I ❤ NYC on them. She looked like her hair had been set, and he wore a baseball cap. The old man smiled at me and I welcomed the opportunity to speak and take the focus off the butterflies in my stomach.

'Is this your first time?' I asked him. 'Up the building, that is?'

'Oh no,' he said. 'We come here every year on our anniversary. It's where I proposed.' And he kissed his wife on the cheek.

'That's so romantic.' I had a chill up my spine at the thought of such pure love. 'And *every* year, that's a lot.'

'We just live in upstate New York, so it's not far. We get the train and make a little trip out of it,' the woman said. 'It's like a mini-honeymoon each year.'

They were so cute I was truly inspired. The queue moved ahead as the lifts took groups of people. I looked around to see if Adam was in the queue but couldn't spot him and was glad. I wanted to get there early, to position myself where I could see him arrive without him seeing me. I wanted time to fix my make-up and my hair. I wanted the moment to be perfect. There had been enough imperfection in our past to last a lifetime.

I was bothered by the endless lines, roped-off areas and maroon-suited staff all in the way of me getting to the top of the building and getting on with my life. I had spent too many months waiting for this moment. I had nearly gone insane with jealousy and insecurity. I had slept with a man I didn't love, and I had behaved like a stalker with Adam. But perhaps it hadn't been for nothing. Perhaps it would be my turn to have something wonderful like the couple in front of me.

'Are you going up alone?' the lady asked.

'I'm meeting my boyfriend up there. It's kind of like a reunion, and a new start.'

'Sounds promising,' she said.

In an old-fashioned act of chivalry the man removed his cap, revealing a bald head, took my hand and said, 'He's a lucky man. If I was twenty years younger and not married—'

'You'd still be too old.' His wife rolled her eyes. 'I fell in love with him in spite of his bad attempts at flirting.'

When it was our turn to get in the lift, I stopped still in fear.

'What's wrong?'

'I need a minute. You go up, I'll see you up there,' I said, and stepped back.

'Ma'am, are you coming in?' the lift attendant asked.

'No, not yet.'

'Ma'am, you can't stand there – you either step into the lift or move through to the exit.'

'Come on, love,' the wife said, sympathetically. The couple reminded me of Mum and Dad, and so I got in the lift. There were two English tourists, a German backpacker, an Australian couple and the attendant. My stomach felt unstable as the lift took flight to the top. I didn't know if I was nervous about the ride, the distance I was travelling towards the top of the tower, or the fact that the moment I had waited so long for with Adam was about to happen, just as I had planned. And then the lift stopped and I was desperate to get out – sweat had broken out on my brow and upper lip and my mouth was dry. But the attendant wouldn't let me out. He wanted to talk about the history of the building, even after we'd arrived on the 86th floor. I couldn't listen – I didn't have time and I was feeling claustrophobic. I had my own affair to remember waiting to begin.

'Excuse me, I feel a little faint, can I get out, please?'

'Me too,' the old lady said.

'Sorry, ladies, of course.'

I stepped out first and there were couples and families but I couldn't see another single girl by herself. There were a few guys by themselves, though. I wondered if they were having affairs to remember as well. I walked around the cramped observation deck and didn't know how it was going to be romantic. I took in the view, looking for what I could recognise – Central Park, 5th Avenue, the Chrysler building, Times Square and the George Washington Bridge. I was entertained by the site of hundreds of yellow cabs moving around town, like little yellow bugs.

It was hard to tell from so far up how hectic life was down below in the city. I wanted to get a glimpse into a telescope but I couldn't stand still long enough, and people were queuing for them anyway.

The space was not how I had imagined it to be. There was a small area outside the lifts so you could stand inside, and then the observation deck. It didn't look like it did in the movies. And it was cramped like Libby said – not cosy, just cramped. And there was really nowhere to sit or to hide while I waited for Adam. The sun was setting and it was meant to be the best time to be up there, but I couldn't really focus. I was sick. What if he didn't show up? What if he did?

I tried to stand still outside but couldn't. I tried to enjoy the sunset but couldn't. I felt sick, but it wasn't nerves or excitement. I didn't know what it was. I didn't feel the warm and romantic rush I thought I would standing there.

I waited and I watched people come and go. Two looked like a honeymooning couple in their late twenties. They were perfectly matched in height and had similar features, with smiles that radiated love to all around them. I was inspired just looking at them as they shared a telescope, touching each other affectionately, taking photos of each other. Smiling, laughing, loving. I was envious even before I noticed their wedding bands. They pecked each other on the cheek spontaneously as they walked one length of the deck. I realised I was staring at them and I felt a pain in my heart, knowing they were the couple that Adam and I had never been. We'd never been out like that, enjoying each other in Canberra like a normal couple. Even here in

New York he was only interested in sport. He had ignored me all these months and now he was jumping on a plane the minute an offer was made. But then, I knew all along what he wanted. He'd at least been honest on that front. The only liar was me, to myself, believing that things had changed, that he had changed, that we had a future together. I shook my head in disappointment in myself; there I was all dressed up at the top of the Empire State Building waiting for a man I had got over months ago. How had I let him back into my life?

I looked at my watch and Adam was already fifteen minutes late. Then he was half an hour late.

When he was an hour late I decided to leave. I wiped a dignified and disappointed tear from my cheek, took a deep breath and turned around.

I gasped as he walked towards me. 'Hello,' he said.

'Hi.' I was shaking my head in confusion.

He put his hands on my waist, then around me, pulling me gently towards him. He kissed me softly on the mouth and I was shocked at the electricity between us. It wasn't what I normally felt. I'd felt lust before, but this was a deeper feeling; it was love and lust and friendship and possibility all in the one kiss. I was surprised at how firmly he held me, as if he wasn't going to let go, or let anyone cut in, or let me stop him. But I didn't want to stop him anyway, I wanted more of the kiss, I wanted to feel his arms tight around me, I wanted the kiss to make its way down my body and I never wanted to open my eyes in case I was imagining it. The moment I'd been waiting for was a moment of feeling like I belonged with someone, that they belonged with me, that we belonged together. And his kiss made me feel that.

I didn't understand, and I couldn't speak. I was confused and turned on. I could feel a strength in his body that I had never considered before. Every sense was alert. I could hear my own heartbeat and feel his against my chest, I could smell his cologne and I could taste him. His breath was sweet like M&Ms, and I thought of the jar on my desk. I opened my eyes slightly and I could see the reflection of us together in the lift doors behind him.

We walked out of the building and I felt unbalanced, like when Dad would spin me around like an airplane as a kid and it would take me minutes to walk upright again. My world had been knocked off its axis just like that, by Wyatt.

We sat in the familiar surrounds of Easy's, and it was so easy to be with Wyatt, cosied up in a corner with a bottle of champagne. We'd never drunk champagne together – we'd never been so intimate before. It was all foreign territory, exciting and heart-warming at the same time.

'I don't understand. How did you know he wouldn't be there?' I asked, head dizzy from the kiss and the bubbles and the realisation that I was in love with Wyatt.

'I had an inkling he wouldn't show up,' Wyatt said wisely.

'You did?'

'Yes, he's an idiot.'

'Because he's a footballer?'

'No, because he let you leave Australia in the first place. He doesn't deserve you. You deserve to be treated with respect and warmth and love.'

'I thought he might be able to give me that.'

'He could never give you that. I think in your heart you know that.'

'Yes.' I felt embarrassed and stupid. Wyatt placed his hand on mine and I thought how easy it would be to just melt into his dreamy eyes and stay there forever.

'I can give you that.' He looked straight into my eyes. 'I want to give you that.'

'I'm confused. I still can't believe we just kissed. God, I feel like an infatuated teenager.'

'I've felt like that since the day we met.' I watched Wyatt's mouth move. I'd never noticed his full lips before, they were luscious and I wanted to lick them right there and then. I wanted to kiss him again.

'You have? You hid it well.'

'It wasn't easy . . .'

I was gobsmacked. My dear friend, Wyatt, not-gay Wyatt, had wanted to kiss me since the day he met me. I must have looked confused.

'What's wrong with me, not macho enough for you because I don't play sports?'

'Don't be silly, nothing's wrong with you. And having just felt your arms around me, you've hidden those muscles well until now.'

'Then what? I'm not rich enough for you? Or tall enough? Come on, Lauren, I know you well enough by now to know you don't care about those things.'

'No, Wyatt, I *don't* care about those things, it's just that I— '

'You what?' He took his hand off mine.

'I thought you were . . . I thought you were . . . gay.' Wyatt spat his drink out and laughed hard.

'Gay? What gave you that idea?'

I wasn't going to make the same ridiculous statements that Adam had, but I wanted to be honest.

'Well, you work in the arts and most of the guys back home in the arts are gay.'

'You work in the arts, and you're not gay.'

'I know.'

'What else then?' He was enjoying watching me make a fool of myself.

'You live in Chelsea, which is pretty much a quintessential gay neighbourhood.'

'Come on, Lauren, *you* live in Chelsea. Again, does that make *you* gay?'

'You come here a lot and there's always heaps of cute gay guys here.'

'God, Lauren, I come by here because *you* drink here. I'd never been here until you mentioned it, and I only pop in on the off chance that I can see you outside of work.'

'What about all those photos of guys on your desk?'

'Most of them are relatives I've got scattered across the continent. You've got photos of Libby and Bec and other women, but I never for a minute thought you were a lesbian.'

'But you never talk about girls. I've never even seen you with a woman. You're hot, why don't you date?'

'I go on dates, but none of them were worth talking about. No-one else stood a chance while I had you in my head and I saw you every day. In a way, I felt like I was the man in your life, except when *Cash* and *Adam* were around.'

I was grateful for the hint of jealousy in Wyatt's voice. 'But all this time, why haven't you done anything?'

'You said you didn't want a relationship and I could tell you weren't over Adam. I didn't want to be a substitute. I sent you the roses on Valentine's Day, but you didn't even consider that I might have done it. At least I now know why.'

'And now? Tonight? Why the Empire State Building?'

'Because I know your contract is nearly up, and I don't want you to go back. Or if you do, I want to go with you. I love having you in my life every day. I hated it when you were away for Christmas and hanging out with Cash. But there was nothing I could do, and I didn't want to try competing with him. He could give you more than I could materially.'

'I don't care about material things.'

'I know, I knew that when you broke up with him. And then Adam turned up and I couldn't stand it. But I knew that jerk wouldn't show up tonight – men like him never step up to the plate. To me it was the perfect moment to tell you how I felt. I waited all these months, and I hoped every day and at every function and with every date you went on that you wouldn't fall in love with someone else.'

'You waited for me?'

'I waited, yes. Didn't you know that love needs faith? I thought that maybe you could eventually love me back.'

'I think I already do.'

'I have something for you.' He passed me a little box. 'Open it.'

Inside was an elegant hand-sculpted clay cherry blossom pendant with freshwater pearls linked together by fine gold wire.

It dangled from a black cord. It matched the earrings Wyatt had given me for my birthday. I took my 'Love needs faith' heart pendant off and replaced it with my new cherry blossom piece.

'I think I need to talk to Maria about extending my fellowship.'

Acknowledgements

Manhattan Dreaming would not have been possible without the assistance of staff from the National Museum of the American Indian at the Smithsonian in New York City way back in 2008/09. They gave of their time not only in showing me their cultural workspace, but in reading drafts as well. Lauren and I remain forever grateful.

For 'on location' research for the original edition and help on the ground in New York, I need to thank Vanessa Rodd, Matt and Nicole Astill, Matilde Busana and Bronwyn Guthrie, Soni Moreno, Loida Garcia-Febo, Roberto Mukaro Borrero, Lily Brett and David Rankin. In fact, the title of this book is a variation of a suggestion by David, who said over the phone, 'You should write *Downtown Dreaming*.' And I thought, 'Yes, I should!'

I'd like to thank Cheryl Tan and Manny Colon for helping me research this new updated edition.

Special thanks also to the countless number of Manhattan men who smiled at Lauren and me in the street, enquired as to our marital status, asked for our numbers and offered to buy us dinner, drinks and coffee. Twenty years of self-esteem work done in five weeks on the ground in the city that never sleeps, worthy of documenting in a book.

For 'on location' research in Canberra, massive thanks to Kirsten Bartlett, Rachel Clarke and Carol Williams. If only the fellas in our capital were as assertive as those in Manhattan I could thank them also. Alas, no credit necessary here.

To the professional women who guide my career and sit and talk as friends also: my agent Tara Wynne (Curtis Brown), my Simon & Schuster publisher Cass Di Bello, and my incredible publicist Anna O'Grady. Thank you also to my editor Elizabeth King and all the team at S&S for making my writing dreams come true.

Writing this novel originally involved brainstorming on Facebook for character names and song titles and so I'd like to thank all those whose suggestions I used: Kevin and Warren, Kim Merritt, Sally Murphy, Bill Chant, Katie Shortland and Vanessa Raine. For relevant songs related to Adam Full-of-himself, thanks to: Judith Ridge, Rhonda Jacobson, Lauren Dower, Georgina Nash and Emma Joel.

For tips here and there, thanks to Michael McDaniel and Cathy Craigie, and to all the individual Indigenous artists who gave feedback on certain aspects of the novel.

This book is about relationships, but it's also a tribute to the strong Aboriginal women working in the arts around Australia and the globe. You inspire me daily.

Finally, I wake up every morning and count my blessings for the enormously supportive family I have. Without them, my characters and I wouldn't be able to dream at all.